# Secrets of the Nire

# Secrets of the Nire

Anne Durand-Athy

| Library of Congress Control Number: | | 2019900185 |
| --- | --- | --- |
| ISBN: | Hardcover | 978-1-9845-7588-3 |
| | Softcover | 978-1-9845-7587-6 |
| | eBook | 978-1-9845-7594-4 |

Print information available on the last page.

Rev. date: 01/08/2019

**To order additional copies of this book, contact:**
Xlibris
1-888-795-4274
www.Xlibris.com
Orders@Xlibris.com
779389

# Contents

To my dear, loving husband, Thomas. You made my lifelong dream of seeing Eire come to fruition, which set in motion the creation of this book.

And to my mother, Elaine Johnston, for leaving her children such an amazing book of heritage, from which *Secrets of the Nire* characters were drawn. I miss you.

And to my daughter, Candace: thank you for working so diligently on the illustrations for Secrets of The Nire. You are amazing.

# Preface

After my mother died in 2008, my brother gave me a small black binder filled with Athy family history and genealogy. She was given the book by her mother, my grandmother, Cora Athy.

My brother was given the book since he was my mother's oldest son. Knowing he would never pursue the contents himself, he gave it to me. As I read it, I was amazed at the magnitude and rich history of the Athy family.

Then, in 2017, my husband and I traveled to Ireland, my family's genealogy book tucked safely in my suitcase, to embark on the most fascinating trip of my life. While I was in the country of my ancestors, *Secrets of the Nire* was born. And although fictional, the names and characters are drawn from my family tree.

I hope the reader enjoys this story as it unfolds and I hope it leaves you wanting more, as this is just the beginning of the adventures of the Athy family.

It was a wet, dark Irish evening in the Nire Valley, not untypical by any means for this ancient part of the world. The North Atlantic was treacherous and unforgiving, as were the islands that seemed to float in its deep, dark waters. The rain and wind were sometimes unrelenting for days on end, blowing and pelting the fertile ground of the Nire, along with its inhabitants. Patrick Athy Jr. had had enough of the political banter and drunken ramblings of the regular Thursday night Guinness club attendees. He called last call over an hour ago, and finally, they filtered out one by one, mumbling to each other, "It's only midnight, Paddy!" Pat Jr. was washing out the last of the beer from the sink when the front door of his pub flew open and she staggered in, soaked to the bone and shaking like a leaf from obvious exposure to the brutal storm outside. "Is there a phone?" she asked in a shaken, hoarse voice.

"On the back wall." Pat nodded toward the back of his establishment, where a phone sat on a small table, next to the back door. He watched as she walked shakily to the table and picked up the phone. Not more than a few seconds later, she dropped to the concrete floor, out cold.

Chapter One

Strangers in Town

Three months earlier

It was an ongoing joke in the Athy Family that all good Irish families should live up to their reputation around the world of being from a land filled with four-leaf clovers, pots of gold, and leprechauns.

He was as close to eight-year-old Fiona's face as he could possibly get without waking her. The whispers came out ever so quietly and slowly at first. "Will ya be wuntin' tha Freench toooast, or shood I geev it to ya brutha?" Gradually, the whispers turned into a low, mocking rendering of the Lucky Charms leprechaun: "Ya betta git oop befur ya brutha eats all yer Luckay Charms Freeench toooast, Li'l Sis!" Fiona largely ignored what had become a morning ritual for her, namely her father, bad breath and all, waking her up by putting his unshaven, scruffy face within an inch from her own. Normally, she would have just rolled over and continued to ignore him, but there was one difference this morning.

"My *brother* will eat *my* French toast?! I'm up, I'm up! Ian, you better not eat my Freeench toooast!" squealed Fiona.

"Well, hello dare, sunshine . . . up so soon?" laughed William Athy.

"Daaad!" Fiona oozed back. "Don't let Ian eat my Freeench toooast."

"I will do my best, but the boy is like a ravenous wolf," said William.

"What's 'ravenous' mean again?" replied Fiona.

"*Hungrrray!*" growled William as he scooped up his daughter in his arms and pretended to be a hungry wolf.

"Da, stop . . . hahaha . . . yer cray-cray!" screamed Fiona.

"Cray-cray? What in God's name is 'cray-cray'?" asked William.

"Y-o-u are c-r-a-z-y!" Fiona said as she crossed her eyes and twirled her finger in a circle motion by her right ear.

"Well, at least you're learning to spell in that school of yours!" replied William.

Fiona bounded to the kitchen to find her older brother, Ian, already on his second helping of Lucky Charms French toast. His plate was filled almost to the brim with syrup.

"Where is miiine, Ian?" Fiona said in a fearful voice, half expecting him to say, "All gone!"

"It's in the oven, Li'l Sis . . . no worries!" yelled William from the back bedroom.

"Thanks, Da!" Fiona yelled back in her best sweet voice.

"I'll get it fer ya, Fee. The oven's still hot," Ian said as he grabbed the oven mitts, opened the oven door, and retrieved his little sister's breakfast.

"T'anks, Ian." Fiona replied as she ran over to give her brother a morning hug.

"Yeah, yeah, yer welcome, Fee . . . now sit down and eat. I'll get ya some syrup," Ian said as he patted his little sister on the back and pushed her gently toward her chair at the same time. "Da, come and eat!" Ian yelled down the hallway of their four-bedroom cottage.

"You two go ahead. I have to get this," William said as he picked up his chirping cell phone, his face still half covered in shaving cream.

"Hello," William said into his phone.

Silence.

"Hello?" William said again.

"William," a voice said on the other end, "it's me. Can we talk?"

"Who is this?" William asked.

"It's Colin Wohl, Will, your best friend," he replied.

"Colin Wohl? I haven't talked to you in—" William started.

"Years, I know. It's been years," replied Colin, sounding agitated.

"Uhhh, it's been *ten* years, Colin. What are ya callin' for now?" William said awkwardly with a slight tone of anger.

"Will, I am sorry I haven't called. I really am. Listen . . . William, I need your help," Colin said, bordering on panic.

"Ummm, what's happening, Colin? I don't hear from you for *ten* years, and now, you want *my* help?"

And with that, the line went dead.

"Hello . . . Colin? You there? Colin, you there?" pressed William.

Nothing.

Colin Wohl had been the star rugby player at Tipperary Secondary School in Clonmel, Ireland, for three straight years. After graduation, he went off to Oxford, where he pursued a degree in law. After his second year at Oxford, Colin dropped off the face of the earth. He simply vanished, only to be talked about in local rumors as living somewhere in California, working for a production company. He and William had been inseparable since the first grade, growing up together, as close as brothers do. So when Colin just dropped out of university and disappeared without so much as a phone call, William was hurt, but not completely surprised. Colin had been complaining about school to William for the better part of a year and would not stop rambling on about wanting to just pack up and leave for a whole new life somewhere new, somewhere warm, somewhere other than England—California.

---

William brushed it off as the usual Colin rantings, until he was gone. William did not hear from him once in ten long years.

Until today.

William finished his shave and wiped the remaining foam from around his ears as his cell phone chirped yet again.

"Yes, hello?" he answered.

"Hello, Will. It's Dad," Pat Athy said.

"Da! How are you this fine morning?" William replied.

"Good, son. And you?" Pat said.

"I'm upright and clean-shaven!" William joked back.

"Good, son. Good," Pat replied.

"What can I do for ya, Da?" William asked.

"Will, I need you to come down to the pub just as soon as you can, son," said Pat.

"Okay. Can be there at half past, after I take the wee ones to school," replied William.

"Dat'll be good, son," said Pat.

"What is the matter, Da? Is Mum all right?" asked William.

"Oh, she's fine, son, ornery as ever. I need you to come down here because there are half a dozen strangers in me pub, and one of them says he's Colin Wohl!"

"I, William Patrick Athy, take you, Emma Fiona Lehy, to be my lawfully wedded wife." It had been eleven years since William had spoken those words to the love of his life, Emma.

---

"Eleven years tomorrow. I miss you every day, Em," William whispered to himself as he sat in his old Range Rover, waiting for Fiona and Ian.

"Ian, Li'l Sis, let's *goooo*! Yer gonna be late again!" William yelled out the Rover window.

"Comin', Da!" Ian shouted back with a laugh.

"What's so funny, boy?!" William asked.

"You'll see," replied Ian.

Just then, Fiona bounded from the cottage, slamming the door behind her.

"Oh, good Lord have mercy, what are ya wearin', Li'l Sis?" William blurted out, in a loud laugh.

"It's pretty! Boys don't know anything!" Fiona said sternly while shaking her index finger at her father and brother.

"If you say so, Fee." Ian laughed.

Fiona was dressed to the hilt in her best Christmas dress, a red velvet number with white lace bows on the sleeves. Underneath, she had decided on her purple sweatpants and a striped green-and-white long-sleeve shirt, and on her tiny feet, she opted for her bright yellow rain boots. Upon her head, she wore an orange knitted hat her grandmother had made for her, covering the pigtails William had worked so hard to perfect that morning.

"Yer coverin' my beautiful pigtails, Li'l Sis!" whined William.

"They're still there, Da, just a bit smooshed!" Fiona said with a giggle.

William gave a dramatic sigh.

With both of his children safely inside the Rover, William set out for Tipperary Elementary School.

"Will! There ya are, son!" shouted Pat Athy.

"Good mornin', Da," William replied as he let himself in the front door of Athy's Pub, his father's establishment, which had been run by an Athy since it was established in 1674. The first pub was in the original building that was built in 1670, but after that building caught fire and burned to the ground in 1832, the present building, erected in 1834, replaced the original.

"Mornin' it is, Will! Good? We shall see!" huffed Pat.

"Where are they?" William asked.

"In the billiard room, son," replied Pat.

William took off his coat and hung it on the coat rack by the front door and walked slowly toward the billiard room at the back right of the pub. He heard voices, the sound of clanging beer mugs and billiards being played coming from the room.

As he entered, William saw six people, all drinking and playing a game of pool and chatting away as if it were completely normal. The smell of cigars permeated the air of the pub, which was old but stylishly appointed. There were twelve booths and eighteen tables scattered throughout the large room. Every wood table and chair was handmade by Patrick, and the seat cushions, made from the family tartan, were sewn by Grace. The walls were filled with old Guinness and Jameson posters and vintage art from all over Ireland. On the back wall of the billiard room was a floor-to-ceiling mural of the Athy family tree, painted by Emma Athy, William's dearly departed wife. It was a beautiful rendering of every member of the Athy family since the twelfth century until modern day, each name written out in the original Gaelic, with a small bust likeness of that family member. Emma painted their ancestors as she saw them in her mind's eye and how they were described in the Athy family Bible. More recent members had photographs, which made their portrait likeness more authentic but did not change the brilliant continuity of this incredible work of art. At each end of the great room were two fireplaces, which were roaring and crackling, keeping the place comfortably warm. The floors were fairly new, polished concrete, since the old wooden ones were too damaged to keep.

"Awfully early to be drinking and making merriment, don't ya think?" William said, oozing sarcasm.

"Not if you're from California! It's midnight for us, ole chap!" And with that, Colin Wohl spun around to face William, grinning from ear to ear. "Will, you haven't changed a bit!" poked Colin as he crept toward William, arms stretched wide open. "Do ya have a hug for yer ole friend?" he said apologetically.

"Colin, it's been a long time," Will said unapologetically.

The two old friends embraced, and William suddenly remembered just how much he truly did miss his old friend.

"It's good to see ya, Sire," whispered William.

"Sire! Hahaha, I haven't been called that in—"

"In ten years," William interrupted, with more sarcasm.

"Yes . . . ten long years," said Colin in a genuinely sad voice.

Colin wrapped one arm around William's broad shoulders, led him to the far corner of the room, and began speaking to him in a low voice, obviously not wanting the others to hear him.

As they reached the far corner of the billiard room, they turned around and gazed back over the group of people Colin had obviously brought with him: five in all, three men and two women, all looking to be around the same age as Colin and William, early to mid-thirties. William hadn't seen anything particularly noticeable about the group until she turned around and flashed him a shy smile. William did a double take as he locked eyes with the loveliest woman he had seen in years. Her eyes were a pale blue-green, and she had long light hair with shocks of red streaming through it. Her stature was tall and thin but curvy in all the right places. William was immediately attracted to her, a feeling he had not experienced in over four years. He quickly snapped his stare away from the beauty across the room and told himself, *What are ya doin'? Absolutely not, Will!* But he could not keep from glancing back every few seconds.

Colin had been rambling on for several minutes, but William had not heard a thing.

"I'm truly sorry, Sire . . . could you repeat that?" William said to Colin.

Colin, obviously frustrated at having to repeat himself, sighed—but then saw William's obvious interest in his companion, Jennifer Sweeney.

"Ohhh, I see you have noticed the divine Miss Jenn?" smirked Colin. "You always did have good taste in women, Will. Sorry about Emma, by the way," said Colin in a somber voice.

William had met Emma at a rugby match when he was twelve years old. She was the most beautiful creature William had ever seen, and he loved her from the very first moment he saw her.

She had light, wavy brown hair with blonde highlights, and when she became a woman, she stood five feet seven with a trim, athletic figure. Her eyes were an intense green-blue color that caught people off guard when she flashed them. In their youth, Emma was attending St. Mary's School for girls and William was at Tipperary Secondary School, a bit over a kilometer away, across town. Emma's parents were killed in a car accident when she was nine, and her uncle had raised her. William and Emma grew up together, along with Colin, whom they nicknamed Sire because he acted like royalty during the rugby season. The three were inseparable, meeting every day halfway between the two schools, at the local ice cream parlor, where Emma eventually worked during the summers. Colin was never jealous or envious of Will and Emma; it was like everyone just knew they were meant to be together. Then, the day came. On a warm June afternoon, William and Emma were married in an old country church in William's hometown, in the Nire Valley. Colin was so very pleased to be Will's best man. That day was filled with absolute joy, love, and laughter as they celebrated the beginning of a marriage. Little did they know at the time, Colin would soon disappear from their lives.

Three years passed, and William and Emma were at that country church again, this time for the dedication of their firstborn, a son, Ian Patrick Athy. It pained Will that Colin had just dropped out of their lives. But life goes on and instead of Colin being Ian's godfather, William's older brother, Patrick Jr. stepped in.

Two more years passed, and the Athys were dedicating their baby daughter, Fiona Emmanuelle. Life was busy for William and Emma. With two young children, William attending night classes and working full-time for the family businesses, and Emma teaching first grade at Tipperary Elementary School, there was never a dull moment in the Athy household. Emma had become the daughter Will's parents had always longed for, and they cherished her as their own. Her uncle had passed away after Ian was born and left her a sizable inheritance, part of which they used to buy a charming Irish cottage on the Nire River, the home Emma had always wanted.

It was a Monday afternoon in late November four years later when they got the call. Emma stood at the back of their kitchen, where the telephone hung on the wall. William heard the ringing from outside, where he was splitting wood for the evening fire.

"Em? Who's calling? Emma?" William yelled from the side yard, near the kitchen door.

No answer.

"Em?" William said as he entered the kitchen, covered in wood chips.

There she sat on the kitchen floor, facing the wall, phone receiver still held to her ear.

"It's cancer, love. Will, it's cancer," Emma whispered, eyes glazed over as she stared at the wall in front of her.

---

William's heart sank as he fell to his knees next to his beloved wife.

"We will beat this thing, Em," Will said through his tears.

Three months later, Emma died.

"Will, you know the Nire Valley better than anyone around," said Colin as he and William stood together across the room from Colin's group of companions.

"Yes, I believe I do. What are you asking me that for, Sire?" William replied. "And who are these people you are with?"

Colin pulled a pack of cigarettes from the breast pocket of his jacket, took one out, lit it, took a long drag, and began his story.

"After I left Oxford, I roamed around the streets of London for close to a month," Colin began.

"Why on earth didn't ya call me, Colin?" William snapped.

"Will, shut up and listen, please," Colin snapped back. "Anyway, after Oxford, I was wandering around London, trying to figure things out. My father would soon find out I had dropped out and the money would dry up. I had to find my way, on my own. I knew I didn't want to practice the law—that was for sure. But my dreams were nowhere to be found in Jolly Ole England. So when I received the last allowance check from me da, I cashed it and bought an airline ticket to LA, California. One way. I'm tellin' ya, Will, California was so different from England! It was warm. There was so much to do and see. And the women, Will! William Thomas Athy, I have never seen so many gorgeous women in my life! I thought I had died and gone to heaven. But the honeymoon was soon over when Da's money ran out. I was evicted from the apartment I had let that was right on Manhattan Beach. I had no way of getting more money since my loving father excommunicated me after the news came to him I had up and quit school. So I had to do something and I had to do it quick. That's when I saw the ad in the local newspaper: 'Proofreaders needed for production company, minimum wage to start.'"

"From Daddy's 5,000 euro a month to minimum wage? You poor little rich boy!" William snarled.

"Yes, it was a shock, Will. T'anks fer the sympathy," Colin snarled back.

"Yer welcome, Sire . . . continue." Will motioned to have a seat on two padded barstools next to them. So the two old friends sat down and Colin continued.

"I applied for the job as proofreader that Friday and got it. Started working for Star Gaze Production Company the very next Monday. I was finally living my dream."

"Yeah, livin' the dream on minimum wage!" William blurted out in a laugh.

"Okay, okay . . . it was more like a nightmare at first. But I learned quickly and soon, I was promoted to production assistant!"

"Production assistant? That was really quick indeed," William said.

"Well, my official title was assistant to the production manager," Colin said faintly as he glanced across the room at his colleagues.

"So ya were the coffee boy?!" exclaimed William, laughing out loud and slapping the table in front of him with his hand. "You were a coffee boy . . . hahahahahahaha! The star rugby player, Sire of the Nire . . . a *coffee boy*? This is too good. Da, I'm gonna need a Guinness!" William yelled to his father in the next room.

"A Guinness? It's nine o'clock in the mornin', William!" Pat yelled back.

"I know, Da. Please, just bring me one!" William said, out of breath from laughing.

As Pat Athy delivered a pint of Guinness to his son William at the table in the billiard room, he noticed that he was wiping his eyes.

"What's the matter, son? Crying?" Pat said.

"Yes, Da, I am cryin'. The tears are flowing on account of the uncontrollable laughter." William managed to get out before he burst into another laughing fit.

Pat just shook his head and set the pint on the table in front of William then said, "Glad to see you two boys gettin' along again."

"Thanks, Mr. A," Colin said.

William gulped down half a pint, wiped his mouth with his sleeve, and said, "Okay, Sire. Sorry for the outburst. Please, by all means, continue."

Colin retrieved his beer from the table across the room, returned to sit with William, and continued.

"Okay, so where was I? Oh yes, I was promoted to coffee boy! Ha-ha, very funny. I had better make this long story short. After a year, I indeed became assistant production manager. That chap o'er there," Colin pointed in the general direction of his group of colleagues. "That is our production manager, Larry Davis. Larry, wave to William!" Colin yelled across the room.

A short, balding man nodded at William, then continued his conversation with the lovely Jennifer Sweeney.
William nodded back and said to Colin, "What does all this have to do with me, Sire?"
"Well, William. We want to do a movie here, in the Nire Valley. And you're going to be our local technical expert!" exclaimed Colin.
William was not amused. "What?" William said as he downed the rest of his Guinness.
"We want you to be our expert." Colin said.
"Expert? *Ha!* Expert of what, exactly?" Will asked with a hint of sarcasm.

"William, come on . . . you know! Expert on the area, the customs, the way of life here in the Nire," Colin replied impatiently.

"Why can't *you* be *the* expert? You grew up here too!" William said bluntly.

"I haven't lived here in—" Colin started.

"*Ten years!*" grumbled William.

"Yes, Will . . . ten long years. I need your help. Will you do it?" asked Colin.

"Sire, I have no time to be yer expert on anything. I have two kids, a family business to run, and no wife to help me!" William said as he got up and took his empty beer mug to the bar.

Colin followed and again asked, "Will, we will help you in any way we can, if you would only be our advisor. Be our expert. Please, Will, for old times' sake," Colin grabbled.

"What's this? An expert of what?" Pat asked.

"He wants me to be their expert on the Nire, Da," replied William.

"Well, if there ever were an expert on these parts, it'd be you, son!" exclaimed Pat.

"There. It's settled. You'll do it!" Colin said with finality in his voice.

"No, I didn't say that, Sire," Will corrected.

"Will, I need you to do this for me. Please," Colin said, holding out his hand.

William shook Colin's hand and replied, "I will think about it. That is the *best* I can do, Sire. So stop askin'!"

"I'll *take it*!" replied Colin with a deep sigh.

# Chapter Two

## Three Against One

William Thomas Athy had his hands full. He was a single father of two active children, ran a household and his family's horse-breeding business, as well as working at his father's pub when his dad and brother needed a break from bartending. So Sunday dinners at his parents' place were a welcome respite for the weary single father. He had dropped off Ian and Fiona early at church, said a short prayer, and left them in the care of his dear mother, Grace Athy. He had a meeting to attend at the horse stables with the local veterinarian. The Athys had several properties located at various places in and around the Nire Valley. The stables were within walking distance to the family pub and were made up of four long rows of stalls, a tack room, four grooming stalls, an enclosed arena as large as a soccer field, kitchen, two bathrooms, and three offices. The grounds were kept immaculate, with dark green, manicured lawns surrounding the complex and flowers lining the sidewalks and filling the garden beds. The buildings were painted bright white with black trim around the doors and windows and bright green painted shutters and doors. As you approached the main entrance, to the right, there stood a bronze statue of a thirteenth-century Athy family patriarch, Thomas William Patrick Athy, atop his steed, an impressive, life-size statue erected in the late nineteenth century by William's great-grandfather, Ian Thomas Athy.

As William approached the main entrance to his family's stables, he nodded toward the statue, oblivious to the fact that it looked remarkably like him. As he opened the giant green doors, the smells of leather, fresh cut hay, and pine cleaner all mingled to awaken his sense of smell. The stables staff was bustling around, attending horses, cleaning stalls and mopping floors. William was pleased to see such dedication and extra effort from his staff of twenty: eight women and twelve men, all working diligently to maintain and see to the smooth running of his family's business. As Will made his way past his large office and into the main stable area, several employees greeted him with "Hello and g'mornin', Mr. Athy!" He smiled at each of them and said loudly, "Top o' da mornin' to you all as well!" as he walked to the third stall on the left and quietly let himself in the half door, which had a plaque mounted on it with the name Lily of the Valley engraved on it.

"How is she, Doc?" William asked as he bent down to gaze at the mare's left hind leg.

"I think she'll be fine, Will. Just needs to rest it. Keep her in her stall for a few days," replied Dr. Samantha Lehy. "It is just a slight sprain. I put a splint on it, just as a precaution and to support that ankle."

"Thanks, so much, Sam," Will replied and the two embraced. "I don't know what we'd do without ya," William said in an appreciative voice.

"Oh, Will. Anything for you, love," Samantha replied.

Samantha Lehy was Emma Athy-Lehy's older half sister. After Emma died, Samantha became a sort of mother figure to Ian and Fiona. She was two years older than William and Emma. She studied veterinary medicine at the University of Bristol, where she attended on an academic scholarship at the same time Colin attended Oxford. There were rumors she and Colin were an item, but nothing ever came of it. Samantha, called Sam by the Athy family, was a bright, lovely woman a little on the masculine side but very much a lady. Unlike her sister, Sam had a full head of dark chestnut hair with auburn highlights that cascaded down her back in wild, uncontrollable curls. Her skin was pale and kissed by many freckles, making her seem much younger than she really was. She stood five foot eight and was fit and athletic in stature. She and Emma were both runners in school, and between the two of them, they had won many blue ribbons. Their long legs and slight builds helped them to excel in sports, and they competed in national and European track and field events in Ireland as well as all over the EU. Her eyes were a striking, very light green, and she had full red lips but never wore a drop of makeup. William had always marveled at the pure, humble, kind, and modest attitudes of his dear wife and sister-in-law, two women who had no idea how truly beautiful they were.

Sam had always had a love for animals, so no one was surprised when she came home from England a doctor of veterinary medicine. She opened a practice in Clonmel, a short distance from the Nire Valley, where she also owned a river cottage one kilometer from William and the kids.

"Well, we should get going if we don't want to miss Grace's bangers and mash!" Sam said.

"Amen to that, Sam! See ya tomorrow, Lady Lil," William said, as he patted his prize mare, Lily of the Valley. "You heal quick now, gorgeous." With that, Will stood, opening the stall door for Samantha, and they both exited and made their way out of the stables to their cars.

By the time Will and Samantha arrived at Pat and Grace Athy's, there were several cars parked outside. Their house was large but modest and kept very tidy. It was painted much like the family stables and pub, bright white with black trim and green doors and shutters. The lawn was mowed, edged, and manicured, and flowers were planted in great abundance in beds and brightly painted ceramic pots. The Athys took great pride in keeping their home and businesses tidy and well appointed.

"Who in God's name do all these cars belong to?" William asked as he and Sam made their way down the long driveway on foot.

"Guess we'll find out!" said Samantha.

Before William could even reach for the handle, the front door to his parents' home swung open wide, and there stood Colin Wohl with a tall drink in his hand, adorned in a frilly apron.

"Hellooo there, you two! Welcome to Gracie's Sunday feast!" cried Colin as he hugged both William and Samantha on their way in.

"Uhh, hello?" said Samantha in the form of a question.

"Hello. Glad you two are finally here. Rough time down at the OK Corral?" Colin smirked.

"Uh . . . great to be here. Question is, what are *you* doing here, Sire?" replied William as he glared, wide-eyed, at Colin.

"Here to see your lovely mum, whom I ran into at the farmers market, ole chap. She invited me for Sunday dinner. I could not refuse. It's been a long while since I had a taste of Mrs. A's bangers and mash! Mmmm," Colin said as he grabbed his stomach and headed back toward the kitchen. "Then, she immediately put me to work! Brought a few friends along—yer mum said it was okay!" Colin shouted over his shoulder as he hurried back to the cutting board where he had been chopping mint leaves for mojitos.

"Okaaay," said William, shaking his head and removing his coat as he slowly walked, looking at the crowd of people.

There, in his parents' living room, sat Larry Davis the production manager and his two colleagues, all in a row on the couch. They looked like birds on a wire! William laughed to himself at the sight of them. In his mother's chair sat Lillie Adams, Larry's present assistant. There were ten or eleven others scattered around the room, standing by the fireplace and sitting at his father's makeshift bar, in the corner. William nodded and made his way to the kitchen with Samantha on his heels.

"Who are all these people, Will?" asked Samantha.

"Colin's production company," answered William.

"What are they doin' *here?*" Samantha pressed further.

"They are—" But before William could finish, Colin chimed in.

"They are here to produce a movie in the Nire Valley, Sam. And Will is our technical expert and advisor!" said Colin enthusiastically.

"I *never* agreed to that, Colin. I said I'd th—" said William before Colin again interrupted.

"You would *think* about it. I know, I know. Well, you *have* to do it. We have already arranged for you to have help with your kids and jobs, " Colin said firmly.

"*You what?!*" William shouted angrily.

Colin continued. "We arranged for—"

"How dare you presume to *arrange* anything regarding *my* children, Colin! You had *no* right to do that without my permission!" William snapped.

"Will, hear me out before you shoot me down," Colin pleaded.

"Willie, at least *listen* to what Colin has to say," piped Grace Athy over her shoulder as she stirred something in a pot on the stove.

"Mum, seriously. You don't un—"

It was then that William saw her, standing next to his mother: Jennifer Sweeney, also adorned in an apron, hard at work chopping something up on a cutting board. She turned briefly to smile at William and Samantha. William stopped midsentence when he saw the beautiful woman he had met two days earlier at his father's pub. He tried to regain his composure but fumbled with his words. William was smitten.

"Uh, Mum . . . uh, you don't understand . . . I . . . ." William struggled.

"What don't I understand, Willie? Colin wants to make a movie here, in the Nire Valley. And he wants *you* to be the technical advisor so they get everyt'ing right! And they're willin' to pay you over a hundred thousand euro for yer advisin'! I think I understand just fine, son," Grace replied boldly.

Grace Athy was a fifty-seven-year-old Irish-Scottish woman from Belfast, Northern Ireland. Her family moved to Clonmel when Grace was a teenager. She attended Tipperary Secondary School, where she met Patrick. They married young and had six sons, two of whom were still living in the Nire. The others were scattered throughout the British Isles: one was in Dublin, one in Edinburgh, Scotland, and the other two were in England. Grace looked young for her age and kept herself in great shape, helping her family with both the horse breeding and pub-keeping businesses. She also took care of her six grandchildren regularly. Her sandy, reddish blonde hair was kept tidy in a bun, and her eyes were deep green with a hint of blue. Grace was a slight woman, only

5'3" and weighed only 110 lbs. soaking wet. Her stature mattered not, however. Grace Elizabeth Athy was a force to be reckoned with who kept six sons and a feisty husband in line with little problem! Her cooking was renowned all over the region and had actually been featured in the *Cuisines of Ireland* magazine, which was published globally. The entire Athy house was filled with the aroma of browning sausage, vegetables, and seasoning, making everyone's mouth water in anticipation. Their home was warm, inviting, and decorated elegantly yet modestly. All the wood furniture was handmade by Patrick Athy in rich cherry and cedar tones. The couches and chairs in the living room were cream colored, with brightly colored throw pillows scattered about. The polished, dark, solid wood floors were stunning and made the entire home look like a picture from a home and garden ad. White storm shutters framed every window, and pure-Aran-wool area rugs added just the perfect splash of color and texture to their lovely, cozy family home.

"You understand *perfectly*, Mrs. A. Perfectly!" Colin responded as he raised his eyebrows at William.

"Yes, but I haven't decided yet, Mum. And you hush, Sire!" snapped William.

"Willie, what else do you need to t'ink about? Miss Sweeney and I will help with the wee ones," said Grace.

"Wait. What? Who?" William said as he held up his hand.

Grace continued, "Miss Sweeney. You've met, right?" Grace asked as she looked back and forth between William and Jennifer.

"Yes, ma'am, we met down at the pub," Jennifer replied with a half-smile.

"Please, call me Grace, love," Grace said as she smiled back and winked at Jennifer.

"Yes, we've met," William said as he felt himself flush.

"Good. So like I was sayin', Miss Sweeney and—" Grace started.

"Please, call me Jenn," Jennifer interrupted.

"Jenn and I will help you with the wee ones, Willie," said Grace as she returned to her pot stirring.

"Mum, even if I did agree to this and I *haven't*, what do you mean 'help'?" William asked.

Grace explained, "We would have them with us while you were doin' yer advisin'. We would make sure they were fed, doin' their home studies, and such. Jenn has volunteered to take them to school and pick them up . . . She even—"

"Wait a minute!" exclaimed William. "I don't even *know* Jenn . . . no offense," William said with a nod toward Jenn.

"I *know* Jenn, Will," Colin piped in. "I have known her for over seven years now. She is a wonderful person who loves kids and—"

William interrupted, "I'm sure she is lovely, but *I* don't know her at all. No offense again," said William, again nodding to Jenn.

"That's okay," Jenn said. "Can I say something, please?"

Everyone stopped. Everyone nodded.

"Go ahead, love," said Grace.

"I totally understand William's concerns. I mean, he doesn't know me at all. May I suggest we treat this like I am applying for a job as a . . . as a nanny? William should interview me, ask for references, the whole nine yards," Jenn said while looking at William.

"Whole nine yards?" said Grace.

"That means 'everything possible', Mrs. A," replied Colin.

"Got it," Grace asserted.

"Well, William?" Colin asked.

"Willie, what do ya t'ink, son?" Grace also asked.

Jenn looked at William with those drop-dead gorgeous eyes, searching his face for an answer as well.

"Okay, okay, I will interview Jenn. But I'm not guaranteeing anything yet!" William finally replied.

There was a collective cheer in the kitchen. Then, Grace yelled, "Supper is ready. Let's eat!"

# Chapter Three

## The Interview

William was nervous and sweating profusely as he waited for Jenn to show up at Athy's Pub. It was seven thirty on Friday evening, and the pub was already crowded with locals who just got paid. William told himself, "This is a *job* interview, *not* a date," as he watched the front door attentively and checked his cell phone clock every few seconds. *Why did Jenn ask to meet at the pub, at seven thirty, on a Friday night?* William wondered. But all the questions and wondering ceased when she appeared in the doorway at seven forty-five. William's heart pounded in his chest as he gazed upon the sheer perfection of this beautiful woman. As she walked toward him, she flashed that smile again and William felt himself flush all over.

"Hi, sorry I'm late, William, there was traffic in Clonmel," Jenn said as she leaned over to give William a peck on both cheeks.

"Oh, yer late? I lost track of time . . . hah," William said as awkwardly as a teenager on a first date. "Please, call me Will," he continued, clearing his throat nervously.

"Okay, Will," Jenn said with a smile.

As she gazed back into Will's eyes, Jenn noticed just how very handsome this man was. He had large, very light-blue eyes that seemed to shine no matter how the room was lit, and an absolutely gorgeous face that held most women captivated. His hair was sandy blond with a hint of red, like his mother's. He stood 6'1" and had an athletic, strong build with broad shoulders like his father's. He also looked younger than his age of thirty-three, a family blessing. Jenn had also noticed this man had no idea just how beautiful he was as he wore his humility on his sleeve as well. Grace had told Jenn a little bit of her middle son's history: married once to the love of his life and childhood sweetheart, widower of four years, devoted father of two amazing children, earned his degree in business, only had a few dates in four years but had no real interest in any of the women she and Samantha had introduced to him. The attraction was there. He seemed to like Jenn, and Jenn was utterly speechless most of the time when Will was present. But tonight was all about the *job* interview. So Jenn ordered a pint of Guinness, much to William's surprise and delight, and the two began the interview.

Will pulled from his coat pocket a folded sheet of paper. He unfolded it and placed it on the table in front of him.

"I jotted down a few questions to ask you. I hope that's okay?" said Will, as he took a long sip of his beer.

"That's fine, no worries," replied Jenn. "But, can I ask . . . what is that mark on your left forearm? It looks almost like a horse's head!"

"Oh, I'm not worried and this? It is just a birthmark . . . had it all me life long." Will smirked.

"It's an expression," Jenn replied, smiling.

"Oh, okay. So let's get this over with," Will said a bit too loudly.

"Sure. Okay!" Jenn replied, just as loud.

"Sheesh, these two are like two middle school kids that are talking to the opposite sex for the very first time," whispered Larry Davis to Colin Wohl as they sat at a corner booth, watching the "job interview" unfold. Larry's cell phone rang out loud and they both thought they were caught, but neither Will nor Jenn even looked away from the other.

"Helloooo," Larry whispered. "No, darling, no news yet . . . I will call you just as soon as I know anything . . . I know, I know. You are waiting with breath that is bated! Kisses back. Buh-bye." Larry hung up and sighed.

"That was Lillie," Larry said.

"I thought she was just your assistant, Larry!" said Colin, with one eyebrow raised.

"She *is* my assistant. And, as of yesterday, my fiancée!" Larry said with a huge exhale.

"Well, congrats, Larry. I am very happy for you both," Colin said. "Let's order two more pints, chap!" and with that, Colin turned to spy on the job interview in progress, only to find two empty barstools and two empty Guinness pints sitting on the table.

"What is it, Colin?" asked Larry.

"We've been duped," whined Colin. "They're gone."

William and Jenn were laughing out loud as they sped off in Will's Range Rover. "Those two couldn't spy their way out of a paper bag!" laughed Will.

"They were a bit obvious!" Jenn said, laughing.

"Are you hungry? I know a great place in Clonmel. Em and I used to g—" Will said but stopped himself. "I'm sorry, Jenn. I didn't mean to mention . . ." said Will apologetically.

"Will, there's no need to apologize at all. I am so sorry for your loss. It must have been so hard," Jenn said sympathetically.

"It was . . . still is," Will replied.

"I'm sure it is," Jenn said as she rested her hand on Will's shoulder.

"Hey, let's go get some fish and chips. I know a great place in Clonmel!" William said, with a half-smile.

"Sounds great, but what about the interview?"

"What interview? I looked at your references, you got the job! Besides, my mum likes you!" said Will.

"Does that mean you will be our advisor for the movie, Will?" asked Jenn.

As he looked at Jenn sitting next to him in the Rover, William knew he was in trouble. He had only known this woman for a short time, and already, he wanted to spend more time with her. A lot more time with her.

"I suppose it does, Miss Sweeney!" Will smirked as he turned the Rover into the Chipper's Fish-n-Chips parking lot.

"That's great, Will!" Jenn grinned.

"You say that now, but will you still think it's great when my kids are driving you crazy? By the way, I'm curious, what is your job title?" asked Will.

"Oh, I'm not worried about your kids at all. I babysat my siblings a lot when I was younger. My job title? I guess *you* would call me the coffee girl?"

## Chapter Four

### Let's Make a Movie

Colin Wohl was more than happy to hear that William Athy was now on Star Gaze Production Company's payroll as technical advisor. Will put up a good fight, but ultimately, he was no match for the Divine Miss Jenn, as Colin called her. Production would start in six weeks, now that a team had finally been assembled and completed with William.

"So what exactly is this movie about, and what's the title, sire?" asked William as he drove Colin, Jenn, Larry, Lillie, and himself to the main site for the film, Jarvis Ranch. A spectacular setting with its green, rolling hills, Jarvis was a working ranch. The owners Roy and Sue Jarvis were hard-working, salt-of-the-earth kind of people, generous to a fault. They had agreed to let Star Gaze use their property and gave them permission to film a movie on location anywhere on their ten thousand acres the production company wanted. The Jarvises were good people but not stupid. Their lawyers negotiated a fair price with Star Gaze for the use of the ranch.

"I made a copy of the script for ya, Will. It is a story set in the late thirteenth century about an Irish family who settled here in the Nire Valley," explained Colin.

"Hmm. Sounds interesting to me, but why would anyone else care about an ancient, fictional Irish family?" Will snickered.

"Well, the family is not fictional. The writer actually has records and proof that this family indeed existed and lived right here, in the Nire," replied Colin.

"Really? Well, I know everyone in these parts, and I've never heard of . . . uh, what is the name of this family?" Will challenged.

"Athy. And that is the author's name as well," Colin replied.

"What do ya mean Athy? That's my na—" Will started and then stopped midsentence, jaw dropped, eyes as big as saucers.

"Will, this movie is about your family, the Athy clan. And the author is someone near and dear to you. The author is your father!" Colin explained.

"What are ya talkin' about, Sire? My da hasn't said a word about this to me!" exclaimed Will, shaking his head.

"Will, your da is the one who sent the story to *us!*" replied Colin.

William, stunned into silence, pulled his Range Rover up to the Jarvis horse stable, and all four passengers and driver piled out, looking around purposefully as they walked up the hill behind the stables. Roy and Sue Jarvis, along with their four children and six ranch hands, were waiting at the top, under a shade tree.

"Hello, welcome!" shouted Roy, with a wave. "Welcome to our family ranch," Roy repeated as the Star Gaze crew made it to the top of the hill.

"This place is amazing, Mr. Jarvis," said Larry.

"Thank you very much, we think so! Please, call me Roy," replied Roy Jarvis.

Just then, two passenger vans pulled up next to Will's Rover, and a dozen people piled out of each van.

"Crew," said Larry.

Roy welcomed the crew to the top of the hill and then started his spiel. Earlier, Colin had arranged for the Jarvis family to take the team from Star Gaze on a tour of their ranch. Waiting on the dirt road thirty meters from the shade tree were four well-used convertible Jeeps, eight four-wheelers, and an old International Scout.

"My kids will drive the Jeeps. You all can figure out who will ride where among yourselves. There is bottled water in the stables—help yourselves.

We will all meet back here in thirty minutes. Ladies, there are no toilets where we are goin', so feel free to use the facilities in the stables or barn. Oh, and the Scout is mine!" shouted Roy so everyone could hear him.

Everyone scrambled to get water, use the toilets, and grab a means of transportation. Thirty minutes later, with Roy leading the pack up the road, there were three accidents involving four-wheelers! So Roy and his kids had to give a twenty-minute lecture on how to use all-terrain vehicles to the Star Gaze Production Company.

Twenty minutes after that, with a few crew members bandaged up, they were on their way to the first site, where they would begin filming: the Meadow. This place reminded Larry of the Hidden Valley Ranch salad dressing commercials—an absolutely stunning three-hundred-acre meadow surrounded by magnificent trees, with the Nire River snaking along its edge.

Roy stopped his Scout alongside the river and motioned to everyone to stop as well. As they all gathered and parked their vehicles, not one person made a peep, not even as they all disembarked from their various vehicles. The unspoiled beauty of this place left them all speechless— green, rolling hills, wildflowers adorning the meadow sporadically and abundantly. The Nire River was crystal clear and flowing slowly through this heaven on earth and lent a blue contrast to this magnificent green paradise. Pine trees and several redwoods had been planted along the southern hillsides, brought all the way from America, planted on the ranch and all over Ireland in the nineteenth century. Their presence added even more majesty to the scenery as they stood in regal dominance over the rest of the vegetation. Black-faced sheep were grazing in the meadow along the river, as well as several cows, horses, and even a dozen peacocks strutted about. The meadow air was filled with the sweet fragrance of honeysuckle and gorse, which caused several to breathe in deeply as they scanned their amazing surroundings.

The silence was suddenly broken by the sound of someone walking through the forest area, only fifty meters away from the convoy. That area was so densely wooded nobody could see who it was.

"More than likely a deer," said Roy.

Just then, Lillie pointed and yelled, "There's something over there, at the edge of the woods, Roy!"

Roy walked toward where Lillie was pointing. William, Colin, and two of Roy's sons followed. They reached the edge of the forest and saw it. A spear was stuck into the ground, tip up, with a piece of parchment paper hanging off the point. Roy and Will approached the spear, looking around intently for whoever left it. They saw no one. Roy removed the paper, read it, and handed it to Will. By this time, most everyone else in their party was gathered around Will and Roy.

"What is it?" a crew member asked.

"What does it say?" asked Jenn.

"It's in Gaelic," Will said. "It says,

> Beware agus aire a thabhairt
> ó ghaoth na hÉireann.
> Deireadh seo anois
> sula dtosaíonn sé."

Translated:

> Beware and take heed
> from the Irish wind.
> End this now
> before it begins.

"What do ya make of it, William?" asked Roy.

"Sounds like a familiar warnin' to me, Roy," replied Will.

"More than likely kids, looking to have a little fun and mess with the Americans," Colin piped in.

"I'd have to agree with Colin," said Roy.

Will nodded and shrugged his shoulders. But to be on the safe side, he, Roy, and Roy's sons hiked through the surrounding woods to look for anything else suspicious. After an hour and a half, they emerged with news they found nothing out of the ordinary and that no one should worry. Just kids.

The business of moviemaking started after the all-clear. The entire production team scoured the area, measuring, taking photos, and writing down every little detail.

As everyone was busy doing their assigned duties, Jenn and Will had stolen away for a walk by the river. It was a beautiful day, mostly sunny with the occasional rain shower that is expected in Ireland. As they walked, Jenn lifted her head upward to catch the sun on her face. Will slowed and watched her as she smiled at the simple pleasure of the sunlight on her face. William was staring now. The breeze picked up and blew Jenn's light, glistening hair around. The light blouse she was wearing slipped off her left shoulder to expose her bare skin. She licked her bottom lip to moisten it and turned her head to look back at Will, flashing her brilliant blue-green eyes at him with a smile. It was almost too much for Will to take. He gently grabbed Jenn by her wrist and drew her into him. She gazed into his deep blue eyes and surrendered to a warm, wet kiss on her full lips.

Abruptly, a car horn sounded.

"Time to head out, people!" yelled Larry.

Will and Jenn looked at each other and laughed.

"Well, nothing like a horn blast to jolt ya back to reality, eh, Jenn?" Will said as the two turned and walked back to the gathering.

As the entire crew and the Jarvis family congregated, Roy Jarvis began another spiel.

"Well, I think that was a very productive first day. You all got the lay of the land and a good idea of the terrain here at Jarvis Ranch. Sue and I would like to thank you all for respecting our land and leaving everything as you found it. There are dumpsters back at the stables to use as you wish. Keeping this place clean is a priority for us. And don't ya worry none about the message that was left at the edge of the woods. It seems we have a prankster or pranksters stirring up trouble," said Roy.

"Much ado about nuthin'!" Sue Jarvis chimed in.

And with that, the crowd dispersed, and everyone mounted their various vehicles and headed for the stables, except Roy Jarvis, Sue Jarvis, Colin Wohl, Larry Davis, Lillie Adams, Jenn Sweeney, and William Athy. The group stood in silence for several moments, then Roy finally spoke: "Not sure what that message on a spear was about, but that was not the act of a bunch of kids. That spear is an ancient weapon, used in battle to defend clan land. Whoever left it there also knows history because the Gaelic message they left I've seen before."

"The burial site on Waterford Peak," William said, squinting his eyes in thought.

"What? What are you talkin' about, Will?" asked Colin.

"There are ancient grave sites all over these parts. But there is one that has that exact Gaelic inscription on a large stone marker at Waterford Peak. It's about five kilometers south of here," William explained.

"Yes, I vaguely remember that from our childhood. Let's go have a look, Will," replied Colin.

"Wait. Is that a good idea? I mean is it safe?" asked Larry.

"I think it will be fine. We just need to keep our eyes and ears open," Roy answered.

And with that, they all piled into their rides and headed south, to Waterford Peak.

Minutes later, they were all standing at the foot of Waterford Peak.

"This place gives me the creeps," Lillie said as she crossed her arms in front of her chest with a shiver.

"There was a major battle fought here several hundred years ago. Hundreds of men died," Will explained.

"There's the stone, up there." Roy pointed.

They all hiked up to the top of the peak. At the back entrance to what was an ancient graveyard for the Gaelic people stood an enormous stone, sitting perfectly upright. It measured over fifteen feet high and eight feet wide and four feet thick. It had been placed there centuries ago at the back of the burial ground. Chiseled upon the polished face of the massive stone that seemed to stand guard over the dead buried in the hallowed ground before it were these words in Gaelic:

An talamh, bhuaigh muid
ar chostas den sórt sin.
Thit an oiread sin
An oiread sin caillte.
Caitheann na carraigeacha amach
le pian searbh.
Bhuaigh cathanna
gan aon ghaois a fuarthas.
Cuireadh an spear cogaidh
Ar an talamh coisithe.
Creeps sa bhás
gan fuaim.
Beware agus aire a thabhairt
ó ghaoth na hÉireann.
Deireadh seo anois
sula dtosaíonn sé.

Translated:

The land, we won

at such a cost.
So many fell
So many lost.
The rocks cry out
with bitter pain.
Battles won
no wisdom gained.
The war spear planted
on hallowed ground
creeps in death
without a sound.
Beware and take heed
from the Irish wind.
End this now
before it begins.

# Chapter Five

## The Cast

Marie Maxwell boarded the private jet that was parked in the private hangar at LAX. Following close behind her were three members of her usual fifty-person entourage. Zach Smith was already seated in the Learjet, reclined in his seat and on his fourth rum and Coke.

"Well, there she is! The Madonna herself! Just the Three Amigos today? Where's your other forty-seven ass-kissers? Pardon my French. Ha!" slurred Zach as he waved his left hand that had his drink in it, spilling half in his lap.

"Oh, great," snapped Marie. "They put us on the *same* plane?"

"Yup! Aren't you *thrilled*, baby? You know you always wanted to join the mile high club!" Zach replied, moving his eyebrows up and down.

"You're disgusting! How many of those have you had already?" Marie said, motioning to the half-empty drink in Zach's hand.

"Not nearly enough!" Zach spat back.

Marie found two seats next to each other, four rows in front of Zach and proceeded to unpack her carry-on bags, placing the contents carefully about her seating area.

"Eye mask, lip balm, lotion, mints, face mister, latest issue of *Elle* and *Vogue*, slippers, cashmere blanket, chew toy for Princess Di, down travel pillow, and a bottle of Xanax. Voila!" said Marie as she sat an animal carrier on the seat next to hers.

"How's my little sweet baby princess?" chirped Marie in a syrupy-sweet baby voice.

"Dear god! You brought that walking pain in the ass with you? Are you f-ing nuts?!" yelled Zach as he attempted to stand up but fell back into his seat.

"Of course I brought her. She's my baby," Marie replied, eyes squinted in disgust.

"Hope she doesn't 'accidentally' disappear while you're getting your beauty sleep, Madonna!" Zach said in his best slithery, Captain Jack Sparrow voice.

"Zach! Shut up, you washed-up, irrelevant drunk!" Marie snapped back.

"Ouch! That hurt. I'm no drunk, Madonna!" Zach replied as he waved at the flight attendant and pointed at his now-empty glass.

"Darling, I'm E-M-P-T-I-E!" he slurred, his eyelids beginning to blink slower.

"What a moron," Marie said under her breath.

"I heard that, Madonna!" Zach said as he laid his head back and promptly began to snore loudly.

"I meant for you to, jackass!" Marie replied.

But Zach had already passed out. The flight attendant hurried down the aisle with another drink in her hand.

"Oh, yeah. That's a greeeat idea. Let's keep giving the obnoxious, already polluted drunk *more drinks*!" Marie snapped loudly.

The flight attendant shot her an angry look as she set the drink down in front of Zach. She then proceeded to buckle his seat belt for him and took the drink away after closing his tray table abruptly, shooting Marie another look of disdain.

"Yeah, give *me* attitude, sweetheart! Brilliant," Marie seethed.

The Three Amigos surrounded Marie, fluffing her pillow, unfolding her blanket, taking Princess Di out of her carrier, and gently putting her onto a down pillow on the seat next to her. One poured her a glass of champagne and opened her pill bottle to retrieve three Xanax, setting them all on her tray table. Marie downed the pills and the champagne. The other amigo put a blanket over the toy poodle and then the three of them retreated to the back of the plane.

"Good evening, ladies and gentlemen, this is your captain, Dan Scott. We will be towed out of the hangar here in just a few minutes. Then, we will begin our preflight checks. Estimated time of departure is 19:30. We expect a smooth flight tonight to JFK and then, on to Dublin, Ireland. If you need anything, don't hesitate to ask one of our top-notch flight attendants, who are happy to meet your every need. So sit back, relax, we will be airborne in approximately twenty minutes."

"*Ha!* Top-notch, my ass," mumbled Marie. She was interrupted by another announcement.

"Please turn your attention to the flight attendants who will now go over the safety instructions."

Before another word was spoken, Marie was out.

In the back of the Learjet sat five people: the Three Amigos, as Zach Smith called them, were Marie's sister, LeAnn Levitz, and two of Marie's old friends from high school, Jenna Brink and Benjamin Willits. Across the aisle from LeAnn sat Matt Roberts, Zach's personal assistant, and Cassie Lidster, Zach's massage therapist.

Across the airport, at the LAX International Concourse, sat the rest of the main cast for Star Gaze Productions' new film, *The Nire*, twelve actors and actresses all reading over their scripts as they waited to board their flight to Dublin—eight men and four women.

| Angus McCulloch | Rita McShera |
| Douglas Fairchild | Molly Taggart |

| | |
|---|---|
| Rodney Jones | Virginia Sloan |
| Mark Eubanks | Christine Nicolls |
| Lawrence Whittaker | |
| Charles Emerson | |
| Sean Ryan | |
| Lee O'Neal | |

Angus McCulloch, Douglas Fairchild, Sean Ryan, Rita McShera, and Molly Taggart were all well-known, accomplished, A-list actors with Irish ancestry. The others were also Ireland-born, well-known character actors, respected and admired in Hollywood and the world, except for Lawrence Whittaker, a native Californian with distant Irish relations, and Angus McCulloch, who was born in Scotland to a Scottish father and Irish mother.

Colin Wohl and Larry Davis had moved mountains to assemble this mega-cast, and there was a lot riding on *The Nire*'s success. Colin and Larry knew this and were very much aware that this film could make or break Star Gaze Productions. They had arranged for the main cast to be flown first-class together. The purpose of this was to forge a relationship among these twelve who were playing the supporting roles of the Clan Athy—a family.

In order to pull this enormous task off, Larry had pulled some major strings in Hollywood. He spent the better part of a year drumming up enthusiasm and support for the Nire project, and he believed he had a diamond in the rough. He believed in Patrick Athy and his family's amazing true story. Word of mouth is a powerful tool in Hollywood, and when that word falls upon the right ears, anything can happen. And it did. Larry and Colin were able to secure a financial backer that was all in to make sure this movie was made, and they had to make sure it was a wise investment by doing everything they could to make *The Nire* a smashing success.

Angus McCulloch believed in the script as well. And after reading it nonstop during the flight to Dublin, he flung it in the air and yelled, "Holy crap, people! Now, this is a *movie!*" The rest of the cast hushed him, as they were still reading it enthusiastically. Angus was a sixty-two-year-old Scottish-Irish actor from Edinburgh. He was a mountain of a man, 6'4" and 250 pounds with a full red shock of hair and beard with gray streaking throughout. He drank a lot, he cursed a lot but was a kind, generous soul who loved his craft. He had played in numerous movies, several of which were opposite major, big-league Hollywood stars. He had one Oscar and two Golden Globes under his belt for supporting actor roles.

"Doug, whattaya think?" asked Angus.

"What do I think? I think this has the potential to be the *Braveheart* of this decade!" replied Douglas Fairchild as he finally finished reading *The Nire*'s script and removed his reading glasses.

"Whoa! That is a bold statement, Doug. But I can't say I disagree!" Angus said as he took the last sip of his Jameson over ice and then said, "I think it has the potential to be a classic, indeed."

The Learjet carrying the two lead actors of *The Nire* touched down at Dublin International Airport at one o'clock in the afternoon. Marie Maxwell had been undergoing an in-flight makeover for the better part of two hours. The Three Amigos had erased the signs of her Xanax-induced coma and were packing up all the "necessities" of life for a starlet, including her pampered poodle, Lady Di. Marie was hydrating herself with a liter of French mineral water and popping "wake up" pills as they taxied toward two brand-new Range Rovers that were waiting to shuttle her, Zach, and their entourages to their hotel for the night.

Zach Smith had already had two Bloody Marys and was puffing on his e-cig as he finished reading *The Nire*'s script. He was unshaven, with a pair of sunglasses on, his clothes wrinkled and smelling like stale whiskey. His assistant, Matt Roberts, handed him a wet nap and a piece of gum as the Learjet came to a stop next to the two waiting Range Rovers.

"Good to go?" Zach muttered in a hoarse voice.

"Good to go, boss," Matt answered.

Larry Davis and Lillie Adams were the welcoming committee for Marie and Zach's arrival. As the two stars and their entourages departed the plane, Marie asked, "Where's the press? Where are all our fans?"

Larry simply answered, "Welcome to Ireland."

Angus McCulloch was startled awake by the announcement that they were on their final approach into Dublin International. He shook off the fatigue and headed for the bathroom. After splashing his face with water and running his fingers through his long hair, he looked in the mirror and said, "Here we go, lad."

The twelve cast members for *The Nire* departed the Aer Lingus plane together. As they left the secured area, they were delighted to see a crowd of people numbering close to two hundred welcoming them and snapping pictures. There were also two men holding signs that said, "Star Gaze Productions," who motioned to the group to follow them. After signing a few autographs and taking a few selfies with their fans, the group headed to their waiting limousines, two stretch Cadillac Escalades.

"Welcome to Dublin!" one of the drivers said enthusiastically.

The group split into two groups of six and were soon headed for their hotel, the Belvedere, in the center of downtown Dublin. They again were met with a large crowd outside the front of the Belvedere, and again they stopped to let fans take pictures and to sign autographs. The press were also on hand to greet the twelve megastars of *The Nire*, with flashes from their cameras and questions galore. But the twelve were asked to keep any and all information about the movie hush-hush, partly because Larry Davis felt it brought more intrigue to the Nire project and partly because the press had a tendency to skew everything said by the famous. This was mostly true of Zach Smith, who arrived as the last of the twelve entered the Belvedere.

"Zach, what is this movie about? Are you looking forward to working with Angus McCulloch? How was rehab? Are you and Marie an item again?" asked several reporters.

"None of your f-ing business. Yes. None of your f-ing business. Hell no!" Zach replied as if he were reading a list. "Get out of the way, you bunch of piranhas!" Zach snapped as he pushed his way through the crowd and disappeared into the hotel.

Marie arrived twenty minutes later, as per her usual fashion of being late, and exited the Range Rover to a crowd of only four reporters and a few leftover fans. She made her driver stop for a decaf fat-free Splenda soy caramel macchiato along the way, which caused a major traffic delay on the busy streets of Dublin, since the only Starbucks along their route was on a main thoroughfare.

"Where is everybody?" snapped Marie to the Three Amigos.

"We were late, so everyone probably thought you were a no-show . . . again," her sister and assistant, LeAnn, replied.

"LeAnn, did I ask *you* for your opinion?" seethed Marie.

"Well, actually, yes," LeAnn answered as they climbed the stairs to the hotel entrance.

As Marie shot LeAnn a look of disdain, she stopped where two reporters were standing, busy on their cell phones.

"Would you like an interview?" Marie cooed.

"Nah, I'm good. Thanks," one reporter replied.

"Already got what I needed," answered the other reporter.

Marie then turned to ask the remaining fans if they would like selfies with her, but they were already walking away as they showed each other their cell phone pictures of Angus McCulloch.

"Well, I never!" snapped Marie as she stormed through the doors of the Hotel Belvedere with the Three Amigos following closely behind her.

---

# Chapter Six

## The Conception

William Athy thought he knew his father, Patrick, but with the new revelation that he had not only written a book and script for a movie and sent both to Colin Wohl, it was a wake-up call that seemed to say he didn't know his da as well as he thought. In the afternoon, before the Friday evening crowd shuffled in, Will sat down with his father and his brother, Pat Jr., at their family pub, Athy's. Pat Jr. was behind the bar, as it was his night to tend. Patrick and William sat next to each other on barstools that were newly refurbished the week before.

"Pour us a pint, Patty," said Patrick to his oldest son. "I have a lot of explaining to do to ya boys."

"That's an understatement if I've ever heard one!" replied William.

Patrick nodded and patted Will on the back.

"So out wit' it, Da!" Pat Jr. said impatiently.

Patrick drew in a deep breath with a half-smile on his face, arose from his barstool, holding his Guinness, and walked toward his office, across the pub, in the front corner of the building.

"Follow me, boys. Bring yer pints!" said Pat over his shoulder.

Pat Jr. motioned to the other bartender and said, "Watch the place. I'll be back in a bit."

William got up and raised his eyebrows to his older brother and said, "This should be good."

The three walked into Patrick's office and shut the door behind them. It was an impressive room furnished with a mahogany desk and chair in one corner, two overstuffed leather chairs and a couch in the opposite corner, and in the middle of the room sat a conference table with twelve chairs. On the walls hung oil paintings of the Irish countryside and several painted portraits of family members, long since gone. There were several bookshelves filled with books and boxes containing ancient manuscripts, all labeled and organized chronologically. In the corner, behind Patrick's desk, sat a large curio cabinet displaying several Athy family heirlooms: a dagger, a swath of cloth that was made with the Athy family tartan woven into it, a chalice, several coins, various pieces of jewelry, a sword with an inscription etched on its blade in Gaelic, and an Athy family Bible believed to have been blessed by Saint Patrick himself in the seventeenth century. On a long side table, next to the curios, there were several framed photographs of Athy family members past and present. On the wall opposite the only door to the office was an enormous picture window that allowed those inside the office to take in the view of the Nire countryside and a beautiful pond that sat just twenty meters away.

"Have a seat, boys," Patrick said while motioning toward the conference table. "Patty, fetch that satchel o'er there on my desk for me, son."

Pat Jr. grabbed the satchel from his father's desk and laid it on the conference table. Patrick went to the large safe that sat upon the floor in a corner of the office, squatted down, dialed in the combination, and opened it. He then reached into the safe and pulled out a large manila envelope that looked stuffed full of whatever its contents were. Patrick carefully laid the envelope on the conference table, pulled a chair out, and sat down. His sons sat across from him, looking ever so curious at the manila envelope and pile of papers that sat on the table before them.

"What is all this, Da?" asked Pat Jr.

"Patience, Patty, patience," replied Patrick. Then, Patrick Athy grabbed his pint of Guinness, raised it, and said, "To the Clan Athy and to Ireland!"

Both sons responded by repeating the customary toast. All three clanked together their glasses, and all three took a long drink simultaneously.

"We have a rich history, boys, filled with stories of battles won and lost, filled with intrigue and mystery," began Patrick. "So much to tell of a family that forged a rich future here in the Nire with their blood, sweat, and tears. This envelope is filled with the personal journal of one of those family members, the patriarch of the thirteenth-century Clan Athy, Thomas William-Patrick Athy," explained Patrick as he rested his hand upon the envelope. "In this envelope is only a small section of the blueprint I used to write both the book, the script, and what is now going to be the movie *The Nire*."

William and Pat Jr. sat spellbound as they watched their father open the envelope and carefully pull out its contents, an ancient-looking leather-bound book.

"This journal is a translated, handwritten copy of the original journal, which is kept in a safety box in the basement of our family home. It was transcribed by the county clerk in 1864. The original journal was partly burned in the 1832 pub fire but saved and stowed away under lock and key by Madeline Athy four generations ago. The journal of Thomas William-Patrick dates back to 1170, when he was approximately thirty years old," explained Patrick.

William carefully picked up the journal, set it down on the table in front of him, and opened it to the first page. There, in the original Gaelic, it said, "This is an account of the life of Thomas William-Patrick Athy, chieftain of the Clan Athy." Below that was a drawing of the Athy family crest and coat of arms, the same coat of arms that hangs in Patrick's office in the form of a large oil painting. Below them both was printed the Athy family motto: "Duetus non Coactus" (May be led, not to be driven).

"Da, why have ya never shown us this before?" said Will as he continued to turn the pages of his ancestor's journal.

"I did show it to ya when ya were younger, Will. Ya looked at it and said, "Dat's cool, Da!" and left in a hurry to meet Emma and Colin somewhere," replied Patrick.

Will thought for a minute and realized his father was right. As a kid, he never thought much about the old journal of some dead guy. But he was paying close attention now.

"Like I said, that copy of Thomas William-Patrick's journal was translated from Gaelic to English in 1864. It had to be an important historical document for the clerk of the county to take the time to copy it into English," Patrick said. "Now, hand me the satchel, Patty." Pat Jr. slid the satchel across the conference table, directly in front of his father. "I made you both a thumb drive containing the entire journal. I want ya both to take them home and read them," said Patrick as he laid the thumb drives on the table. William and Pat Jr. grabbed them and looked at their father in amazement for several seconds.

Then William broke the silence: "Da, I still wanna know why ya didn't tell me ya had written a book and a screenplay! *And* why you said nothin' about talkin' to Colin!"

"I wanna know how he knows what a thumb drive is! I usually have to do all the computer work for ya, Da!" said Pat Jr.

"I didn't want to tell anyone I was writin' a book, boys. I had no idea if it were even good enough for *me* to read!" Patrick replied. "I was scared, I suppose. Scared of being laughed at, scared of being called an old fool," Patrick continued. "But yer mum was the one who sent the script to Colin, Will. She read it and had faith it was worth everyone reading. We didn't even go to a publisher! Yer mum said she trusted Colin to do the right thing. Colin has gotten the book deal finalized and asked me to write a screenplay last year so he could start working on getting a movie made. After he read a rough draft of the book, he was overwhelmed with excitement. And, I had someone do the computer work, Patty. Samantha is a whiz on those darn things!"

"This was all happening for the last *two years*, and ya said nuthin' to me or Pat Jr., Da? Nuthin' about talkin' to my long-lost *best* friend that I haven't seen or talked to in *ten* damn years, Da?" William said angrily.

"Wait. You had *Samantha* doin' yer computer work?" said Patty.

"I'm sorry, boys. Colin asked that we say nuthin' until he made the deals. That way, nobody gets disappointed or embarrassed if things fell through. And yes, Patty, Samantha. But she had no idea about the book or movie.

She simply helped me copy and paste and send documents," Patrick replied.

"Well, I think it was selfish and basically lyin' to keep something like this from Pat Jr. and me, Da! Dun't ya agree, Patty?" asked William.

Pat Jr. had sat down at Patrick's desk and opened his thumb drive on the desktop computer to read his copy of the journal, oblivious to the conversation between his father and brother.

"Pat?" William said again.

"Will, ya need to get o'er yourself, brother. This has the potential to be huge, and you need to get on board!" Pat Jr. said without even looking up from his copy of the journal.

William's jaw dropped. How could his brother, who barely said two words to anyone, suddenly become the pillar of wisdom? It was like someone flipped a switch in him.

"Will, yer bruther's right. I am sorry I didn't tell ya about all this. But I had my reasons, son. Now, we need to get on with it and come together as a family to make sure that this movie is done right. So go home. Read the journal. Then, you will see the importance of getting our family's story on film. It is important to our family and our country to see this through." And with that, Patrick downed the rest of his Guinness and got up from the conference table.

Pat Jr. looked at this watch and also got up to prepare for the busy night ahead, behind the bar. Patrick motioned for his sons to come closer. They moved next to their father, and Patrick put a hand on each of their shoulders. "Boys, I love ya, and I hope I can make ya proud."

"We have been and will always be proud of ya, Da," replied Pat Jr.

Patrick and Pat Jr. then looked at William expectantly.

"I'm proud of ya, even if ya are an old fool!" replied William.

There was silence for a long minute and then all three broke out in laughter.

William lay in bed that night, reading the journal. Without realizing it, he had read until three in the morning. As he closed his laptop and set it on his side table, he was astonished at all that had transpired in the last week. He thought about his father and how he never knew what a talented, insightful man he was until now. He thought about Thomas Athy's journal and was also astonished at the magnitude of the content. *This journey the Athy family has begun will most certainly be an adventure!* thought Will as he fell asleep.

Patrick Athy sat in his basement study, drinking two shots of his one-hundred-year-old brandy from his great-grandfather's Waterford crystal snifter. As he sat, he reflected on the conversation he had had with his sons, William and Patrick Jr., earlier in the afternoon. He hoped that his boys would forgive him and understand his reasons for keeping certain things from them. He stared at his mahogany bookcase that took up the entire east wall of his study. *Behind that bookcase is a story beyond anyone's imagination*, he thought. Patrick arose from his armchair, pulled a book from the bookcase, and opened it to retrieve a key from its hollowed inners. He then walked to the fireplace, where he pulled at the carved stone lion on the hearth. Slowly and quietly, the large mahogany bookcase opened inward, exposing the stone wall and door behind it. He set the book back in its place on the shelf as he walked to the door. Patrick unlocked it and pushed a button that was located on the wall just beside the door. The giant bookcase closed slowly behind him. A motion sensor light came on immediately upon Patrick's entrance and illuminated the long, bare hallway that led to a hatch-like door at the end. As he reached the second door, his cell chirped alive in his cardigan pocket. He retrieved it and said, "Hello, love."

The voice of his beloved Gracie asked, "Where are ya, Pat? I'm freezin' here alone in our bed!"

Patrick beamed and said, "After all these years, ya miss me warmin' yer toes, Gracie?! I'm in the study—be up in a bit, love."

"Okay fer you if ya'd rather spend time with those ole moldy books than me! See ya in a bit, my love," Grace Athy replied. And with that, they both hung up.

Patrick then stopped five meters from the second door, at a fire extinguisher case that was mounted on the wall to the left. He raised a lever on the right side of the case, causing the entire extinguisher case to open. Behind it was a keypad. Patrick typed in a code that unlocked the door then he turned the large wheel mounted on the front and pulled the hatch open. The lights went on as he entered to illuminate a large warehouse-like room, filled with shelves of ancient artifacts of all kinds. Books, maps, art, jewelry, clothing, coins, historical documents, deeds, certificates, marriage licenses, birth certificates and records, death certificates, bills of sale, and more. The shelves were large, over ten meters high and chock-full of various artifacts all incased in sealed, waterproof containers. Patrick strolled to the southernmost corner of the warehouse, where he stood in front of a smaller shelving unit. He reached onto the middle shelf and lifted the lid of a small wooden trunk, causing the entire unit to slide to the right, exposing a staircase. He took the staircase down the equivalent of three flights, where there lied the door to a large vault: the Annals, just 20 meters below the Athy Pub and 100 meters from his study. As with the other rooms in his lair, this one too was illuminated automatically upon Patrick's entrance. The Annals looked like a scene from an adventure movie, another large warehouse-like room with rows and rows of precious art pieces, carefully stacked in between large metal boxes filled with coins of solid gold and silver. There were solid gold crowns, goblets, plates, and assorted items as well, some in sealed containers, some stored in safes along the northern wall. Patrick walked to one of the safes, squatted down, and dialed the combination that opened it. He reached in and pulled out an old wooden box. He then closed the safe and spun its dial to lock it, stood up, and exited the vault. Safely back in his cozy study, Patrick set the old wooden box on his desk and whispered to himself, "It's time to tell them."

Patrick then pulled a document from his desk drawer: a copy of a written study done by Professor M. G. Rohan, chairman of the Irish History Commission. It read:

"Our best authority states that the Irish name Athy, is from the Birminghams of Warwickshire, one of whom came over with Strongbow in 1170. A descendant of his was Richard of the Battles, and a descendant of his was Thomas, who commanded and won the Battle of Atheney and was thereon created Baron Atheney, from which the name Athy. The word, however, is purely Irish from the name of the battlefield Atha-na-riogh, the Ford of the Kings, three kings having been slain at the battle."

This document and many others were proof that the Athy Family were indeed the first noblemen in Ireland, a fact that had deadly consequences for generations of Athys, including the present one.

Chapter Seven

Let's Do This!

William was already awake after his cell phone alarm sounded well over ten minutes ago, but he lay in his bed, pondering the conversation he had the night before with his father and brother. Suddenly, he heard giggling outside his bedroom door, so he closed his eyes to act asleep. "Let's see what those two goofs are up to." Will laughed to himself. Fiona crept in and climbed up on the bed. She put her face close enough to her father's for him to feel and smell her breath.

"Da, do ya want yer Lucky Charms Freeench toast?" Fiona whispered.

William, although awake, remained silent with his eyes closed.

Fiona then put her head on William's chest and said quietly to herself, "He's still breathin'."

(It was all Will could do not to burst out laughing.)

She then made her way up to William's ear, where she again whispered, "Da? Are ya in there? Do you want yer Freeench toast? Better hurry befur Ian eats it!"

At that, William sat straight up and yelled, "Yer always afta me Luckay Charms, Ian!" making Fiona scream and then laugh uncontrollably. William arose from his bed, lifted up his daughter onto his shoulders, and galloped like a horse to the kitchen. As they entered, William stopped abruptly at the sight of Jennifer Sweeney, standing in front of the stove and Ian standing next to her.

"Well, hello there, Princess Fiona! Are you and your horse hungry?" said Jennifer in an animated voice.

"Jenn, what on earth are ya doin' here?" William blurted out as he took Fiona down from his broad shoulders.

"She was at the door, Da!" said Fiona loudly.

"The kids let me in. I hope you don't mind," said Jenn as she couldn't help but glance at Will's bare chest, as he stood there in only pajama bottoms.

"Oh, okay. And now yer makin' us breakfast?" asked Will.

"Ian asked if I wanted to learn how to make Lucky Charms French toast. I couldn't resist!" Jenn answered.

Will excused himself as he rushed back to his bedroom, threw on some jeans and a T-shirt, then ran a brush through his hair. He returned to the kitchen to find his two children and Jenn sitting, waiting for him at the table, which was set for four, with a huge plate of Lucky Charms French toast sitting in the middle. Will felt his heart beating faster as he glanced at Jenn. She was dressed in a white knee-length summer dress that hugged her slender body perfectly. Her hair was put up in a clip with strands of it escaping to fall around her face and neck. Her cheeks were flushed as she stared back at Will from across the table.

"You changed your outfit. You didn't have to do that on my account," Jenn said as she shot him a sultry look and then looked away.

William blushed and cleared his throat, glancing at both of his children, who were staring at him.

"I needed to put a shirt on for dining . . . for breakfast." Will stammered.

"Da, why are yer cheeks so red? Ya feelin' sick?" asked Fiona.

"No, I'm fine, Li'l Sis. Let's eat!" William managed, as he lifted the plate of French toast and held it for Jenn to serve herself. Jenn grabbed a fork and put three pieces on her plate, making a "mmmmm" sound.

"Ya like Lucky Charms French toast, Jenn?" asked Fiona.

"Don't know but it looks delicious!" Jenn said as she again glanced at William, who was watching her every move.

"Da? Da? *Da!*" Fiona cried. "Are ya gonna take some?"

William jolted himself back from his thoughts, hoping no one could read his mind and took four pieces of French toast.

"Oh my . . . this is sinful!" Jenn said, in between bites.

"It is a family favorite," Will said as he winked at his kids.

"Listen, Will, there is a reason I'm here, besides the Lucky Charms French toast. Today is the meet and greet at the Jarvis Ranch. I thought you might need help with the kiddos. The entire cast and crew are meeting to go over the game plan."

"Yes, I know. I'm actually lookin' forward to it," replied Will, with a smile.

"Wow, you've changed your tune, Mr. Athy!" Jenn said with a hint of sarcasm.

"I have. Let's just say I have been persuaded this movie needs to be made," said Will.

"Hmmm. I guess you don't need my help, then," Jenn replied with a fake pouty expression.

"No, no! I could use *your* help any day of the week, Miss Sweeney!" Will said with a wide grin on his face.

"Are you sure? Because I can go," Jenn teased.

"I'm positive!" Will replied.

After everyone had finished breakfast, it was time to take the kids to their Grandma Grace's house on the way to Jarvis Ranch. Jenn escorted Fiona to the guest/kid's bathroom where she helped the eight-year-old clean up and do her hair. William took a quick shower while Ian waited in his dad's room, looking at old family photos of his mother that sat on the dressing table. Will finished and yelled, "Yer turn, son!"

Ian entered the shower and said to Will, "Da, I think it's time ya moved on."

"Huh, what ya say, buddy?" Will managed as he shaved his upper lip.

"I said, I think it's time ya moved on, Da!" Ian said louder.

"Move on? Whatcha mean 'move on'?" Will questioned.

"I think it's time ya found someone, ya know, to date," Ian said carefully.

Will finished shaving, wiped his face, and threw open the shower curtain and said, "Ya do, do ya? Well, now!" Will said as he snapped Ian gently on his legs with a towel as the two broke out in laughter.

After the father and son were dressed, Ian let himself back into Will's room. Ian approached Will, who was standing by his bedroom window, holding a wedding photograph of him and his dear wife, Emma. He heard Ian and quickly wiped tears from his face.

"Are ya all ready, son?" asked Will quietly.

"Yes, Da," said Ian as he took the photograph, set it back on the dresser, and said, "Are *you* ready, Da?"

The two embraced, Will kissed Ian on his forehead and asked, "How'd ya get so grown-up, son?"

The four all met in the family room to gather up coats, coloring books, and various toys to bring with them. Will took one look at Fiona and Froze, jaw opened, eyes widened.

"Sweet Jesus, Mary, and Joseph! Is *that* me daughter?" Will said, sounding astonished.

"Yes, Da. It's me!" Fiona answered as she gently touched her hair. "Jenn made my hair into a Freeeench braid! Isn't it fabilis?"

"I'm sorry. Did you just say 'fabulous'?" Will said as he shot a wide-eyed look at Jenn.

"Sorry, I may use that word from time to time," Jenn confessed.

Will face-palmed himself and rolled his eyes. "Hollywood much, Jenn?" Will said, oozing sarcasm.

"Ya look beautiful, Li'l Sis, absolutely *bea-u-ti-ful*! A word we Irish use from time to time," Will mocked, with a wink.

"She *does* look *bea*-you-ti-*full*!" Jenn said in an exaggerated voice. "That's how we say it in Hollywood!" She winked back.

Will, Jenn, Ian, and Fiona all piled into the Rover and headed off to Grandma Grace's. When they arrived, Grace Athy was in her yard, trimming roses and fussing over flower baskets.

"There's my *beautiful* grandbabies!" Grace yelled with joy, her arms wide opened, awaiting her grandchildren, who were running full steam ahead toward her.

"He-he, me mum taught me vocabulary!" Will teased and brushed his hand over Jenn's arm.

"You're a funny guy, William Athy!" Jenn shot back.

"Hello, everyone! How are ya all doin' this fine mornin'? Good to see ya, Jennifer," Grace said with a nod toward Jenn as she hugged and kissed Ian and Fiona.

"Come 'ere and get a smooch for yerself, Willie, my boy!" Grace said as she reached for her son.

William embraced his dear mother, a hug that lifted her off the ground. "I love ya, Mum!" Will said as he kissed her cheek.

Jenn looked on, and her heart melted. *This man is one in a million*, she thought.

Ten minutes later, Will and Jenn were en route to Jarvis Ranch, cruising down an Irish country road with music blaring as they sang along. William felt utterly happy for the first time in a long while. He reached over and grabbed Jenn's hand, brought it up to his lips, and kissed it, putting a huge smile on her face.

"You are something else, William Athy!" Jenn said as she looked out her window at the Irish countryside. "This place is stunning," she said.

"You're stunning," Will blurted out, which made him blush immediately.

"Haha. Are you blushing? You are, you're *blushing*!" Jenn teased as she held Will's hand ever so tightly.

"Noooo. I'm not!" Will laughed and checked his face in the rear-view mirror. "Okay, okay, maybe I am blushin' just a wee bit," he concurred.

As the two lovebirds pulled into the long driveway of Jarvis Ranch, Will was surprised to see not only several passenger vans but also a large assortment of other vehicles as well: cars, trucks, limousines, catering trucks, trucks pulling trailers, and more. As they pulled into the stable area, they looked out across the once-open field to the right of the stables. It was jam-packed full of trailers, semitrucks, and motor coaches.

"Sweet Lord! Look at that, will ya?" Will said as he nodded toward the trailer city that used to be the Jarvis field.

"LeAnn! I asked you for a latte an hour ago, what *is* the holdup, girl?!" Marie screamed from her vanity room in her huge set-trailer.

"Marie, we are in bum-f Ireland! The closest Starbucks is forty kilometers away!" snapped LeAnn, frustrated with her spoiled sister's whining and demanding attitude.

Marie let out an overexaggerated sigh and rolled her eyes. "What kind of backwoods, hillbilly place is this?" Marie complained as her makeup artist put the finishing touches on her face.

Zach Smith had made quite an entrance at Jarvis Ranch. He had bought a Harley Davidson motorcycle in Dublin and rode it to make the two-hour trek to the Nire. He parked it in the barn and was making himself at home, especially with ladies who were hired as extras. He hadn't been in the Nire an hour when he and a "local lovely," as he called them, were rolling in the hay!

Angus McCulloch had arrived with the other eleven cast members in the same two limos they took from the airport in Dublin. He found his set-trailer and made himself disappear from everything, if only for an hour. Each trailer was set up according to the preferences of the actor. So Angus was pleased to see his trailer had a full-size refrigerator stocked with his favorites: Guinness, Irish ginger ale, Evian bottled water, various cold cuts, cheeses, fresh fruit, and a vegetable tray. He also had a fully stocked bar, where he poured himself a two-shot of Jameson. In the back of the trailer, there was an amazing media room furnished with two recliners, tables, and a huge flat-screen television on the wall, equipped with surround sound. Angus eased back in a recliner and closed his eyes. As he drew in a deep breath, he envisioned himself as Thomas Athy. He let his imagination take over, and soon, he had a clear idea of how he wanted to portray this interesting character.

Roy and Sue Jarvis loved Ireland, but both weren't natives of their beloved island. Roy was actually born in Dallas, Texas, in 1947. His family migrated to Ireland when Roy was ten years old. His mother was born in Galway, Ireland, where her family had a sheep farm. After the Second World War, Roy's father struggled to provide adequately for his family, so Roy's mother's folks offered them the sheep farm, as it was too much for them to handle in their old age. At age thirteen, Roy got a job at a horse ranch near Galway where he thrived as a ranch hand. He adored horses and wasn't afraid of hard work. He met and fell in love with Sue at age eighteen, and the two were married three months later, much to the dismay of the ranch owner and Roy's boss, Sue's father. Sue was an only child, so she inherited her father's ranch as well as his property in the Nire

Valley, where they eventually settled and raised a family of their own. Roy was a tall, thin man with leathery skin and gray hair that was kept in a buzz cut. He was a no-nonsense kind of man who prided himself on being honest and trustworthy. Sue Jarvis was tall, thin and kept her salt-and-pepper hair in a braid that reached all the way down to her waist. She was a striking woman who knew her mind and wasn't afraid to speak it.

Roy and Sue walked out onto the large deck located on the south end of the stables. Sue climbed up into a small bell tower that was at the end of the deck. She began to ring the bell vigorously, calling all hands on deck!

Over a PA system, Larry Davis' voice rang out across the entire ranch: "Good morning, everyone, and welcome to Jarvis Ranch, our home away from home for the next several months! I hope you had a good journey to this beautiful place and that you enjoy this experience of making *The Nire*. Cast, I hope your accommodations are satisfactory, and if there is anything else you need, each of you have been assigned a go-to person, whose sole job is to provide your every need. Now, if you will all join us at the south side of the stables, we will begin our meet and greet! All cast, crew, and Star Gaze staff to the stables! Thanks."

The crowd numbered over two hundred, including all support staff as well as cast, crew and production company members. Everyone needed to be there to get the printed schedule of shoot times and to learn about ranch safety. The script and all other pertinent information had already been sent out via e-mail two weeks prior. Larry and Colin led the meeting, Larry was all business. Colin provided the comic relief and fun, which was "just as important as the business portion of the program," he stated, which made the crowd applaud. Colin had the charisma of a seasoned politician and a wit that drew people to him instantly. Of course, the fact that he was handsome didn't hurt. Colin Wohl stood 6'3" and maintained a healthy weight of 175 lbs. There was no doubt he was Irish, as he had dark red hair, intense green eyes, and was covered in freckles. He maintained his star-athlete physique by running ten kilometers every day, lifting light weights, and eating healthy. The ladies in the crowd of over two hundred were paying close attention as he spoke, and when he shot them all his infamous Prince William smile, there was a collective sigh.

After the meeting, the crowd broke up into smaller groups according to job title. The crew met in the barn to go over the practical aspects of location filming. The cast met in an old ranch-hand dining hall across from the stables to discuss their schedule as well as get fitted for costumes. Each group had assigned a leader to facilitate all meetings.

"Well, that went swimmingly," Larry said as he and Colin walked toward the production-administrative trailer.

"Yes, I agree. I think everyb—" Colin started but was interrupted by a loud commotion coming from the barn where the crew was meeting.

A crew member came running out of the barn and yelled, "Call an ambulance—we have an injured man in here! Hurry, something fell on him!"

As Larry and Colin rushed into the barn, they could see a man lying on the ground with some sort of large contraption next to him.

"What happened?" Larry asked.

Just then, William, Roy, and Sue rushed in. "What on earth? What happened?" Will said.

The crew chief, Ward Haskle, who was attending to the injured man, stood up. "That contraption fell on him, barely missed hitting him on the head but caught his shoulder and knocked him down. I think his arm is broken."

"What the devil! That's my old hand plow! How did it fall on him?" said Roy as he leaned over to check the poor guy lying in obvious pain.

"It fell from up there," Ward replied and pointed up to the hay storage area.

"*Fell?*" Roy said, shooting a look at his wife and Will.

"Yes, it coulda killed him!" Ward said as he returned to tending his crew member.

Roy asked everyone to exit the barn until they could figure out what happened. As the crew vacated, an ambulance team entered.

Roy, Sue, Will, Larry, and Colin all gathered in a far corner of the barn as the injured man was hauled off on a stretcher to the nearest hospital in Clonmel.

"Whatdaya make of it, Roy? Do you usually keep old hand plows up in the hayloft?" asked Will, knowing the answer.

"Hell no! That plow is normally stored in my shed, behind the house. How it got up there, in the loft . . . well, I haven't a clue, Will," Roy replied as he took off his hat and shook his head.

After everyone had left the barn, William climbed up the ladder to the hayloft first, followed by Roy and then Colin. Everyone else went on about their duties for the day.

"You can see here that something was dragged across the floor," Will said, pointing out the drag marks.

"Dragged, or more likely, *pushed*," Roy said, squatting down to get a closer look.

"Yep, somebody did this, all right . . . but why?" asked Colin.

# Chapter Eight

## The "Enlightening"

Patrick Athy was just finishing up some paperwork for the pub from the night before, when William and Pat Jr. entered their father's office, talking about the accident that happened the day before at the Jarvis Ranch and the ensuing police investigation.

"Mornin', boys. Thanks for coming. Whattaya talkin' about?" asked Pat.

"Someone pushed a hand plow off the hayloft and onto a crew member's head yesterday at the Jarvises'!" Pat Jr. replied, sounding worried.

"Patty, I told ya, it missed his head but broke his arm!" Will said, shaking his head.

"Yes, I heard about that last night from Colin. I guess everyone o'er there at the ranch is pretty shaken up, eh?" said Pat.

"Yes, but we're tryin' to keep everyone calm. We don't know nuthin' yet," William said in a reassuring voice.

"'Cept someone tried to kill one er ya crew members with a hand plow!" exclaimed Pat Jr. loudly and sarcastically.

"Well, I hope they get to the bottom of it!" Pat said as he sat down at the conference table and motioned for his sons to join him. Sitting in the middle of the table were scones and fresh coffee, which all three men helped themselves to. And when they had finished eating, sipping their coffee, and chatting, Pat got to the reason they were summoned.

"Okay, boys, let me get to why yer here. First, did ya read the journal?" said Pat.

"Yes, I couldn't stop! Read the whole t'ing, Da," Pat Jr. said proudly.

"Yes, I did too. Quite a character, our great-great-great . . . grandda!" Will said as he poured another cup of coffee.

"Good. Glad you both read the journal, and yes, Thomas Athy was indeed a character!" Pat replied, looking like the cat that ate the canary.

"So . . . why are we here, Da? Is it about Thomas Athy and his journal?" asked Pat Jr.

"Yes, Patty. Partly. I have something to tell ya both, and I needed the pub empty so as to not be interrupted," Pat replied.

"Partly? Whattaya up to now, Da?" pressed Will.

Patrick picked up the wooden box he had brought up from the Annals, set it on his desk in front of him, and opened it. He removed a black velvet pouch and handed it to Pat Jr.

"Open it, Patty," said Patrick.

Pat Jr. untied the strings of the pouch and pulled out a medallion. Both boys examined the medallion closely with obvious curiosity. It was two inches in diameter with two openings in the middle and made entirely of silver. Engraved on its face were the words "Duetus non Coactus" (May be led, not to be driven).

"Okay, Da. What is this, and why are we looking at it?" asked Will snidely.

"That, son, is a chieftain medallion—a Clan Athy chieftain medallion, to be exact," replied Patrick.

"Aaand?" pushed Will.

"Boys, that is *my* Clan Athy chieftain medallion. Your father is the chieftain of the Athy clan. My father was before me and his father before him. That medallion is over a thousand years old. It signifies that the one in possession of it is indeed the leader and chieftain of Clan Athy, that being

_____

me," Patrick said as he held out his hand and motioned for Pat Jr. to hand him the medallion.

"I dun't get it, Da . . . What are ya tryin' to tell us . . . yer some clan big shot? Okay . . . good fer you . . . what is the big deal? Clans are not exactly relevant today," said Pat Jr. as he shrugged and glanced at William.

"I agree wit' Patty, Da. What is the big deal about an old medallion and a title? I mean, it's kinda intriguing on a historical level, but why all the mystery and why haven't ya told yer sons?" Will questioned, with a hint of anger still in his voice.

"William, finish yer coffee, and both of ya, follow me." And with that, Pat got up from his chair and walked over to the bookcase, removing the hollowed-out book that held a key. He then pulled the lion statue, activating the bookcase to open, revealing the door behind it.

"Sweet Jesus, Mary, and Joseph! What the hell is happenin'?!" Will shouted and jumped from his chair to his feet abruptly, knocking over his chair and spilling the last of his coffee on his chest.

At the same time, Pat Jr. sat motionless at the conference table, mouth opened and eyes as wide as saucers. "What just happened?" was all Pat Jr. could manage to get out.

"Boys, I have somethin' to show ya. Follow me and watch yer steps!" Patrick said as he disappeared behind the bookcase.

Will and Pat Jr. looked at each other in utter disbelief and then bolted toward the bookcase opening, Will getting there first to edge out his brother.

As they followed their father through the door, all the boys could say was "Holy crap! Sweet Lord! I dun't belieeeeeve this!" and "How can this be?"

Patrick stopped at a fire extinguisher that hung on the wall and turned a lever, which exposed the keypad. William and Pat Jr. shook their heads and glanced at one another.

"Okay, boys, welcome to the Annals," Patrick said quietly as he opened the door and the light went on in the large warehouse.

William and Pat Jr. walked into the Annals with eyes wide and mouths opened. They moved through the giant warehouse silently, looking in utter disbelief at all that was stored on the shelves. A long ten minutes went by before any of the three men spoke.

Pat Jr. finally broke the silence. "Da, what is this place? Where'd ya get all this stuff? How . . . why . . . what is all this?" he stuttered.

"You are standing in the Annals, boys. This place has been in existence for over a thousand years, modified in the 1800s, remodified in the 1950s, and recently, completely remodeled and updated with state-of-the-art security systems and climate control," replied Patrick as he slowly walked to a desk and chair near the main entrance and sat down. "I know it's a lot to take in, boys, so I will let you process it all for a bit. When yer ready, ask away."

William continued to walk slowly through the entire warehouse, marveling at the sheer magnitude of what was stored there. Rows and rows of sealed containers all labeled and neatly placed in chronological order. "Clan Birth Records 1590–1690 . . . Clan Land Deeds 1480–1580," he read as he meandered among the annals of Clan Athy history. He stopped abruptly at a container that was labeled "Patrick Thomas Athy: Patrick Thomas Athy II, Desmond John Athy, William Patrick Athy, Thomas Ian Athy, 1982–1989."

"Wait, what?" William whispered to himself. "That's us . . . that's our family, my brothers and me."

William had discovered the container of his and his brother's records, everything from their birth to their marriages, mortgages, divorce decrees, bills of sale, health records, dental records—basically all information pertaining to himself and his four brothers.

Finally, Will spoke up loudly. "Patrick Thomas Athy, you've been busy!"

"Yes, son. But I didn't do all this. This is the work of generations of Clan Athy members as well, your ancestors. And the work of many more . . . many who still stand guard over this place and the contents herein." replied Patrick. "You are standing among the Annals of the First Tribes of Galway, boys. You are standing on hallowed ground. The history contained here and the cache of priceless heirlooms have been secretly stashed away for centuries, sealed and guarded."

"I am speechless," said Pat Jr.

"I am feckin' pissed!" snapped Will. "How could ya keep this from us, Da? Your sons! Why didn't ya tell us?"

"Will, my bonnie boy. I was sworn to secrecy until the timing was right to tell ya," replied Patrick.

"*Timin'* was right? Are you kiddin' me, Da? You've been sittin' on a feckin' warehouse full of treasure and *our* family history and you didn't tell us cuz the timin' wasn't right?!' Will shouted as he shook his head, glaring at his father.

"William, this place is filled with more than just *our* family history, son. It is filled with the First Tribes of Galway history. Come sit down, Will, and I will tell ya the story now. And I hope when I finish, that chip on yer shoulder will be gone!" replied Patrick as he motioned to both boys to sit on a bench that was against the wall near the desk.

Patrick continued, "Athy, Blake, Bodkin, Browne, D'Arcy, Deane, Font, French, Joyce, Kirwan, Lynch, Martin, Morris, and Skerrett—these are the original Tribes of Galway. They were so named by Cromwell's forces, as a term of reproach against the natives of the town who banded together as one during the time of their unparalleled persecution, but later, the term was used as an honorable mark of distinction among themselves and those cruel oppressors. They were the first. They laid claim to the land from the sea to the hills that surround and settled they did by the river they named Corrib. Some migrated to the east and south. Our direct ancestors, the Athys, came to settle in the Nire Valley. As the English oppressors increased their attacks, the Galway Tribes sent portions of each clan throughout Ireland, taking with them important documents and treasures of the era. When these caverns here in Nire were discovered, the original Tribes of Galway chieftains saw to it that all the possessions of all fourteen tribes were accumulated and stored away in three main hideaways: under the Cliffs of Moher, where enormous caverns are hidden and modern-day Clan Lynch members keep watch. in a catacomb of caves near the Giant's Causeway, watched over by descendants of Clan Skerrett, and here in these caverns in the Nire Valley, where I and your Uncle Sean Athy, along with our cousins from County Tipperary, have stood guard." Patrick paused. "Are ye following me, boys?" he asked.

Pat Jr. and William simply nodded as they stared at their father in sheer amazement.

After a few minutes, Will cleared his throat and shook his head quickly as if to wake himself up from a daze.

"Da, I am still not getting not telling us. And why all the fuss about some old documents, heirlooms, and books?" William remarked.

"Good question, son," Patrick replied. "You weren't told because to know means your very lives would be endangered. Now, before you scoff, come with me."

Patrick got up and retrieved a key from his vest pocket and walked to a door that was labeled "Storage." Once inside, he flipped on the light and asked Pat Jr. to shut the door behind them. As the three stood there, in what was a small room with several boxes stacked on a set of shelves, Patrick walked to the far side of the shelving unit and yanked on the steel handle at the back. It swung open slowly to reveal another room, chalked full of stacked boxes that were unlabeled. In the middle of this interior room was a large, round table with fourteen chairs placed around it.

"Sit," said Patrick as he motioned to the table and chairs.

Pat Jr. and William sat down slowly and quietly, watching their father retrieve a box from a shelf.

"We are not guarding only old documents, heirlooms, and books, son." Patrick said as he glanced at William. "We are guarding priceless information that could bring down the entire British Empire. We are guarding treasures that were taken from the British oppressors over the centuries. Our ancestors did not take the English occupation lightly, and while they could not completely defeat the British Army, they indeed could organize systematic covert operations to take hundreds of thousands of pieces of jewelry, precious gems, gold coins, art, and other valuable assets from the British they viewed as compensation for the brutality the English waged upon the Irish people. They would cross the channel under cover of night, and with the help of servants and locals disloyal to the Crown, they stole an enormous amount from the British hierarchy, who blamed the thefts on marauders. They also robbed many, many caravans filled with gold from the Catholic Church, which caused great disputes among the clergy and the monarchy, as neither had any idea who these thieves were and the British authorities could never catch the perpetrators. But beyond that, we are guarding information—documented information that proves, beyond the shadow of a doubt, that the British monarchy was an utter sham and that Irish aristocracy were the rightful heirs to the entire British Empire, which should be rightly called the Celtic Empire."

With that, William raised his hands and said, "Whoa . . . hold on . . . *What?* How is this possible? What proof do you have, Da?"

Pat replied, "William, you are sitting among the proof!" as he opened the box in front of him. He then pulled out a rolled scroll that had a gold ribbon tied around it. Pat set the scroll down and said, "Boys, this document is the definitive proof that Clan Athy are the rightful heirs to the throne of what is known today as England. But that is not the original name of these isles . . . no, these are not the British Isles! These are the Isles of the Kingdom of Athanariogh, the Isles of the Celts!" Then, Patrick read aloud from the document: "Is iad seo na cúnaint a bunaíodh ag na chéad chinn. Na h-oidhrí cearta le Na hOileáin Cheiltigh, Na Ceithre Thrí Déag de Ghaillimh, Éire. An Monarchy Ceilteach ceart, De Áth!" Translated: "These are the covenants that were established by the first ones, the rightful heirs to the Celtic Isles, the Fourteen Tribes of Galway, Ireland—the rightful Celtic monarchy, De Athy!"

After several minutes, Pat Jr. stood up and walked to a water cooler near the door to the Annals and poured himself a small cup of water and drank it down in one gulp. He crushed the paper cup in one hand and tossed it in a nearby trash can then turned to face his father and brother. "So now that we know this information, Da, what er we supposed to do with it?" asked Pat Jr. "I mean, this is all a bit overwhelmin', to say the least!"

"It is a lot to take in, son," replied Pat. "It has been a heavy burden and difficult task to keep it all from you boys too."

"Not to mention, a powder keg waitin' to blow and we're now a part of it!" said William as he too made his way to the water cooler. "Now what, Da? What are we to do with this, this history lesson?"

"Well, boys, I needed to tell you now because my book is due to come out next week and we are about to blow history as we know it right out of the water!" replied Pat as he made his way to a shelf that held a bottle of Jameson to have a drink of something a bit stronger than water.

# Chapter Nine

## Back to the Beginning

William sat quietly in front of his computer, staring at the screen in front of him in utter amazement. The words from his ancestor, Thomas William Patrick Athy, washed over him like a flood, overwhelming him at times. The enormous amount of information he had just read left William battling exhaustion, but his curiosity and excitement were winning that fight thus far. If it wasn't for his eyelids slamming shut every few minutes, Will would have continued poring over Athy family historical documents. But alas, fatigue took over, and he barely made it to his bed, where he fell fast asleep as his head hit the pillow. Once asleep, William Athy's dreams took him to a place and time he had just read about, a time when Thomas Athy was the commander of the Battle of Atheney.

It was August 15, 1249, and Thomas Athy was commanding his small but fierce army against the hordes from the south in a bloody battle on the Field of Athanariogh near Galway, Ireland. Thomas was victorious and, after defeating the enemy, became Baron Atheney. The Clan Athy had established itself as one of the most affluent and influential of the fourteen original Tribes of Galway. And though there was fighting among the clans from the south and north, the Fourteen were closely knit and worked together to defend their land. Mostly tradesmen, fishermen, and merchants, the fourteen Tribes of Galway had quite a reputation as fierce warriors as well. In fact, they were known as the Tribes of Galway, first as an expression invented by Cromwell's forces. It was a term of reproach against the natives of the town of Galway, for their singular friendship and attachment to each other during the time of their unparalleled trouble and persecutions, then later, as an honorable mark of distinction between themselves and their cruel oppressors. But the Tribes of Galway were much more than a rebellious group of clans who fought bravely against their enemies; they were the original inhabitants and rightful heirs to the Celtic Isles. Long before the Norman invasions, long before the British established their monarchy, the ancestors of the members of the Tribes of Galway had inhabited the land—their land. Thomas Athy knew this well and was determined to protect and preserve the evidence that proved it. He knew full well that overthrowing the British ruling class and the established monarchy was an impossibility. The ravages of war with them, as well as the other Celtic clans, had taken a toll in both lives lost and territory stolen. The land had dwindled down to an area no larger than a tenth of the size of Ireland itself. Maintaining their territory was crucial to their survival, but so was preserving the proof and documentation of a terrible injustice that could one day bring down an entire empire.

As he stared out over the Field of Athanariogh, Thomas was ever so aware of the importance of the task before him. He summoned his brothers Liam and Ailan to his home, which was one of the first grand stone houses ever built in Ireland. The stone wall that snaked along the green pastures, drawing a line as far as the eye could see, was a witness to this ancient family's presence in Galway. Thomas watched as his brothers approached on horseback. Liam, seven years his junior, was Thomas' exact likeness. His reddish-blond hair that came to the middle of his back was tied with a string of woven sheep's wool. He seemed to always have a smile on his face, especially when riding his beloved horse, Cadarn, whose name meant "mighty," which he was. At the Battle of Athanariogh, Cadarn saved Liam's life by running over and trampling several of his enemies. Cadarn was a large white stallion with a long silver mane and tail. Ailan was trying his best to keep up with his brother but had neither the desire nor the competitive spirit of Liam. He was the thinker of the family. Although as handsome as his brothers, Ailan favored his mother and what he lacked in stature, he made up for in brilliance and wit. With a shock of almost-white blond hair, Ailan scowled as he once again heard Liam yell, "I win again!" while the two rode through Thomas' gate. "Must you always declare victory o'er everythin', Liam?" Ailan said with disgust.

"Yeah . . . yeah, I do, cuz *I won again*, Wee One!" Liam bragged back.

"Dun't call me that, Liam!" Ailan yelled.

"Okay, okay . . . calm down, Ail!" said Thomas as he held up both hands motioning for calmness from both his brothers. "Da chuldrun are asleep—quiet wit' da both of ya!"

Liam and Ailan both slid off their horses and handed the tie-downs to Thomas' caretaker, an older man named Snead.

"What's dis all about, Thom?" asked Ailan.

"Yeah, why do we have to meet now? I had a lassie ready to take a ride on Cadarn wit' me when da messenger came!" agreed Liam as the three headed toward a smaller building toward the back of the house.

"We have some t'ings to discuss, lads, and it couldn't wait," replied Thomas.

Behind Thomas' home was a smaller stone building that abutted the hillside. The structure was actually built into the side of the hill and was more of an entranceway than a building. As they entered, all three men paid homage to their family crest that was carved into the stone above the door, by kissing their right hand and touching the stone as they passed under it. Liam was the last one in. He closed and bolted the door behind him. The room was dimly lit by the fire burning in the fireplace, and the aroma of food cooking filled the room.

"What is cookin', Thomas?" asked Ailan.

"Dat is rabbit stew. Hannah was kind enough to make sure we were fed before she left for her mum's," replied Thomas.

"What she doin' goin' to her mum's?" asked Liam.

"Her poor ole mum is suff'rin' with da consumption . . . it's not good," Thomas said, visibly sad.

"Sorry to hear that, Thom . . . I hope she'll be all right. She has always been good to us," said Ailan as he reached out and grabbed his older brother's shoulder.

"T'anks, lad. It's in the Almighty's hands," Thom said as he walked toward the fireplace. "Come, eat."

The three Athy brothers filled their bowls, poured some ale in their cups and gathered around the table in front of the fire. As they thoroughly enjoyed the stew, Thomas began.

"Lads, we need to prepare for the transfer of all we have *acquired* from our enemies and prepare for the next *withdrawal* from His Majesty's bounty, which is rightly ours. There is a possibility that the King of Scots is planning to return from London, where he met with King Henry, to Edinburgh in six days. We need to plan accordingly and make ready the clansmen. Liam, you are in charge of planning the exact location and best time to ambush the king's convoy. Ailan, you are in charge of the usual: archers' positions and plan of attack." Both Liam and Ailan nodded with enthusiasm.

"I dun't have to tell ya that this has to be like the other justice runs: move swiftly, no unnecessary killing, and take only what is rightfully ours. Aye?" said Thomas as he raised his cup in a toast.

"Aye!" yelled all three.

"Sire, the royal carriage awaits. May I suggest you wear this overcoat for today's journey?" asked Reginald, the royal valet to King Alexander II.

"Reginald, what would I do without you?" Alexander retorted in exasperation. "This journey has not even started yet, and I am exhausted. I am having to travel all the way to the Isle of Kerrera to speak to that mongrel Scot, Ewen! I could not care less that he is the Lord of Argyll! But I must persuade him to sever his allegiance to Haakon of Norway. So we will journey. Hand me my *medicine*, Reginald. I must remain calm, and it does the trick." Reginald scampered across the room, retrieved the medicine so as to obey his master's command, and handed it to him. Alexander took a large gulp from his silver flask filled with a tonic of Scotch whisky and opium and gasped loudly. "Awww, the nectar of the gods, Reginald, the nectar of the gods!"

"Yes, Majesty," Reginald replied with a half bow.

"Off to the Highlands we go! Furst? Come here, boy!" Alexander shouted, summoning his dog, a pug given to him as gift from the Wu Ding Dynasty of China. Furst came running. Alexander grabbed him up and stashed him in a velvet sack as he and his entourage headed to the waiting carriages.

The next morning was cold and damp as Alexander's royal carriage and four other carriages containing his servants, closest friends, concubines, and staff meandered through the narrow country roads of Scotland. Most all were asleep except for the carriage drivers, footmen, and royal guards who were escorting the king. Before any of them could react, they were surrounded by masked horsemen and archers, all training their bows directly at the royal guards.

"Stop where ya are, or weel unleash hell upon ya!" yelled one of the masked horsemen.

All at once, all five carriages came to an abrupt stop, causing their occupants to be jolted awake.

"Wha—who . . . what in the name of . . . what is happening?!" Alexander yelled out as he grabbed his beloved pug and peered out the window.

"I'm not sure, sire, but I think we are being attacked by those masked men!" answered Reginald.

Alexander plopped Furst into Reginald's lap and tumbled out if the carriage wildly.

"Who are you and what do you want? Do you know who I *am*?!" screamed Alexander.

"Top of da mornin' to ya, Yer Majesty! Yes, we know who yeh are!" said the same horseman.

Just then, two of them grabbed Alexander from behind and slipped a sack over his head. "We know who yeh are, Majesty," whispered the tall one as he forced Alexander to the ground next to the carriage.

The masked men had no problem disarming the royal guard, whom they blindfolded and tied up alongside the road. Then they forced the rest of the king's entourage to follow suit, tied them up, and forced them to sit on the ground, facing away from the carriages.

"Take what is ours, lads!" shouted the man who seemed to be the leader of the masked brigade.

And with that, they proceeded to take three large trunks from one of the servant carriages, mount their horses, and ride away as quickly as they appeared, less the leader, who knelt next to Alexander and whispered, "T'ank you, sire. We only take what is ours. Ya have a nice journey now and watch out for doze thievin' Celts!"

Alexander sat for a moment and then realized he was no longer bound. He tore off the sack from his head and stood up in a panic, thrashing around. "Where are they? Where are my guards?!" he shouted.

"We are all over here, Your Majesty!" shouted Reginald in a high-pitched voice. "The thieves are gone, vanished into thin air! I was the only one they did not blindfold!"

Alexander staggered over to Reginald, untied him, and fell to the ground on his back. "Reginald, untie everyone! Guards, *find those men*!"

Thomas, Liam, Ailan, and the rest of the Clan Athy rode hard for hours until they finally met the boats to take them all back to Ireland. They unsaddled their horses and loaded them on the large ship first and then boarded the remaining boats for home.

"Open them," said Thomas to his brother Liam.

Liam opened the first of the three large chests, which was filled to the top with gold coins. Then, he moved to the second, opening it to reveal the same. As he opened the last of the three chests, several clan members gasped. The third chest was filled with the royal jewels, including the crown of Alexander, the King of Scots.

Alexander was in a fury as he set foot upon the Isle of Kerrera. After a four-day journey in which they were robbed and made to look like fools, the King of Scots was not in the mood for diplomacy.

Ewen, Lord of Argyll, met Alexander at the harbor and escorted him to Ewen's castle, which was built along the ocean shore. After a week of diplomatic meetings, long discussions, and even bribes, Alexander was readying himself for the journey home. On the evening before their planned departure, Reginald made his king the usual bedtime hot brew, a concoction of tea, whiskey, milk, sugar, and opium. But as he delivered it to His Majesty's bedside table, Reginald could not rouse the king.

"Your Majesty? Sire? Your Majesty, are you all right?" asked Reginald. "Oh my, he is burning hot!" he cried as he felt the king's forehead.

Ewen, Lord of Argyll, summoned the healer of the realm. But despite the healer's best efforts to save him, Alexander II, the King of Scots, died.

Three days after his death, Alexander's seven-year-old son, Alexander III, was named king.

And that same day, in England, a great king trembled.

"What is the meaning of this? How does a small band of thieves steal three trunks filled with gold, precious jewels, and priceless information and not fire so much as one arrow?!" screamed Henry III, King of England. "And they managed to also kill Alexander, the King of Scots, as well? They must be found and brought to me . . . *now!*"

Liam Athy had finished stashing the last of the gold and precious jewels in the basement of his brother Thomas' outbuilding. He bolted the basement door behind him and bounded up the stairs, to join Thomas and Ailan at the supper table. In his hand, he carried a thick cloth-wrapped package, which he laid on the table in front of Thomas.

"That is them, Thom. Those are the signed papers taken from the traitor!" spat Liam.

Thomas removed the cloth that covered the highly important documents, stood and declared, "Is iad seo na cúnaint a bunaíodh ag na chéad chinn. Na h-oidhrí cearta le Na hOileáin Cheiltigh, Na Ceithre Thrí Déag de Ghaillimh, Éire. An Monarchy Ceilteach ceart, De Áth!" Translated: "These are the covenants that were established by the first ones, the rightful heirs to the Celtic Isles, the Fourteen Tribes of Galway, Ireland— the rightful Celtic monarchy, De Athy!"

Just then, there was a loud knocking at the door. Liam, Ailan, and Thomas all grabbed their swords. Thomas motioned for his brothers to be still as he approached the door silently. As he drew closer, the loud knocking stopped.

"Who is knocking?!" yelled Thomas.

"Open the door!" a voice said loudly.

"I say again, who is knocking?" Thomas repeated.

"Thomas Athy, open the damn door, lad! It is I, yer da!"

Thomas, Liam, and Ailan breathed a sigh of relief then Thomas yelled, "What is the password?!"

"The damned password is 'Christblood.' Now open the door before I knock it down, son!" replied Dermot Athy, Thomas, Liam, and Ailan's father.

Thomas nodded, and Liam unbolted and opened the door. Dermot Athy bounded in with James and Sean Athy, his brothers, and the Reverend Patrick Ralaghan. All four men were obviously shaken. After greeting one another with handshakes and brotherly embraces, the Athy men and Reverend Patrick gathered around Thomas' table. Ailan brought two bottles of port and a bottle of local whiskey from the kitchen and set them on the table as Liam brought seven cups. Thomas grabbed the whiskey and began to pour as his father, Dermot finally spoke.

"My sons, I bring news. We must move the stash now . . . tonight. There is word that King Henry has ordered every house in Galway to be searched. His men are on their way across the channel now! Thom, you know what to do. Do it now, son. Liam, Ailan, you also know what needs to be done. The knights will be here before dawn. Let us drink and begin our task," said Dermot soberly.

The men all downed their whiskey and hurried to prepare the precious cargo to be relocated. Reverend Patrick poured another and drank it down as well and said, "God be with us!"

# Chapter Ten

## Roll Cameras!

Day one of filming *The Nire* began at six o'clock in the morning. It was a brisk, clear Irish morning, and Angus McCulloch padded down the steps of his RV with a large mug of coffee in hand. As he headed out for the costumers', he met Molly Taggart who was walking slowly toward the costume trailers as well.

"Top of the mornin' to ya, sweet Molly! Or should I say, 'Orlagh' or 'wifey'?" Angus said with a laugh.

"You can call me 'darlin' wife' or 'goddess divine'!" Molly replied as she locked arms with Angus.

The two strolled slowly arm in arm together and morphed into their characters with each step. Molly became Orlagh Athy, the kind but cantankerous wife of Dermot Athy and mother of Thomas, Liam, and Ailan Athy. Angus became Dermot, the strong, loud, imposing patriarch of Clan Athy. By the time the two reached the costume trailers, they were no longer Angus and Molly.

"After you, me dear!" Angus said to Molly with a gesture of gallantry as he opened the costume trailer door.

"Why, t'ank you, me fine husband and luver!" Molly replied as she patted Angus' chest on her way up the trailer steps.

Angus was a bit caught off guard by Molly's forwardness but then realized she was playing the part and playing it well. "This is going to be an adventure!" Angus thought to himself as he followed Molly into the trailer to get in costume and then makeup.

The entire cast was lined up like birds on a wire after they were in full costume. Their hair and makeup were being inspected by the director of *The Nire*, Rudy Gallo. He was a short, stout middle-aged man with salt-and-pepper hair and beard. As he strutted back and forth, examining the cast, he mumbled to himself, "Looks good, looks good . . . not bad, too much rouge on her . . . he needs more dirt under his nails . . ." A young man attempted to follow Rudy as he made his rounds but was lagging behind as he tried to keep up and make notations on an iPad. "Kevin, pleeeasssse try to keep up!" snapped Rudy with a large sigh. "We must get this right!"

Rudy then stepped up onto a small makeshift stage that was erected in the middle of the large meadow on Jarvis Ranch. Kevin handed Rudy a megaphone, and Rudy addressed the cast and crew: "Okay, people, welcome to the first day of filming for *The Nire*! By now, you have all read the itinerary for the week. So, actors, take your places! Crew, ready yourselves for the scene 'Nire Valley Meadow Battle, scene one take one. Horse handlers, be ready. Extras, are you ready?" As everyone took their places, Rudy made his way to his director's chair.

"*Quiet on the set!*" yelled Rudy's assistant director.

"Okay, people, let's do this! Places . . . aaaand *action!*" Rudy yelled.

And with that, the first day of production started for *The Nire*.

After twelve long hours of filming that included fifteen breaks due to inclement weather, Angus was ready for his recliner and three fingers of Jameson. *After a hot shower,* he thought to himself. Just as he was pouring his favorite whiskey, his hair still wet, a knock came from his front door. Angus slipped on his spa robe, compliments of Star Gaze Productions. He opened his door to find Molly, also donning her spa robe. "Thought ya might like to share a nightcap," she said as she brought a bottle of Jameson from behind her back.

Angus, without hesitation, stepped back and motioned for his leading lady to join him. "Welcome to my humble abode, lass!" he said.

Molly giggled as she saw that Angus had already poured himself a whiskey. "Great minds think alike," she said as the two made their way to the back of the trailer, where two recliners awaited their cold, tired bones.

"Well, that was certainly an *interesting* day." Molly sighed as she lay back in the overstuffed easy chair and stretched.

"Indeed, it was," replied Angus as he also relaxed back into his wonderfully soft recliner. "I wonder if Red Rudy will survive the week?" he said, dripping with sarcasm.

The two laughed out loud.

"If that man's face turned any redder . . . well, I don't know . . . ha ha!" laughed Molly.

"I thought he was goin' to keel over when my horse took out his director's chair! *Ha!*" said Angus, now crying with laughter.

"Oh, his face was as red as a tomato," laughed Molly. "Poor man may have even shat himself!"

With that, Angus spit out his drink with an enormous, deep roar of laughter. The two sat in their heavenly recliners for hours, drinking, laughing, and talking over each and every moment of their day until exhaustion took over and they drifted off into a sound sleep.

Colin Wohl was in full panic mode as he stared at the note that was slipped under his door. After the incidents at Jarvis Ranch, he was already on edge, but now his nerves were overwhelming. Thoughts of the note on the spear and the near-fatal "accident" in the barn ran through his mind.

*What on earth is this about?* he thought to himself. He picked up his cell phone and dialed William's number.

"Hello, Sire. What can I do fer ya dis fine mornin'?" William said after only one ring.

"Will, you need to come over here to the inn. I—you—Will, I need you to come now!" replied Colin hastily.

"What's goin' on, Sire?" William asked, sensing the urgency in Colin's voice.

"There's another note, William. What is goin' on? Who could be doin' dis, Will?" Colin replied.

"I'll be right there, Colin. Sit tight," William said as he grabbed his keys and hurried out the door.

When William saw Colin's face as he stood in the doorway of his room at the River Inn, he knew something had really shaken him.

"Sire, are ya okay?" asked Will quietly as he entered the room.

"No, no, I'm not okay. Not at all okay, actually," Colin replied as he walked to the window and looked out upon the Nire River. "Someone does not want this movie to be made, William, and that someone has made it clear just how much."

"Where's the note, Sire?" William asked somberly.

Colin walked to the desk across the room, picked up a sheet of paper, and handed it to Will. "Here. Please tell me that the Gaelic part does not say what I think it says, Will," said Colin in a hoarse voice.

William took the sheet of paper as he looked into Colin's ashen face. "Be calm, Sire," William said quietly as he fixed his eyes on the message written on the paper:

> Cuireadh an spear cogaidh
> Ar an talamh coisithe.
> Creeps sa bhás.

Translated:

> The war spear planted
> on hallowed ground

creeps in death
without a sound.

William knew instantly what the Gaelic message meant, and he knew that it was a continuation of the message left on the spear tip by the woods at Jarvis Ranch. He also knew where the message was taken from: the old burial site stone. William paused to glance at Colin, who was staring out the window again. Then, he read the note in his hand, in its entirety:

Cuireadh an spear cogaidh
Ar an talamh coisithe.
Creeps sa bhás.
This is your third warning! Stop production of
*The Nire* NOW or next time, we will not miss!

William drew a deep breath and took out his cell phone. "Mr. Jarvis . . . Okay, Roy. This is . . . yes, hello. Roy, I need to meet with you ASAP. No, I mean *now*. Can you call Larry and tell him it's urgent that he meet with us as well? T'anks, Roy. I will call me da. Let's meet at the pub. Okay, see ya in a bit."

"Come on, Sire. Pull yourself together. We need to get to the bottom of this now," William said to Colin, prodding him to get his shoes on.

The two were headed out the door when William's phone rang.

"Hello," Will answered. "Da, I was just goin' to call ya. I'm on my way o'er to the pub now with Colin. Roy and Larry are meeting us there. I will explain when we get there," Will said as he ended the call abruptly.

"Let's go, Sire. We will get to the bottom of this, dun't ya worry!" And with that, the two longtime friends headed to William's Range Rover.

Patrick Athy was wondering why his son William had sounded so mysterious on the phone and why he insisted on a meeting at the family pub with Roy Jarvis, Larry Davis, Colin Wohl, and the two of them. *It's not like Will to act in such a way,* Patrick thought as he finished up balancing the books for the pub.

Ten minutes later, William and Colin sped into the Athy family pub parking lot. Right behind them were Roy and Larry in Roy's Scout.

"Mornin', boys." Roy greeted them as they all walked toward the front door.

"Wanna tell me what this is all about, William?" asked Larry.

"You're about to find out," replied Will. "Let's get inside first. Da should have the coffee on."

The five men gathered in Patrick's office, around the large conference table. William retrieved from his breast pocket the note that was slid under Colin's door. After he read it aloud, there was not a peep from anyone for several minutes. Then, all at once, the questions flew!

"What the hell is going on here? Do we have a serial killer on the loose?" Larry gasped.

"What in da name of all that is good is this about?" said a concerned Colin.

"This is shaping up to be a real mystery," said Roy as he took off his cowboy hat and scratched his head.

"I know you all have questions, but I know as much as you do—nothing. Nothing except the obvious. The note is clearly from the same hand as the other note that was found on the tip of the spear, and even clearer is that someone or some people do not want this movie made," William offered.

"That *is* obvious," spat Larry. "Sorry, William, I didn't mean—"

"It's okay, Larry. We are all concerned," Will interrupted.

Just then, the office phone rang out, making Colin jump.

"Athy's Pub," answered Patrick. "Oh, hello, Constable O'Brian. What's that? What?! Oh, well, he is here . . . but . . . yes, Finn, I will. But what is this about?" There was a long pause. Patrick turned as white as a sheet.

Samantha Lehy was still and silent as she sat on the ground of Lily's stall. Lily of the Valley was a prized champion jumper, and at eight years old, she was the first Arabian cross that had won four consecutive titles. Now, the beloved creature lay motionless in her stall, a large pool of blood surrounding her head.

*How could someone do this?* Samantha thought as she reached over to caress Lily. "Who could hurt such a wonderful animal?" she whispered.

William burst into the stable entrance. "Sam, *Sam*! Samantha, where are ya, lass?!" he cried.

"Here, Will, I am here, in her stall," Samantha answered.

"Tell me what Finn said isn't true, Sam," Will said in desperation as he slowly approached the entrance to Lily's stall.

When William saw Lily lying on the stall floor with Sam sitting by her side, he gasped for air and let out a moan. "Oh, no . . . God, *no*!"

William fell to his knees by his mare's lifeless body and began to weep uncontrollably. He grabbed the knife that was protruding from her chest and tried to pull it out, unsuccessfully. He laid his head upon her side and stroked her mane. "Who could have done such a thing, Sam?" William said, weeping.

Samantha had no words; all she could do was shake her head and point. Will didn't notice at first. But then he looked over at her and saw, through his tear-filled eyes, her arm was raised and she was pointing at the back wall of the stall.

"What? What are ya pointin' at, Sam?" Will said, laboring to even talk.

As William wiped his eyes, he looked in the direction of the back wall and saw it. Written on the wall in what looked to be blood was

Cuireadh an spear cogaidh
Ar an talamh coisithe.
Creeps sa bhás.

The war spear planted
On hallowed ground.
Creeps in death
without a sound.

Constable Finnius O'Brian, Finn, was the only law enforcement at the scene. He quietly stepped into Lily's stall, took a knee beside Samantha, and put his hand on her shoulder. "Do either of you need anything? I am so sorry this happened, Will," he said quietly. "When I received Sam's call, I couldn't believe it. Nothing like this has ever happened in this town."

William could only manage a nod as he stared at the back wall with the message on it. "You need to find who did this, Finn. Or I will."

"I will do my best, Will. But now, I need to ask you both to gently and slowly leave this stall. It is a crime scene, and I need it clean for the forensic team," Finn said gently.

Ten minutes later, William's stables were filled with police, friends, and family all wanting to know what had happened, all wondering who could have killed Will's prized beauty

# Chapter Eleven

## The Order of Solomon's Temple

As the sun rose over the rolling hills of Galway, Ireland, Thomas Athy looked down upon Clan Athy land from high above, where he stood on the road that led to the southland.

"It will be a long while before I see 'er again," he whispered to himself.

Following several minutes behind him were 260 well-armed Athy Clan militia, guarded by 130 Knights of the Templar. The horde surrounded each of the twenty-seven wagons as they meandered their way along the road. Each wagon carried precious cargo taken from Thomas Athy's and other Clan Athy members' homes. At the very same time, there were twelve other smaller caravans, all representing each of the thirteen Tribes of Galway, headed to three separate locations, all carrying great riches and documents. They dispersed from Galway into the Irish countryside, headed to three main locations: northeast, to the Giant's Causeway. The southwest, to the Cliffs of Moher. And the southeast, to the Nire Valley.

To the Giant's Causeway traveled clans Blake, French, Martin, and Skerrett.

To the Cliffs of Moher traveled clans Bodkin, D'Arcy, Font, and Kirwan.

And to the Nire Valley traveled clans Athy, Browne, Joyce, Lynch, and Morris.

All had a common mission: to safely deliver the contents of all wagons to the prepared hideaways.

As Thomas said a silent prayer for safety and the success of the momentous task ahead of him, he was startled back to earth by his approaching father, Dermot, and brothers Ailan and Liam, as well as Father Patrick.

"Thomas, my son! All clear?" Dermot shouted.

"Yes, Da. But we need to remain vigilant. They're out there, and they want to not only stop us. They want us dead!" replied Thomas.

"No truer words have ever been spoken, son," said Dermot.

Dermot barely got those words out when an arrow whizzed by Thomas' head and hit Dermot Athy in his left shoulder. They all jumped off their horses and hid behind rocks, including Dermot, who was wrenching in pain.

"Da, you alive? Da?!" yelled Liam.

As Dermot labored to draw a breath, he managed to get three words out: "Kill dem bastards!"

Just then, a horde of British soldiers charged up the hill toward the Athy men and Father Patrick as hundreds of arrows sailed through the air and landed all around them. Father Patrick managed to crawl to Dermot's side.

"Dermot? You still wit' us, dear friend?" said Father Patrick.

"I am, Father . . . but I'm angry enoof to spit fire and brimstone!" growled Dermot.

"Good! I hope your anger spreads to the clans!" replied Father Patrick. "We could use some God-ordained, righteous indignation about now, Dermot!"

Immediately after Father Patrick spoke those words, the sound of galloping horse hooves could be heard. The ground began to shake, and with a force likened to a gale-force wind in a mighty storm, they emerged from around the bend in the road.

"God has answered, Dermot! His army is here!" screamed Father Patrick.

"Praise be to God! The Tribes of Galway and the knights are here!" replied Dermot with renewed strength.

The army numbered close to six hundred. Warriors from clans Athy, Browne, Joyce, Lynch, and Morris all banded together with hundreds of the Knights of Solomon's Order. They bounded by Dermot and Father Patrick, heading directly for the British Army and their archers. As they passed by, Dermot and Father Patrick watched as several of their comrades were hit by British arrows and fell violently to the ground. But they still advanced like a tidal wave upon the formidable army. As they plunged through their front lines, the clanging of swords smashing together filled the air. Liam Athy mounted his beloved steed and joined the rushing forces along with his brothers, Ailan and Thomas. Hand-to-hand combat ensued, and Thomas ran headlong into the battle, grasping his shield and wielding his sword. As he drew closer, he saw a British soldier about to take off the head of his beloved brother Liam from behind. He then, in three lightning-fast moves, returned his sword to its sheath, grabbed his throwing ax, which was strapped to his waist, and hurled it toward the soldier, planting it directly between his eyes. Liam, utterly clueless as to what had just transpired, turned to see Thomas and shouted, "'Bout time ya joined the fun, bruther!" Thomas ran to the soldier he had just killed, retrieved his ax, and nodded at Liam, who suddenly realized what had happened. "Ya saved me bacon, Thomas! I owe ya!" Liam shouted. The two then spotted Ailan, who was struggling as he fought two Brits off with a hatchet and sword. Thomas and Liam looked at each other and, without hesitation, rushed to Ailan's aid. Thomas again threw his ax, this time at the Brit on Ailan's left, severing his right arm as he was raising it to strike Ailan. Ailan then finished the task by running the Brit soldier through with his spear. Liam managed to reach the other Brit before he could strike Ailan and proceeded to decapitate him with one swift pass of his sword. Just then, a mounted soldier ran at the three, attempting to hurl his spear at Thomas, but Ailan, being an excellent shot, produced his sling, grabbed a large rock, and flung it, hitting the charging soldier right below his left eye, which caused him to fall back, off his horse and onto the ground close to where Father Patrick and Dermot Athy were lying against a large rock. Before anyone could stop him, Dermot managed to roll himself close enough to the fallen Brit to plunge his dagger into his chest.

Father Patrick let out a guttural "Dermot, noooo!" But it was too late. Dermot had managed to kill the Brit soldier but was now a sitting duck, out in the open, lying on the ground next to his prey. Just then, three soldiers rushed him. Without batting an eye, Father Patrick stood and threw Dermot's sword at one of the approaching soldiers, hitting him in the left leg. Thomas saw this transpire and took out one of the other soldiers with his ax, planting it in his abdomen, and then finished Father Patrick's victim by slicing him open from ear to ear with his knife. As the third soldier reached Dermot, Ailan hurled a large rock from twenty meters away that hit him right above his right ear, killing him instantly.

"Boys? *Boys*?!" yelled Dermot. "Get this monstrosity off me!"

Ailan had killed the approaching soldier, but he had landed directly on top of his father.

"Ailan, fix your mess!" yelled Liam as he plunged his sword into the Brit he was battling.

And as Ailan yelled back, "I know, Liam!" he grabbed the dead Brit by the back of his head, removing him from Dermot's chest.

"T'ank ya, son!" Dermot said in a matter-of-fact tone.

"Of course, Da! Remember me in yer will, old man!" Ailan quipped back as he grabbed his father gently and managed to get him back to safety swiftly.

Three Athy brothers stood shoulder to shoulder as they continued to fight, wielding their weapons and battling with a mighty spirit, along with their comrades.

The battle was fierce and went on for hours. The clans and the knights fought with unimaginable zeal, driving back the British and causing them to retreat. As the clansmen and knights realized that they had made the British Army flee, a great shout of victory erupted. But the celebrating was short-lived, as the commanders warned, "They will be back . . . and they will bring more soldiers!"

Thomas, Liam, and Ailan returned to where their father was injured. Dermot lay on the cold ground as Father Patrick tended to his wound. His shirt was ripped open and bloodstained, his face ashen from the loss of blood.

"Is he gonna live, Father?" asked Thomas.

"I am!" shouted Dermot, followed by a large gulp of Irish whiskey from Father Pat's silver flask. "But ya better get this priest off me before I run him through!"

"He'll be fine!" said Thomas with a grin of relief. "He's too darn stubborn to die!"

Father Patrick then poured a large amount of whiskey over Dermot's wound and quickly jumped back before he could be the victim of his friend's Irish rage!

"You dirty bastard! You filthy, evil unholy priest!" spat Dermot in pain.

The Athy men looked at each other with eyebrows raised.

"Better you than me, Father Pat!" scoffed Ailan.

"Glad you'll be all right, Da!" said Liam.

"I will be fine, but that priest's days are numbered!" replied Dermot as he slumped forward, out cold.


Thomas Athy climbed atop a large rock and faced out over the massive army of clansmen and knights. He motioned for the chieftains of the other four clans to join him. And as the four gathered around, he addressed them.

"You fought valiantly today. You showed those British bastards that they are no match for a united Ireland!" he shouted.

Cheers erupted as the men raised their swords in victory.

Thomas continued, "But we must make haste and continue onward. We must bury our fallen and see this task through to the end. We must protect what is rightfully ours! Clans of Galway, Knights of Solomon's Order, unite!"

As Thomas climbed down from the rock, the leader of the knights approached and shook his hand.

"You do know they will be back, monsieur? And they will be sending more men than we fought here today!" said Sir Renaud de Vichier, the grand master of the Knights of Solomon's Temple. Sir Renaud and his seneschal ruled over eight Templar provincial masters in Europe: Apulia (Italy), Aragon (Spain), England, France, Hungary, Poitiers (a city in western France), Portugal, and Scotland. He was not a man of large stature, but what he lacked in size, he made up for in bravery and sheer grit. His face was strikingly handsome but also well weathered from years of sun exposure. A scar stretched from his right temple to his right jaw, lending him a battle-laden persona, and he was renowned for being a fierce, unapologetic warrior. The French had even given him the nickname "le féroce guerrier de Dieu"; translated, it means "the Fierce Warrior of God." His hair was black and cut short, and he had a well-groomed black mustache and beard. His reputation for also being a ladies' man preceded him, as women adored him, his ice blue eyes, and his dashing manner. But on the battlefield, Sir Renaud was swift, agile, and deadly.

"Yes, Sir Renaud, I know. We must depart this place and disappear quickly!" Thomas replied. And with that, Thomas whistled for his horse, mounted up, and followed Sir Renaud, who was riding toward the dead and wounded. As the two leaders approached the area where the dead were being buried, they stopped abruptly and were stunned by what they saw.

"I only see five graves!" shouted Thomas.

"This cannot be all of the fallen! Surely there are more?" Sir Renaud replied.

"No, this is all, Sir Renaud!" Liam retorted. "There are eighteen slightly wounded, including me da, who only require their wounds to be cared for. It is a miracle!"

"Indeed! God has seen fit to shine His favor upon us, Thomas. We must give Him thanks!" said Sir Renaud as he knelt on one knee, bowed his head, and prayed. Thomas kneeled with head bowed as well. "Our Father, who art in heaven, thank You for this victory! We ask that You continue to guide us and protect us as we do Your work. Amen." With that, Sir Renaud touched his right hand to his forehead and chest, making the shape of a cross. "Sir Raymond! Make sure we cover all signs of our route. We will journey to our hideaway, only a half a day's ride from here. There we can rest, eat, drink, and prepare for the rest of our journey!"

"Yes, Sir Renaud!" replied Sir Raymond, the knight's second in command.

It was nightfall as the massive army of knights and the Tribes of Galway arrived at the Templar hideaway twelve long hours later; they dismounted their exhausted steeds and gathered inside the giant lair. Once inside the large cavern, Thomas stood in awe of what he saw. It resembled a great cathedral, brightly lit by torches and pit fires. Large stalactites adorned the cavern's ceiling, making it look as though they were placed there purposely for decoration. The walls looked almost liquefied with deep browns, tans, and reds as the many fires bounced light all around. Lamb was being roasted, and pots were boiling over with all sorts of aromatic delights. The smell of roasting meat and herbs filled his nose and nudged his enormous appetite awake. Rows of makeshift tables lined the cavern floor, all filled with bowls of different kinds of food and ewers of wine, water, and ale. The colors were brilliant and inviting, especially after a long, arduous journey. At the entrance, a small group of minstrels were playing stringed instruments, flutes, and drums to set the festive mood. As the men continued to file in, the noise of their voices filled the cavern and echoed around its walls. They formed a line where the lambs were being roasted, and each was given a plate of tender, moist meat. The tables were all filled several minutes later, and the feast began.

Sir Renaud stood upon a chair and addressed the crowd. "Let us give thanks!" he shouted. The cavern went silent. "Our Father in heaven, hallowed be Thy name," he started. And as he continued the Lord's Prayer, the sound of the entire gathering praying in unison moved many to tears. Father Patrick wiped his tears as they all said, "Amen."

"Thank you, Sir Renaud, and thank you to the Knights of Solomon's Temple! Now, eat, drink, fellowship. Minstrels, play your most jovial tunes! Tomorrow, our long journey continues. Tomorrow, we continue our quest to protect, defend, and harbor the proof of the rightful heirs to the Celtic Isles. We *will* succeed! For if God is for us, who can be against us?" shouted Thomas, his voice echoing.

The massive cavern was filled with the shouts and exaltations of the men. An entire army, united for one cause, celebrated together. The sounds of their voices and their goblets clanging together in toasts could be heard for miles.

And only a mile away, a British soldier heard the roar of the Celts and knights' celebration. He was sent by his regiment commander and had followed the enemy while keeping to the shadows. Now, he rode by the light of the moon to report back and inform the British Army of the exact whereabouts of that enemy. He would reach the British encampment right before dawn, and shortly after sunrise, three thousand of His Majesty's finest were in rapid pursuit of the king's enemies.

# Chapter Twelve

## The Whole Truth

Just before the sun began to rise over the Nire Valley, William lay in his bed and listened to the land begin to awaken. The birds began their lively chorus, chirping and busying themselves with their morning rituals. Horses, sheep, cows, and goats all began the brand-new day with a menagerie of sounds that perfectly harmonized with their winged friends. The rushing of water drummed a rhythm that seemed to accompany the fowl and other animals. William drew in a deep breath and enjoyed the amazing song playing outside his window. As his head cleared and he also began the awakening process, a heavy weight of sadness fell upon him. "Lily of the Valley," he whispered to himself. He turned on his side to face the window as the sun began to illuminate the Nire River, which rushed just twenty meters from his bedroom. The grieving process was nothing new to Will, as he had lost his beloved wife to cancer and thought he would die from the heartache of his loss. But life went on, every day a process of one foot in front of the other, one minute at a time, cleaving to his precious children as if they were a lifeboat. And they were, if the truth be told. William dedicated himself to his children, but they were his salvation just as much as he was their protector. Even though grieving for his prized mare was nowhere close to the grief he experienced losing his wife, he felt its sting nonetheless.

The sound of rustling coming from the bathroom jarred William's foggy, half-asleep brain awake. As he threw off the covers and sat up on the edge of the bed, he heard his darling daughter, Fiona.

"Oh, I wish I was a unicorn, pink and purple and blue . . . 'cause if I were a unicorn, there's nothin' I couldn't do! Hmmmm . . ."

"Wow, love the song, Li'l Sis!" William yelled, just as the toilet flushed.

"Da! Yer not supposed to hear it . . . or me! Not yet!" Fiona said with a dramatic sigh.

"Oops, sorry, but it was great, Fee!" William persisted.

"T'anks, Da!" Fiona replied as she flung open Will's bedroom door and bounded in.

"Fee, what have I told ya about knocking first?" said William.

"Sooorry, Da!" she replied with a giggle as she crawled onto her father's bed and then upon his back.

"Good mornin', love of my life!" Will said as he grabbed his daughter's arms and stood.

He galloped to the kitchen where he sat Fiona on the counter and began preparing breakfast. As he pulled a frying pan out of the cabinet, he heard Ian's voice coming from down the hall.

"Yes, Gran, I will tell Da. Yes, I can remember," Ian said.

Will set down the pan and went to peek around the corner into the hallway. He spotted Ian exiting from his father's room. "Ian, what were ya doin' in my room, son?"

"Yer phone was ringin', Da. It was Gran. She wants you to call her . . . ASAT," replied Ian proudly.

William tilted his head. "ASAT? Oh, you mean ASAP?!" He laughed.

Ian handed William his cell phone and shot his father a scowl.

"Ah, son, it's okay! You were very close!" Will said as he took his phone and patted Ian on his shoulder.

But Ian still was not happy and padded back to his bedroom and slammed the door.

William returned to the kitchen, where Fiona still sat on the counter, arms crossed, shaking her head.

"What?" William barked at his daughter.

"You really dun't know how to talk to Ian, Da!" Fiona replied.

As William dialed his mother's number, he gave his seemingly middle-aged daughter a triple take.

"What are ya talkin' 'bout, Fee?" William said, slightly irritated.

"Well, *you* need to pay more attention to yer son, who is havin' giiiirl trouble, William Athy!" Fiona replied as she jumped off the counter and marched to the table, pulled out a chair, and motioned to her father to sit.

William, completely stunned, crept to the table as he set his phone on the counter. He sat slowly down and glared at his eight-year-old daughter from across the table, eyebrows raised and mouth gaping open.

"What did ya say to me, young lady?" William managed, after several seconds.

"I said, you really dun't know how to talk to yer son!" Fiona said in a loud, exaggerated voice.

"Li'l Sis, you had better explain why you are speakin' in this manner to me, yer da, or yer gonna get yer bottom tanned posthaste!" Will responded, his face now showing anger.

"Da, why are ya mad at me? I am only tryin' to help!" Fiona said, tearing up.

"Fiona Emmanuel, dun't even start the waterworks, Missy! You know full well not to speak to me in that tone of voice!" William spat back.

"Yes, Da. I'm sorry. But Ian needs *you*, and ya can't even see it!" she replied.

"Ian needs me? What are ya talkin' 'bout, Fee? What is goin' on?" William asked.

"Da, Ian has giiirl problems!" Fiona repeated.

"What sort of giiirl problems, Fee?" he questioned.

"Okay, so there's this girl in his class at school, Molly. Well, Ian is madly in love with her," Fiona explained as if she were three times her age.

William leaned forward and rested his elbows on the table and narrowed his eyes at his beloved daughter. "How do ya know all this, Li'l Sis?" William pressed.

"Becausssse Gran and Jenn were talkin about it all day yesterday: 'Ian is in love. Ian has a first love.' Trust me, Da, I know t'ings!" she stressed.

"Oh, I know *you* know t'ings, Fee! But you are too young to know *these t'ings*, Li'l Sis!" Will exclaimed.

"Da, I am almost *niiiine!*" whined Fiona.

"I know how old ya are, Sis. You need to stop eavesdropping on adults, and ya need to obey yer da, Miss Sharp Tongue! Do ya hear me, Li'l Sis?!" Will persisted.

"Yes, Da. I mean, yes, sir! I'm sorry, Da, but I only want you to help Ian," Fiona responded in a quiet, apologetic voice.

"All right then, come here, sweet girl. There's nuthin' wrong with caring about yer brother. But ya can't keep listening in on private conversations, Fee. Okay?" William said softly as he reached out his arms to Fiona, who crawled onto his lap.

The phone on the counter chirped, and William kissed his daughter's forehead, sat her down, and answered it.

"Hello. Oh, good mornin', Mum, how are ya this mornin'?" Will replied as he padded into the living room and sat down on the sofa.

"I am as right as rain, son, but I need to talk to ya, face to face," said Grace Athy.

"All right, Mum. I can stop by after I feed the kids and get them ready," replied Will.

"No need to feed 'em, love. I have homemade soda bread in the oven and razers, beans, and eggs on the stove," Grace replied.

"Oh, Mum! Now yer speakin' my language!" Will gushed.

"See ya in a bit, son," said Grace.

William called both of his children to the living room. Fiona and Ian came bounding in and sat on either side of their father.

"So dat was Gran. She has a good ole-fashioned Irish breakfast waitin' for us at her house!" William said.

"Yay!" shouted Fiona as she jumped up and dashed to the bathroom. "We're gunna see Gran, and we are gunna fix Ian!"

Ian's eyes got as big as saucers. "What is she sayin'? Why do I need fixin', Da?" Ian said angrily.

"Son, I have learned o'er the years to not question women when they set their mind to sumt'ing. Do you hear what I am sayin'? When Gran says, 'We need to talk, face to face,' I know better than to question her or argue. It is just not wort' it, son!" William said as he grabbed his son in a bear hug and wrestled him to the floor. "We are mere men and no competition for the Athy women!" William said in an exaggerated, dramatic voice.

"But, Da!" Ian said, bursting out in laughter as his father tickled him.

"There are no ifs, ands, or buts, son! Only "Yes, ma'am" and "Yes, Gran"! We are forever mere pawns in Grace Athy's game of thrones! Do as yer told, mere mortal men!" William said in his best rendering of Sean Connery's 007 voice.

Ian gasped and let out a belly laugh that brought Fiona running, half dressed and scowling at her father and brother. "Are ya two gonna get ready or what?!" yelled Fiona as she spun around and ran back to her room.

"See, see there! We have no say, no power . . . Ian Athy, we are doomed to be their slaves forever and a day! Yes, ma'am, we mere men are obeyin'!" William screamed in laughter as he grabbed his son and kissed him on his cheek.

"We, sir, have the upper hand," William whispered in Ian's ear. "They just dun't know it. Ya see, we may have to get ready and do as Gran says, to keep on livin'. But they, in turn, take care of us men! Now, let's get ready. Grace doesn't like waitin', and she has made us a feast!" William said as he and Ian sauntered down the hallway, his arm over his son's shoulder.

A half an hour later, William, Ian, and Fiona pulled the old Range Rover into Grace and Patrick Athy's driveway. "Time to eat!" William proclaimed as the three entered the Athy family house, the house where William and his brothers grew up, a house that held such fond memories of an amazing childhood, filled with love, laughter, trials, and triumphs. The aroma of Grace Athy's cooking permeated William's senses. The smell brought him back to being ten years old and racing to the table with his brothers to partake in their mother's culinary masterpieces. His mouth watered as he gazed at his parent's table, filled with heaping platters of fried razers or Irish bacon, as tourists called it. Fluffy, fresh scrambled farm eggs, baked beans, and black pudding. Garden-fresh fruit salad stood out with bright red strawberries, green kiwi, oranges, red grapes, and apples. The smell of food was mingled with fresh, brewing coffee aroma. As Will made his way to his mother's kitchen, he heard a familiar sound.

"Aww, yer using the juicer I bought you last Christmas, great!" Will cooed as he hugged Grace, who was making fresh orange juice.

"Yes, I am, son! I love it!" Grace replied as she gave her son a peck on the cheek. "Breakfast is ready, to the table wit' ya!"

"Well, what's this, then? Good mornin' to ya all!" said Patrick Athy with a wink, as he acted stunned to see his grandchildren at his table. "What a wonderful surprise to see me munchkins at the table this fine morn!"

"Papa!" yelled Fiona as she bounded into her grandfather's arms.

"Mornin', Papa!" said Ian as he poured himself a glass of milk.

"Top o' da mornin' to you as well, Sir Ian!" Patrick said with a nod to his grandson.

Patrick squeezed his adorable granddaughter in his arms and kissed her cheeks, one after the other rapidly, eight times. Fiona was a stunning child with her strawberry blonde hair and big green eyes. Her smile and beautiful face that was adorned with freckles lit up any room. And her kind, caring spirit melted her grandfather's heart.

"Eight kisses for the eight-year-old!" said Patrick jovially. "I do love ya to da moon and back, me Fiona!"

"I love you more, Papa!" Fiona gushed. Then, she swiftly made her way to her seat, where she picked up her fork and knife and sat staring at the food in front of her. "Time to eat, Gran?"

"Yes, love, it is indeed time to eat!" replied Grace. "But first, what do we say?"

"*Grace!*" yelled Fiona.

"Indeed!" Grace replied. "Princess Fee, will you do the great honor of thanking our Lord for this bountiful feast that He has provided for us?"

"Yes, ma'am. Dear Jesus, t'ank you fer dis feets and t'ank ya fer me gran who cooks so yummy and good. Amen!" said Fiona.

"Ya mean *feast*, Li'l Sis!" said Ian, with a face-palm.

"I said *feast*, Ian!" Fiona replied with a scowl.

"Ya did jus fine, sis," William interjected.

"T'ank ya, Da," Fiona said and then shot her brother a look, narrowing her eyes.

"Indeed, dat was a beautiful prayer, Miss Fee. And ya know da Lord is smilin' down upon you," Patrick offered, which made Fiona smile broadly. The family then enjoyed Grace's scrumptious breakfast as they ate and chatted about the weather and how the pub was doing. After everyone had finished and Grace had finished cleaning the kitchen, she summoned her family to the backyard, where several baby goats greeted them.

"Children, would you please feed the chickens for ya gran?" asked Grace.

"Yes, ma'am!" replied Ian and Fiona enthusiastically as they ran to the feed barn to retrieve the chicken feed and then into the chicken coop. As the two scattered feed for the chickens, Grace addressed William.

"How are ya, William?"

"I'm okay, Mum," William replied as he stared at his children.

"William Athy, ya can't fool yer mum! It's been over a week since Lily of the Valley was killed, and you've barely said two words about it! Now, ya wanna tell me the truth, son? Please," Grace said as she pulled a chair up directly across from William.

"Whataya wunt me to say, Mum? I was devastated. I was angry. I wanted revenge. But none of those wants will bring my mare back. None of those things will actually help find the culprit, Mum. I know that. So I have tried to focus on my children. They are the most important part of my life, and I cannot set out to take revenge on whoever killed my horse, knowing that I could be put in jail or end up dead! They need their only surviving parent *alive*, at the very least," William replied, tears welling up in his eyes.

"Oh, Willie, I love you, my dear, sweet, wonderful son," Grace said slowly. "But yer cuttin' off your nose to spite yer face, love. Come wit' me, Will. Come on!"

Grace took her middle son by the hand and led him into the house. As she walked toward the back door, she yelled over her shoulder, "Paddy, dear, please watch the wee ones for a bit, will ya, lover?"

"Of course, my bride. It is my pleasure to do your will," Patrick said as he bowed as if he were a court jester, causing his two grandchildren to burst out laughing.

"Oh, Papaw, you are hildareous!" screamed Fiona.

Once inside the house, Grace led William to the study, motioned for him to sit as she took a seat behind her desk. Grace Athy was not only a wife, mother, and grandmother, she was also the head bookkeeper and co-manager of the family businesses. As William sat down, Grace took a key from her top drawer and used it to unlock a drawer in the filing cabinet behind her. She retrieved a large envelope from the cabinet and set it on the desk in front of her. William stared at his mother with one eyebrow raised.

"Yer not gonna tell me there's a secret passage in here too, are ya, Mum?" William said, semi-joking.

"Wouldn't you like to know!" replied Grace sarcastically.

Then she continued, and her voice became more serious. "My dear William, I was goin' to wait till you were older to give you this, but recent events have changed me mind, and I think you should have it now, love."

"What's this, Mum?" William questioned.

"This is your da's and my last will and testament, son," she replied as she slid the envelope across the desk, closer to William.

"And? What does it have to do with me?" Will replied.

"Open it, son," Grace replied with a nod.

William picked up the envelope, opened it, and withdrew the contents. As he read the six-page document, his eyes grew larger, and he shot a glance of surprise at his mother.

"Mum, what is the meaning of this?" William said softly after reading the document in its entirety.

"Did ya not read it, son?" Grace said, bordering on frustration.

"Mum, ya saw me read it. I read it all! It names *me* as executor of yer will. Why? I am *not* the oldest! What will Paddy say about this? Plus, I hardly think we need to be talkin' about this now, Mum!" William said as he arose from his chair and walked to peer out the window.

"William, Paddy knows everything. Who do ya t'ink insisted *you* be the executor?" Grace replied.

William turned to face Grace, shock on his face. "What? Paddy knows? He insisted I be the executor? Why?" he pressed as he returned to his chair.

"Well, love, you are the only logical choice. You are next in line to be the chieftain of Clan Athy," Grace replied as she studied William's face for his reaction.

"Hahaha . . . what? *Me?* How can that be? I am the *middle* son, Mum! I am not rightfully or logically the right choice at all!" William said, shaking his head.

"William, you are the oldest son," Grace said as she returned the envelope to the file cabinet and pulled out another.

As Grace placed another envelope on her desk, William shook his head and sneered at his mother in disbelief. "What are ya talkin' 'bout, Mum?"

"William, you are the oldest of our three biological sons. You see, your two older brothers are actually yer cousins," Grace explained.

Will jumped to his feet, knocking his chair over and let out a loud "What the hell are you sayin', Mum? How could ya have kept *this* from me all these years? How dare you and Da lie to me my entire life! Yer liars and hypocrites!"

"Willie, calm down, love," Grace whispered as she stood.

"Dun't ya dare tell me to calm down! I deserve to be angry! My parents are liars!" William replied.

Just then, Patrick and Patrick Jr. entered the study. "Will, dun't talk to yer mum like that, son! It was not her idea to keep anyt'ing from you. It was necessary and it was my doin'!" Patrick said in a stern voice.

"I'm sorry, Da, but I will talk to ya two any way I choose, considering yer liars and betrayed me!" With that, William dashed from the room, yelled for his children, and left hastily.

"Oh my. I t'ink I mucked that all up, dears," Grace said as she fell back into her chair and began to sob.

"My darlin', you did what you had to do," Patrick replied as he knelt beside his wife and wrapped his arms around her. "He will calm down. And when he does, we will explain it all to 'em, love."

"So ya told 'em the entire story, Mum?" asked Pat Jr.

Grace nodded and shrugged at the same time. "I tried, but there is so much more to say," she managed to say in a hoarse voice. "He needs to hear the whole truth."

The whole truth was proving to be more of a challenge to convey than Grace and Patrick ever imagined. Their dear son William was devastated, angry, and disappointed in his parents, and they knew his emotions were justified. However, their hopes were still high that William would forgive them once he knew the entire story. The story spans centuries and tells a tale greater than any fictional novel ever could—the story of Clan Athy, the rightful heirs to the Celtic monarchy, a family that fought bravely but could not endure the British military's centuries-long brutal onslaught, who held the key to the demise of the farcical British Empire!

As the sun set on what was one of the worst days of William Athy's life, he sat in his porch swing and downed his third bottle of Guinness. The sound of the rushing Nire River brought solace somehow to Will's troubled soul. He watched the horizon turn pink and orange, which made everything take on a rosy hue. His children were inside, watching their favorite show on the telly, giving William time to mull over all that had transpired that day. The sound of vehicles approaching and car headlights cutting through the beautiful sunset colors caused him to be jolted back into his earlier heartache. "Who is this, I wonder?" Will whispered to himself. As the two vehicles drew closer, William recognized his parents' car. "Oh, great . . . they're here to tell me more nonsensical dribble about Clan Athy history!" he continued as he arose and walked out into his well-manicured yard to greet his family.

William glared at his parents, brother, and Jennifer Sweeney as they all exited their vehicles. "Wait, Pat Jr. and Jennifer Sweeney?" he said to himself. "What is *she* doin' here?"

Will was delighted to see Jenn but had no idea why she was with his family. "Hello, stranger!" Jenn said as she approached William for a hug.

"Umm, hellooo?" William replied, one eyebrow raised.

"Sorry to just barge in but your mom asked me to come along to help with the kids," Jennifer replied.

"Help with *my* kids? Why would I need help wit' my kids?" Will said as he shot his mother an angry look.

"Before you start on me again, Willie, I indeed asked Jennifer to come tonight. You will be coming with us, and she will look after the wee ones," Grace replied.

"I am goin' nowhere wit' you!" William spat back.

"William, *do not* talk to yer mum like that! I know yer upset, son, but there is no need for disrespectin' yer mum," Patrick snapped.

"Upset? *Upset?* That is the biggest understatement I've ever heard, Da! Or are you really me da? Or is dat a lie too?" William shot back, now feeling the effects of the three bottles of Guinness.

"William, if ya dun't come wit' us, we cannot explain t'ings properly. You must give us a chance to tell ya the entire story, Willie!" Grace begged.

"Mum, I am not goin' anywh—" William started but was interrupted.

"Will, get in the damn car. All of our lives are at stake, and ya need to stop bein' an utter arse already!" shouted Pat Jr.

"I'm the arse? *I am the arse?*" William replied.

Jennifer had let herself into William's house and was about to prepare a snack for Ian and Fiona, when she heard Pat Jr. shout. In order to keep them calm and divert their attention, she said, "Hey, you two, want to rent a movie?"

"Yeah!" Ian and Fiona said enthusiastically.

"All righty then! You pick one and I will make you something to snack on!" Jenn replied as she peered out the kitchen window at the Athy family conference going on in the yard.

"Who do ya t'ink ya are, Paddy, talkin' to me like that?" Will spat. "And if yer me cousin, why is yer name Patrick Athy Jr., genius, huh? Answer me dat, *Pat Juniorrrr*!

"I am yer cousin, Will. And my name is Patrick Thomas Eugene Athy after me dearly departed father, your uncle and your da's brother! Now, get in that damn car befer I kick yer arse to next Tuesday!' Pat Jr. spat back.

"I said *no!*" Will said firmly. And as he turned to head to his porch, Patrick Athy grabbed him firmly and gently stabbed his son in the arm with a hypodermic needle. William looked at his father in shock. Ten seconds later, he was out.

Grace let herself into William's house to make sure her grandchildren were taken care of. Jenn met her at the back door.

"Ah, there ya are, Jenn!" said Grace. "We will be taking William to a . . . meeting in town. Can you put the kids to bed and stay the night, love?"

"Of course. What kind of meeting is it at this hour?" Jenn inquired.

"Just a business meeting, dear, nothing to be concerned about at all," Grace replied.

"William isn't going to say good night to his kids . . . or me?" Jenn asked, causing herself to blush.

"He is already on his way to the meeting wit' Paddy, love. He will see you in da mornin'!" Grace said with a reassuring nod as she made her way to Fiona and Ian's bedrooms.

"An all-night meeting? Hmmm," Jenn whispered under her breath.

Grace opened the door to Ian's bedroom to find both her grandchildren lying on the floor in a tent made of sheets and blankets, watching a movie on William's computer.

"I see the two of ya are snug as bugs in a rug! Just comin' to say g'night and love ya!" Grace said in the best jovial voice she could muster as she knelt down beside the tent. Fiona popped up, threw her arms around Grace's neck, and kissed her firmly on the cheek.

"Nighty night, Gram! Love ya lots and lots!" Fiona gushed.

"G'night, my sweet princess. Now, just to let ya both know, yer da is having a sleepover at my and Papa's house, just for tonight. He will be back in the mornin'," Grace said.

Ian stopped the movie and hugged his grandmother, kissed her on the cheek, and said, "Da didn't say g'night, Gram. Why? Is everyt'ing all right?"

"Oh, everyt'ing is fine, love. He and Papa just forgot. No worries!" Grace replied as she helped them both back into their tent, tucked them in, and kissed them again on their foreheads. "You will see dem both in the morn!"

"Do you like our awesome tent, Gram?" asked Fiona. "Jenn made it jus' fer us!"

"I love it, Fee! It is indeed awesome! Is that a word ya jus' learned?" Grace asked.

"Yeah, I like the 'merican words, Gram, dun't you? Jenn is teaching us new words." Fiona replied, smiling wide.

"Dat's wonderful, love, but dun't fergit: yer Irish! Hahah," Grace said as she gave her grandchildren a tickle. "See ya in da mornin', loves of me life!"

Jenn watched from the bedroom door as Grace said good night to Ian and Fiona. She thought it was so sweet how close they all were. But she also wondered what on earth was happening in William's front yard. A minute prior, Jenn witnessed William being placed in Grace's car, and he didn't look like he was doing well at all. As Grace exited Ian's room, she pulled the door shut quietly.

"We dun't want them to be disturbed. Now, you can sleep in William's room and help yerself to whatever ya need, love. I will call and check on ya in the morn," Grace said as she hurried to let herself out through the back door.

"But, but, Grace, *wait!*" Jenn blurted out.

Grace stopped abruptly, eyes widened, mouth opened. "Yes, Jenn. What is it, dear?" she asked.

"What is going on out there?" Jenn asked as she pointed to the front yard, where she had just seen Patrick and Pat Jr. load William into Grace's car.

"Love, everyt'ing is just fi—" started Grace, only to be interrupted.

"Please, Grace! I just saw your husband and son load your other son into your minivan, and Will didn't look so fine to me!" Jenn replied, visibly agitated. "I need to know what I am getting myself into, now!"

Grace took her hand off the back-door handle and turned to face Jennifer. "Dear, sweet Jenn, know this: there is nuthin' illegal or underhand goin' on out there. Willie will be fine, but we need to handle a very pressing family matter tonight. Please, you must trust me! You will be told everyt'ing as well in due time, love. Trust me?"

Jenn drew in a deep breath and looked toward the front window and then back at Grace. "Okay, I will trust you, but I need to know that these children and I are not in any danger. I know a lot of weird stuff has gone on here: Will's prized mare being killed and mysterious notes showing up everywhere. I will trust you because I think you are truly good people. But I will need to be in the loop soon, or I'm out!"

"I understand fully, Jenn. You deserve to know and be in da loop! But tonight, right here, right now, is not the time fer it!" Grace then embraced Jennifer and whispered, "All in good time, love, all in good time."

And with that, Grace left, shutting the door behind her.

Patrick and Pat Jr. had carefully lifted William into Grace's minivan, buckling him in, and the four were on the road within seconds, leaving Pat Jr.'s Jeep in William's driveway. Grace was behind the wheel.

"Are ya sure he is okay, love?" asked Grace in a concerned voice.

"He is going to be fine, Gracie. We had to resort to this for his own good, you know that," Patrick replied.

"I know, but it seems awfully drastic," Grace pressed.

"Mum, how else could we 'ove done what we had to do? Will needs to hear the truth. He refused to listen, so we *had* to do what was necessary. All of our lives depend on it!" replied Pat Jr.

Grace rounded the corner that led to the Athy family pub and came to an abrupt stop next to two black SUVs that were parked on the side of the road. Patrick rolled down his passenger-side window.

"We have him, but he had to be sedated. Follow us, park around back of the pub, in the garage. Close the garage door after ya, so no one spots yer cars," Patrick said to the driver of the lead SUV.

With that, all three cars continued together to the Athy family pub. Once they arrived in the parking lot, Grace stopped directly in front of the side door, and the two black SUVs continued on, around the corner of the building, to the garage, where they disappeared into the darkness.

Grace got out of her car, unlocked the side door, and propped it open. Patrick and Pat Jr. ever so carefully carried William from the parked minivan into the pub and placed him on the couch in Patrick's office. Grace then placed a blanket over her son and leaned down to kiss him on the forehead. "Me precious boy, I pray you receive this news well and you will find it in yer heart to forgive us." She then sat down next to William on the couch and let out a long, loud sigh, then placed her hand on William's foot as she closed her eyes and bowed her head. "Father in heaven, be wit' us as we tell this young man the truth of his heritage and rightful place as Eire's true and rightful sovereign."

"Come in, my bruthers, come in!" Patrick said as he, Pat Jr., and thirteen other men entered the office. "Please, sit. Paddy, would ya fetch us a bottle of Jameson and thirteen glasses? And fetch one fer yerself too," Patrick asked, still breathless from carrying William from Grace's car to the couch in his office.

Pat motioned to the men as he asked them to gather around the conference table that sat in the middle of his large office. "Come in, lads. Sit down, please. We'll share in a drink and a toast to God's divine favor in the endeavor that lies befer us." The men gathered around the large table, each looking at William as they found their places. Pat Jr. followed the last man in, carrying a large tray filled with glasses and a bottle of Jameson whiskey, which he set in front of his father, who stood at the end of the large oval table and then took a seat next to his mother, in an armchair. Patrick then opened the bottle of whiskey, poured a measured two fingers in each of the fourteen glasses, and gave each glass to the man on his right, who, in turn, passed each glass to his right until all fourteen had their share. Patrick then cleared his throat and began a toast: "Beannaithe a bheith le Dia ár nAthair agus Íosa Críost a mhac a n-aonar!

"Tá muid, na Cheiftans de na Ceithre Thrí Déag de chuid na Gaillimhe, sula mbeidh an Uile-chumhdach humbled, agus biotáilleacha ag iarraidh teacht ar an bhfabhar sa iarracht atá romhainn. Lig dúinn ár gcreideamh a bhreithniú le chéile:

"Táimid, seirbhísigh Dhia agus Eire, ag iarraidh seasamh le haghaidh fírinne, ceartais, ionracas agus luach. Cosnaimid orainn ár n-Eire beloved go dtí bás agus fírinne dár oidhreacht cheart a thabhairt don domhan. Ní thabharfaimid tarscaoileadh ná déanfaidh muid an chuid eile go dtí go mbeidh ár n-Eire beloved arís agus go deo an náisiún a bhfuil sé beartaithe ag Dia. Ní thabharfaimid tarscaoileadh ná ní bheidh muid ag fanacht go dtí go mbeidh ár Rí ceart ag brath ar an gCúlta Ceiltigh le riail thar na hoileáin seo, Na hOileáin Cheiltigh!

"Lig dúinn anois toast.

"Go Dia agus Eire!"

Translated:

"Blessed be to God our Father and Jesus Christ, His only begotten Son!

"We, the chieftains of the Fourteen Tribes of Galway, stand before the Almighty humbled, with spirits of contrition to ask for favor in the endeavor before us. Let us recite our creed together:

"We, the servants of God and Eire, vow to stand for truth, justice, integrity, and valor. We will defend our beloved Eire until death and bring the truth of our rightful inheritance to the world. We will not waver or rest until our beloved Eire is once again and forever the sovereign, united nation God intended. We will not waver or rest until our rightful king sits upon the Celtic throne to rule over these isles, the Celtic Isles!

"Let us now toast.

"To God and Eire!"

"To God and Eire!" repeated the thirteen men. And they all drank together. "Please, be seated," said Patrick. As the men were seated, he continued, "As you all know, the appointed time has come. The Knights of Solomon's Temple have been summoned here, to the Nire Valley and will arrive at any moment. The attacks have started, as we knew they would, and we will need every clan member to do their part. Now, let us not break with tradition." Patrick nodded to Ciaran Skerrett, chieftain of Clan Skerrett, who arose and pulled a ram's horn from the satchel that he wore across his chest. He drew in a deep breath, put it to his lips, and blew. The sound permeated throughout the Athy family pub—a sound that was mightier, louder, and more earth-shaking than a thousand trumpets. He blew fourteen ten-second-long blasts that sent chills down the spine of every person in the room—fourteen chilling reminders that the Tribes of Galway were alive, well, and ready for battle!

Ciaran Skerrett was a large middle-aged man who was often mistaken for the actor Sean Connery. His grey hair was waist-length and worn in a ponytail that cascaded down his back. His eyes were emerald green, which lent a dramatic flair to the permanent fierce expression on his weathered face. He stowed the ram's horn back in its place and nodded back at Patrick as he sat back down. Patrick stood and said, "Chieftains of the Tribes of Galway, sound off! Clan Athy, present!"

Aiden Blake stood and said, "Clan Blake, present!"

Daniel Bodkin stood and said, "Clan Bodkin, present!" And so it went with all fourteen Clan chieftains.

Clan chieftains Conor Browne, Ryan D'Arcy, Dylan Deane, Sean Font, Stephen French, Darragh Joyce, Robert Kirwan, Patrick Lynch, Thom Martin, Liam Morris, and Ciaran Skerrett.

When Ciaran Skerrett finished the clan roll call, he took the ram's horn and blew three ten-second blasts, and the fourteen all sat down. "Let this meeting be called to order. Chieftain and Chaplain Lynch, please open this meeting with a prayer," said Patrick Athy.

Patrick Lynch then bowed his head and began the benediction, from Saint Patrick's Breastplate:

> We arise today
> Through a mighty strength,
> the invocation of the Trinity,
> Through belief in the Threeness,
> Through confession of the Oneness
> of the Creator of creation.
> We arise today
> Through the strength of Christ's
> birth with His baptism,
> Through the strength of His crucifixion
> with His burial,
> Through the strength of His resurrection
> with His ascension,
> Through the strength of His descent
> for the Day of Judgment.
> We arise today
> Through the strength of the love
> of cherubim,
> In the obedience of angels,
> In the service of archangels,
> In the hope of resurrection to meet
> with reward,
> In the prayers of patriarchs,
> In the predictions of prophets,
> In the preaching of apostles,
> In the faith of confessors,

In the innocence of holy virgins,
In the deeds of righteous men.
We arise today, through
The strength of heaven,
The light of the sun,
The radiance of the moon,
The splendor of fire,
The speed of lightning,
The swiftness of wind,
The depth of the sea,
The stability of the earth,
The firmness of rock.
We arise today, through
God's strength to pilot me,
God's might to uphold us,
God's wisdom to guide us,
God's eye to look before us,
God's ear to hear us,
God's word to speak for us,
God's hand to guard us,
God's shield to protect us,
God's host to save us
From snares of devils,
From temptation of vices,
From everyone who shall wish us ill,
afar and near.
We summon today
All these powers between us and
those evils,
Against every cruel and merciless power
that may oppose our bodies and souls,
Against incantations of false prophets,
Against black laws of pagandom,
Against false laws of heretics,
Against craft of idolatry,
Against spells of witches and smiths
and wizards,
Against every knowledge that corrupts

man's body and soul;
Christ to shield us today
Against poison, against burning,
Against drowning, against wounding,
So that there may come to us an
abundance of reward.
Let us say the following together:
Christ with me,
Christ before me,
Christ behind me,
Christ in me,
Christ beneath me,
Christ above me,
Christ on my right,
Christ on my left,
Christ when I lie down,
Christ when I sit down,
Christ when I arise,
Christ in the heart of every man
who thinks of me,
Christ in the mouth of everyone
who speaks of me,
Christ in every eye that sees me,
Christ in every ear that hears me.
We arise today
Through a mighty strength,
the invocation of the Trinity,
Through belief in the Threeness,
Through confession of the Oneness
of the Creator of creation.
Amen.

# Chapter Thirteen

## Meanwhile, Back at the Ranch

Angus and Molly slept so soundly they never heard Molly's cell phone alarm go off. At 7:30 a.m., both were startled awake by a loud banging on Angus' trailer door.

"What . . . who . . . what in the name of . . . who's there?" managed Angus as he tried to open his tired eyes.

"Mr. McCullough? Mr. McCullough? Are you in there? Mr. McCullough, sir . . . you are needed in makeup ASAP! Mr. Gallo is frantic, Molly is missing! Mr. McCullough, *please open the door*!" a voice shouted from outside the door.

"All right, all right, I'm comin', for shat sakes! Hold on!" Angus shouted with a strained voice. "Molly, love . . . wake up. We're late."

"Huh, what? Oh *nooo*!" Molly squealed. "My darn phone alarm! I didn't hear, did you?"

"Well, obviously no, I didn't," replied Angus sarcastically.

Molly raised an eyebrow and said, "Well, excuse me!"

"No, I didn't mean it to come out like that, love," Angus said as he was now almost awake and headed to his door.

"Well, I should hope not," Molly yelled on her way to the bathroom.

Angus opened his door to find Rudy Gallo's assistant, Kevin, pacing and biting his nails.

"Sorry, lad, we didn't hear the alarm!" Angus offered.

"We? Is Molly in there with you?" asked Kevin as he pushed his way by Angus to enter the trailer. "Where is she? You two need to get to makeup *now*, or my booty is toast!" Kevin said, obviously exasperated.

"I'm here, Kev. We will be there in five!" Molly shouted from the bathroom.

"Okay. But Rudy is really ticked off! He scares me," whined Kevin.

"Okay, like me wifey said, we'll be there in five!" replied Angus as he grabbed Kevin's arm to escort him out.

"Ouch! Whoa, down, boy! I am leaving! But you two need to read the Star Gaze fraternization rules and then get your lovebird asses to makeup!" Kevin said teasingly.

"Yeah, yeah, we'll be on our way. Now, get out! And we are *not* lovebirds nor are we fraternizing!" Angus shouted back.

With that, Kevin hurried out of the trailer, and Angus slammed the door behind him.

"What a pain in the arse he is!" grumbled Angus.

"He's just doing his job, Angus," said Molly as she hurried past her leading man, sporting wet hair, still wearing her robe. "Thanks for the sleepover, love!" she gushed, patting him on the cheek. "See you in a bit!" she sang as she opened the door and disappeared.

"Umm, uhh, okay," was all Angus could manage.


"Where in god's name have you two been?!" shouted Rudy Gallo as Angus and Molly entered the makeup trailer. "You have put production back at least two hours!"

"Sorry, boss," said Molly in her best baby-talk voice.

"Yeah, sorry, Rudy. We didn't hear the alarm," offered Angus halfheartedly.

"*We*? We didn't hear the alarm? Are you kidding me? You two are supposed to be professionals, for Pete's sakes! What were you thinking?" Rudy replied in anger.

"Well, she is me wifey, Rudy!" Angus quipped.

Molly, who had just taken a large gulp of water, let out a roar of laughter and spewed water all over the mirror in front of her, which caused her makeup artist to drop the liquid makeup spray nozzle, which hit the floor and started spraying makeup everywhere.

"For the love of God, grab the nozzle!" Rudy shrieked.

An hour later, Molly and Angus arrived on the set in a golf cart to thunderous applause from the rest of the cast and crew. They bowed and curtsied, overexaggerating every move.

"All right, all right. Places, people!" yelled Rudy. "No reason to applaud bad behavior! We all need to be extra focused today. Today, we shoot the Battle of Athanariogh! As you all know from reading the script and Patrick Athy's incredibly genius book, *The Battle of Athanariogh*, put the Athy family on the map historically. It was a bloody, violent battle with many casualties. But the Tribes of Galway were victorious, and Thomas Athy, who is being played by none other than our amazing leading man, Zachariah Smith, became the Baron of Atheney!" Applause broke out again from the cast and crew as they looked around for Zach Smith. After several minutes, Zach came running onto the set, half-clothed and looking disheveled as he managed to wrestle on his costume shirt. "Thank you, thank you, everyone!" Zach said, as he took bows like a Broadway star on opening night.

"Mr. Smith, thank you for joining us!" Rudy spat. "If you wouldn't mind, we would *like to get started on filming a movie sometime toodaaay!*"

Just then, a lovely young extra made her way to the set, looking ravaged and disheveled herself as she too struggled to get her costume back in order.

"Miss James?" Rudy said in a scolding tone as he shot Zach a nasty glare. "Any more of this, you will both be fired! Understood, Miss James? Zachariah?"

All the poor, mortified girl could manage to say was "Yes, sir, Mr. Rudy, I mean, Mr. Gallo," as she stared at her feet in embarrassment.

"Well, I guess it's no great mystery where our *leading* man was. HA! He was *leading* that poor, innocent girl down the road to trouble!" Angus blurted out, which caused the entire set to erupt into laughter. Zach ran his hands through his messy hair, puffed out his chest, raised one eyebrow, and flashed a broad grin. "Damn straight!" he replied, which caused another eruption of laughter from the large crowd of cast and crew.

"All right, all right . . . *enough*!" shouted Rudy. "To your places, people!" Then he whispered in Zach's ear, "You behave, or *I will indeed* fire you!"

Zach bowed his head and replied, "Yes, my liege."

The crowd dispersed noisily as the cast and crew continued to laugh and discuss the morning's events.

The Jarvis Ranch was bustling with not only movie staff but also several law enforcement officers and security guards who had been hired to keep an eye on things after the events of the past two weeks. No arrests had been made, and no clues had been found to help solve the mystery of the note on the spear, the falling plow in the barn, or the murdered horse. This made Roy and Sue Jarvis very uneasy. Even though they both had great respect for law enforcement and appreciated their comforting presence on their property, Roy and Sue, along with their entire family, were armed to the hilt. The Jarvis children, who included not only Roy and Sue's children but also their nieces and nephews, were transformed into a security force to be reckoned with. Roy had organized a strategic security plan that functioned 24/7 and covered every inch of the Jarvis Ranch. He employed neighbors as well to patrol the surrounding area. If someone or some people wanted to threaten or cause any further havoc, they would be met with more than they bargained for.

After things settled down on the set, filming commenced with no glitches, threats, or delays. In other words, it was an uneventful day. Rudy Gallo was ecstatic as he watched each scene unfold. The horses were even behaving, and the cast and crew worked incredibly hard to make sure every line was done right and every scene was perfection.

"This day may have started out rough, but wow, just wow!" Rudy exclaimed to the small group of cast members enjoying a much-needed break by a set campfire that was built for the last scene of the day. "Bravo to you all! You were spectacular today! Even *you*, Zachariah!" he said with a half-smile.

"Well, somebody pinch me. I must be dreaming! Did Rudy Gallo just pay *me* a compliment?" Zach replied, oozing sarcasm.

Roy Jarvis was patrolling the perimeter of his land, driving his old International Scout along the river. He stopped at the edge of the woods, near where they had discovered the spear with the Gaelic message attached to it. He got out of his vehicle slowly, stretched his tired muscles, and yawned. "What a day," he whispered to himself as he meandered closer to the slow-moving river. Once he drew closer to the edge, he looked out over the lovely setting. The ranch was one of the most breathtaking pieces of property in all of Ireland. With its rolling green hills, crystal-clear river and streams, magnificent ancient oaks, and fragrant pine trees, Jarvis Ranch was Roy's heaven on earth. He continued to walk slowly down the river's edge and came to a clearing where several tree stumps were arranged around a fire pit. He sat on one of the stumps, pulled out his hand-hewed pipe and a small pouch of tobacco from his vest pocket, filled the pipe, and lit it. Roy drew in the delicious smoke and blew it out slowly with a sigh. This was his happy place, his sanctuary. It was where he came to think and clear his head. He then reached into his other vest pocket, pulled out a small pewter flask, opened it, and took a sip of homemade whiskey. The warmth of the whiskey traveled all the way down his throat and into his stomach, which made him realize he hadn't eaten since eight thirty that morning. *I had better get myself some nourishment soon, before I fall over! I don't want to cause my Sue any more worry*, he thought to himself. *Poor woman has had enough worry for two lifetimes.*

Only Roy, Sue, and Roy's oncologist knew of Roy's condition. He had been diagnosed with prostate cancer right before Christmas and had refused any chemotherapy. Sue Jarvis did her best to remain strong but was beginning to lose that strength because of her husband's adamant refusal to receive any therapy. Roy was of the mindset that any radiation would be worse than the disease itself. He had seen his uncle go through two years of horrible suffering because of chemotherapy and wanted nothing to do with it. "If I'm gonna suffer, it will be on my terms!" he had said. But now, Roy had seen the effects of his decision on his beloved wife's face every day. She had aged ten years in just a few short months. Then, when Roy decided to let Star Gaze film a movie on their ranch, Sue became very withdrawn at times, spending sometimes days in the seclusion of her small art cabin on the south end of their land. Roy knew he had disappointed her and upset her badly, and he was deep in thought about what he needed to do to rectify the situation, when a sound of footsteps jolted him back into the present. He looked toward where the sounds were coming from and saw two figures walking toward him, unrecognizable at first. But as they drew closer, Roy saw that it was two of his sons approaching from the back forty.

"Da! What are ya doin' out here by yerself? Ya know there is a murderer on the loose!" the eldest, Robert, yelled, still ten meters away.

"Hello, boys! Yes, I know. I am fine, got my revolver right here in its holster!" he said as he patted his right side.

"Good. But, Da, you really should have someone wit' ya at all times, jus' in case," said the youngest, Samuel.

"Where have the two of ya been?" Roy asked as his two sons approached the campfire site and sat down on either side of their father.

"We were walkin' the property line, up and around the old graveyard," answered Robert.

"Everything okay up there, then?" Roy pressed.

"Yeah, everyt'ing is quiet, Da," replied Samuel.

"But we did notice some tracks up there. Quite a few tracks, actually, and they were all over the place. It looked like several men were up there, around the large stone. And whoever was up there had built a fire and left some items on the ground nearby," Robert explained.

"What kind of items, son?" Roy replied.

"Well, it looked like candles that were almost completely used up and some parchment paper that looked to be burned on the edges. Oh, and it smelled like petrol too," Robert continued.

"Hmmm," Roy said as he removed his hat and scratched his forehead. "Well, I guess we better post security up there, just in case, boys."

"Yes, sir," replied Robert. "Consider it done."

"All right, my boys, we had better get back to the house. Your mother will be worrying after us," said Roy as he arose from his seat. Once standing, Roy began to teeter slightly, then, as he tried to take a step, he stumbled and fell to the ground, hitting his head on a rock rendering him unconscious.

"*Da! Da!*" yelled Robert.

"*Da!* Rob, what's happening to him? Da!" screamed Samuel.

"I dun't know! Go get help. *Now!*" Robert replied frantically as he removed his flannel shirt, tore a strip of material from it, and did his best to bind his father's head wound. "He is bleedin' pretty bad, Sam . . . hurry! I dun't want to move him!"

Samuel jumped into his father's Scout, started it, pushed the accelerator to the floor, and sped away toward the Jarvis house. As he made his way, he dialed 999 on his cell phone.

"This is 999. What is your emergency?" the voice on the phone asked.

"Me da is dyin' . . . please, send an ambulance *now!*" replied Samuel.

As the cast and crew were finishing their long day of filming and heading back to their trailers, Samuel Jarvis came speeding into the parking lot next to the barn and brought his father's Scout to an abrupt stop. "Help! Please help! Me da has fallen and hit his head . . . it's very, very bad! I called an ambulance—they should be here by now!" he cried.

"What? Samuel, where is he? Did you leave him alone?" asked Angus as he approached Samuel.

"He is down by the river. Rob is wit' him," Samuel replied in a concerned voice. "He staggered and then fell, hit his head on a rock and is bleedin' bad."

"Okay, Sam . . . Ah, that'd be the ambulance!" Angus said as the sound of sirens drew closer. "Come on, lad, we will show them where yer da is!" With that, Samuel and Angus jumped into the Scout and headed to the main gate of Jarvis Ranch. Several of the cast, crew, and Jarvis family members had heard Samuel and were already on their way to the river. Samuel and Angus met the ambulance at the gate and motioned for them to follow.

"He is this way, down by the river!" Angus shouted to the EMTs that were driving the ambulance.

"There are more fire trucks and another emergency team coming behind us!" replied one of the EMTs.

"Okay, I will leave the gate open for them!" Samuel shouted back.

By the time the emergency crew, Samuel, and Angus arrived at the scene by the river, there were dozens of people congregated around Roy Jarvis. Robert was still holding his father's head, in an effort to stop the bleeding.

"Please, help him! He has lost a lot of blood," Robert pleaded with the approaching emergency crew.

"We will take it from here, sir. Thank you," one of the EMTs replied.

Robert was visibly distraught as he arose and wiped the tears from his face. "He has cancer," he said as he made his way to sit on one of the stumps that were placed around the fire pit. "He has stage three prostate cancer."

Samuel, who had made his way to his father's side, stood up abruptly. "What? Robbie, what do you mean? How do you know that? How do I *not* know that?" he stammered.

"I found the hospital and doctor bills in Da's desk when I was looking for grain receipts yesterday. I was goin' to confront him about it tonight," replied Robert.

The EMTs stabilized Roy, whose head was drenched in blood and was still unconscious. They readied him for transport to Tipperary General Hospital. Sue Jarvis arrived just as they were lifting her beloved husband into the waiting ambulance. "I will ride with him," she managed.

"Yes, ma'am," the EMT replied as he helped Sue into the ambulance seat, next to Roy. Once safely seated, Sue looked at her husband, who was still seemingly lifeless. The right side of his head was severely swollen and bandaged, but the blood was still seeping through. The sight of him made Sue sob uncontrollably as the ambulance began its fifteen-minute journey to Tipperary General. Samuel and Robert piled into Roy's Scout and followed.

Angus stood on one of the stumps near the river and addressed the crowd: "Can I have yer attention, everyone? Gather round, please. What the Jarvis family needs right now is our thoughts and prayers. And we must do what we can to help keep this ranch running smoothly so the family can be where they need to be, by Roy's side during this most difficult time." Many in the crowd responded with *yeses* and *amens*. "So let's all head back, and I will ask Robert and Samuel what we need to do to help them around here in the mornin'." With that, the crowd dispersed.

Molly Taggart, who was cast as Angus' onscreen wife, sidled up next to him as the mountain of a Scotsman started the rather long walk back to his trailer. The trail was well lit by floodlights that were set up for filming night scenes. Angus was glad to have Molly's arm in his as they made their way in the cool Irish summer night.

"I hope he is okay," Molly said quietly.

"He has cancer, love," replied Angus as he squeezed his leading lady's hand. "From what Robert said, there's not much any of us can do now. Except pray."

The next morning, as the sun rose over the Nire Valley, the cast and crew were awakened by the sound of police asking everyone to congregate in the field by the barn. The PA system was so loud it made Angus jump up and take a battle stance. "What in the name of all that is holy is goin' on?!" he shouted. "Who the hell is shouting me awake at this unholy hour?"

Angus wrapped the bed sheet around himself as he made his way to the window to peer out in the direction of the racket. He became confused when he realized he was not in his trailer. As the fog lifted off his mind, he remembered he had stayed with Molly. "She needed consoling," he whispered to himself.

As he began to search for his trousers among the clothes scattered about the room, Molly shouted from the bathroom. "Angus, is that you?"

Angus froze at first, like a deer in headlights, as if anyone could see him. "Uh, yeah . . . hello there. Yes, I'm here! The police are asking us to meet in the field by the barn," he replied.

"What? Did you say police?" Molly replied as she exited the shower.

"Yes, the police are outside, and they're asking all cast and crew to meet them now." Angus managed as he hopped around Molly's bedroom on one leg, trying to get his pants on.

Molly wrapped a towel around herself and made her way to the bedroom, where she found Angus in a panic to get his clothes on.

"Dun't worry, love. You dun't have to rush off on my account. Nuthin' happened," she said.

"What? I dun't know what ya mean," Angus said as he stumbled over his boots.

"Angus! You drank most of me port last night and passed out on me bed!" Molly snorted.

Angus, now on the floor trying to retrieve his boots and shirt, stopped and looked at Molly. "Ya dun't say. So sorry, love," he managed.

And the two broke out in laughter as Molly helped Angus gather his things.

"Ya daft aper! Get yerself out to the field. I will be there shortly!" Molly said as she shook her head.

As the cast and crew slowly gathered, the police were setting up tables and asking everyone to form lines. Angus strolled slowly toward the surreal scene and came upon Zach and several extras that were at the back of one of the lines. "Top o' the mornin' to ya," Angus said with a nod to the small group.

"Hello there, my large Scottish friend! You're lookin' a bit green around the gills, sir!" Zach replied with a laugh.

"Haha, yes, I might have overindulged just a wee bit last evening!" Angus replied with a sigh. "What's happenin' here? Why the lines and what are the tables for?"

"Well, apparently and according to the scuttlebutt I overheard, Roy Jarvis was poisoned yesterday afternoon, and these fine law enforcement officers are determined to find out who did the poisoning!" Zach replied.

"Poisoned?" Angus said loudly, causing everyone standing in line and the police officers to turn and stare. "Sorry, folks, just found out the news!"

The PA system then came alive with static, and a burly, balding man in uniform stepped up onto the Star Gaze Production stage. He cleared his throat loudly for several seconds then began, "Ladies and gentlemen, can I have yer attention, please? Ladies and gentlemen? Hello, thank you for your undivided attention for the next few minutes. I am Chief Constable Connor Aberdeen. You all are probably wonderin' why we are here and what the tables are for. I have some disturbing news this mornin' . . . Roy Jarvis fell, hit his head, and was transported to Tipperary Hospital last evening."

"Yeah, tell us something we don't know!" Zach offered in his naturally sarcastic voice.

Without skipping a beat, Constable Aberdeen continued, "Mr. Jarvis suffered a severe concussion and is currently in ICU, unconscious. He lost a lot of blood and had to receive a transfusion. The doctors tending to Mr. Jarvis have informed us he was poisoned." A collective gasp came from the crowd. "So local law enforcement, in collaboration with Ireland's best from the Royal Constabulary, our version of the Feds, have opened a criminal investigation and will be questioning each and every one of you. The cast, crew, and Star Gaze administrative personnel, as well as Jarvis Ranch employees, are all being asked to please put your names, job title, country of origin, address, and telephone number on the forms provided on the tables. We appreciate your full cooperation in this matter as we do our best to find the perpetrator or perpetrators who committed this heinous act. As this is an ongoing investigation, I cannot comment on any particulars of the case. This is an active crime scene as well, so please do not disturb the area where Mr. Jarvis collapsed, down by the river. Thank you. You will be updated regularly as the investigation unfolds and information is made available." With that, Constable Aberdeen switched off the microphone and hurried off the stage to a waiting vehicle.

"Wow. This is crazy," said Zach as he put his hand on Angus' shoulder.

"Yes, it is crazy. So is the fact that you are actually touchin' me. Crazy and dangerous," said Angus as he glared at the Hollywood leading man.

"Oops! Sorry, Haus! No harm, no foul, bruh!" Zach replied, still as cocky as ever.

"Son, I am not your damn bruh, nor am I this Haus character! Show some respect, or you'll be Roy Jarvis' roomie at Tipperary Hospital!"

# Chapter Fourteen

## A Battle for the Ages

An evening of abundance had left Thomas, Dermot, Liam, and Ailan Athy exhausted. Father Patrick continued to attend to Dermot's wound, which was already much better. They had made their camp just outside the enormous cavern and hideout and fell asleep quickly, sleeping soundly for more than ten hours.

Archers and lookouts were standing constant guard over the large army of Celts and knights, which allowed a restful night for most, but not for Sir Renaud de Vichier. He had slept only four hours when he was awakened by a bad dream. He arose at three in the morning and fetched some water, paced around their campfire for over an hour, and then decided to check the archers and lookouts. He climbed to the top of the large dome that was the roof of the cavernous hideout and found two of his archers awake, alert and watching for any sign of intruders.

"Good morning, men. All is well?" Sir Renaud said quietly.

The two snapped to attention. "Yes, sir! All is clear!" one archer responded.

"Good, good. Remain vigilant. I have a feeling in the pit of my stomach that trouble is coming," Sir Renaud whispered.

Both archers looked at each other and then scanned the surrounding area, with worried faces.

"If there are intruders, Sir Renaud, we will spot them!" replied the other archer.

"Still, I believe I will wake our army soon. We must set out for the Nire sooner than later!" said Sir Renaud as he started his descent back to the cavern.

Once inside the massive hideout, Sir Renaud poured himself some cognac from one of the many barrels of spirits and ale stored in the Celts' wagons, to calm his nerves.

His nightmare was so vivid he could not return to sleep. In it, he saw a massive British army surrounding him as he stood in a field alone with only a dagger to protect himself. They were giant and armed with every imaginable weapon of warfare possible. When Sir Renaud tried to escape, the Brits drew closer and closer, encircling him and blocking any hope of getting away. He looked into their faces and only saw blackness. Then, the sound of the Royal Guard trumpets rang out; the British Army parted before Sir Renaud, who was now paralyzed with fear. In came a black stallion with what appeared to be a knight atop him. As he drew closer, Sir Renaud saw the coat of arms upon his chest. It was Henry III, King of England, wielding a large spear. In a split second, the English king was coming toward Sir Renaud, in a full gallop, raising his spear and launching it directly at his head. Just before the spear reached his forehead, Sir Renaud woke up in a panic, gasping for air and drenched in sweat.

*What is the meaning of this nightmare?* he thought to himself as he sat down next to one of the campfires, just outside the cavern entrance. He stared into the fire and tried to calm himself in prayer. Two hours later, the sound of a man's voice startled Sir Renaud awake.

"Awaken, my friend. We must prepare to leave right away! Sir Renaud? Wake up!" said Thomas Athy as he placed his hand on his comrade's shoulder.

Before Thomas could remove his hand, Sir Vichier had jumped up, twisted Thomas' arm behind his back and slammed him into the ground face-first, held a dagger to his throat, and yelled, "Arrêtez! Je vais te tuer, les porcs britanniques!" Translated: "Stop! I will kill you, British swine!"

Thomas swiftly reacted by grabbing Sir Renaud's wrist, removing the dagger, managed to stand and was behind his French comrade within a second. He held him in a headlock and whispered in his ear, "Mon ami, c'est moi, votre comrade, Thomas. Est-ce que tu vas bien? Je crois que je t'ai fait peur! Ne tirez jamais un poignard sur un Irlandais, à moins que vous ne vouliez rencontrer votre fabricant à la hâte!" Translated: "My friend, it is me, your comrade Thomas. Are you all right? I believe I startled you! Never pull a dagger on an Irishman, unless you want to meet your maker posthaste!

With that, Sir Renaud let out a laugh. "Ha! My friend Thomas! I thought you were a British swine! Please, forgive me."

Thomas released his friend, straightened out his clothes for him, and then smiled broadly and hugged him. "You had me on the ground before I knew what hit me, you French bastard!" Thomas said as he patted Sir Renaud on his back.

"Yes, but you soon had me in your grip, you filthy Irish animal!" Sir Renaud replied, kissing both of Thomas' cheeks.

"Stop wit' the kissin', Frenchy! Only me wife has that privilege!" Thomas said with a mock scowl on his face.

The two laughed and dusted themselves off. "Why so touchy, Vichier?" Thomas asked.

"Sorry, my dear friend, I had a very real nightmare that shook me to my core. I apologize for my rash reaction to being awakened," replied Sir Renaud.

"Well, you need to tell me about this nightmare while we eat some breakfast and prepare to depart for the Nire, me friend," said Thomas as he made his way toward the cavern entrance, motioning for Sir Renaud to follow.

It was early morning, before dawn. The encampment was now bustling with activity. Cooks were preparing food; men were packing up gear and loading carts. Warriors were sharpening swords, readying bows and arrows. Horses were being fed, watered, and groomed. It was a crystal-clear pre-dawn, yet the dampness chilled the men to their bones. As they got dressed, some warmed themselves and their battle gear by fires. And after everyone was fed and all was packed up, Thomas addressed the men from atop a food cart.

"G'mornin' men!" he said loudly, which caused a silence to fall upon the massive crowd of warriors. "T'ank you for yer attention. We are about to set off on an important journey this morn. It is of the utmost importance that we deliver this precious cargo to the Nire. The British will surely try to stop us, but they must not prevail! We must outfight, outmaneuver, and outsmart those bastards at all costs!"

The crowd erupted with thunderous shouts and the clanging of swords and shields. Thomas raised his hands, and the hordes fell silent again.

"I dun't have to tell ya, this monumental task will not be easy. The British are surely making their way after us now. But we *must* prevail. And we *will* prevail. For if God is wit' us, tell me—"

The entirety of the Celts and Knights then joined Thomas in perfect unison: "*Who can be against us?*"

Thomas raised his sword and shouted, "Amen! Mighty men of God, mount up!" And with that, they set out for the Nire.

The archers were out in front, leading the Celts and knights' army, the best shots and most skilled archers from each of the Galway clans and from the Knights of Solomon's Temple. In equal measure, these skilled ones also brought up the rear, watching for any signs of an ambush. The cargo wagons were directly in the middle, protected in front and behind. Thomas rode directly behind the last wagon, armed to the hilt. His sword was placed strategically in its sheath, on his left, tied to his saddle. In his belt, he kept his knife, and in his left hand, he carried his spear, ready for whatever was to come.

Liam Athy was out in front of the army, riding next to Sir Renaud. Both men were also armed and ready for battle. Dermot Athy managed to mount his steed as well but was forced to ride alongside Father Patrick and close to the supply wagon, where medicine and bandages were stored. Ailan was the very last man. His speed and agility was best used here, as he rode in circles, constantly keeping watch from behind, making sure they were not flanked. He was armed with his sling, a knife, dagger, sword, and a satchel with several fist-sized rocks in it—a dangerous, deadly warrior, as were all the clansmen.

The road to the Nire was narrow and cumbersome in spots. But they could not travel on the main roads because of the danger posed by the British Army. They had traveled for three hours when one of the supply wagon's wheels suddenly split, causing it to tip sideways, spilling several barrels of ale onto the wet ground. It was a clear day, but the ground was still saturated from the previous week's rain.

"*No!* Not the ale!" shouted Dermot. "Save the ale!"

Thomas shouted, "Halt! Halt! We have a broken wheel—*stop!*"

Several men dismounted as the entire convoy came to a stop. Four of them began the arduous task of replacing the wagon wheel.

"Take this time to rest, drink, and stretch! But hurry, men. We have no time to waste!" Thomas shouted as he too dismounted. He let out a large sigh as he stretched his arms up over his head. Dermot was trying to dismount as well, but his foot caught in his stirrup and he let out a yelp in pain. "Da!" Thomas yelled. "Da, wait and I'll help ya!" Thomas reached Dermot just in time to stop his fall. "I got ya, Da. That was a close one," he said.

"Ah, t'ank ya, son. Yer ole da is frail and worthless, I'm afraid," Dermot said with a sigh.

"Nah, yer too stubborn to be worthless and still too fierce to be frail, Da. But ye are old!" Thomas responded with a laugh and nod.

"I expect yer right about dat, son!" Dermot responded.

Father Patrick sidled up next to Dermot as he found a rock to sit on. "Let me help ya, dear friend," Father Patrick said quietly.

They had stopped on the edge of an opening to a large field. The first sixty or so men were actually past the opening and could see the expanse of the large clearing.

Sir Renaud did not dismount. He stayed atop his horse as the animal became increasingly more unsettled. "What is it, mon ami?" he said to his longtime friend and steed. "I sense it too, Cheval de Guerre." Translated: "Warhorse."

With that, Sir Renaud's horse flared his nostrils, snorted, and began to move nervously from side to side, forcing his master to grab the reins. "Calm down, ami," Sir Renaud whispered. "Liam, something is wrong. We must take cover. Now!"

"I don't see anyt'ing!" Liam spat back. Just then, Liam gasped. "Retreat, take cover! The British are here, the British are here!" he shouted, eyes wide open. "*Take cover!*"

In the distance, on the opposite side of the large valley, the British archers could barely be seen on the edge of the woods. There was a mist that was rising up from the valley floor, making the scene dreadful and ominous. The sky began to rain arrows, and before any of the Celts or knights could escape back into the dense forest behind them, the hell fury of the Brit army landed all around them. Sir Renaud tried to jump from his horse, but before he could, he was hit in his left shoulder, which caused him to fall backward off his steed.

Liam was still yelling, "*Retreat!*" when an arrow came down and hit his beloved horse directly on top of its head, piercing through to its brain. The magnificent steed dropped suddenly and violently with Liam still on his back. The impact of the fall caused Liam to be knocked unconscious. Sir Renaud saw Liam drop and managed to grab him by his belt and drag him behind the fallen horse. Those who were still under the cover of the woods jumped from their horses and took cover wherever they could, but the British arrows found several of them as well. Thomas and Ailan made their way to the treeline and spotted Liam and Sir Renaud behind Liam's fallen horse.

"Hurry, we must help as many as we can to safety!" Thomas said to Ailan as he crouched down and ran as fast as he could to his brother's side.

"Liam! Liam! Are you still wit' us, brother?" Thomas said as he dove to the ground, next to Sir Renaud and Liam.

"He is still breathing, dear friend," replied Sir Renaud.

"We need to get you both to safety!" Thomas said as he waved off Ailan and shook his head. "No, Ailan, you need to stay put. We will come to you!"

Ailan had found shelter from the shower of Brit arrows underneath a fallen oak tree, as well as several others from the Celts and knights. Thomas grabbed Liam and slung him over his right shoulder as he yelled at Sir Renaud, "*Run!*" Sir Renaud managed to stagger his way to Ailan's side, and Thomas was close behind, with Liam over his shoulder, head bobbing. In an instant, four arrows hit Liam in his back and buttocks before Thomas could reach the safety of the fallen tree.

"He's hit, he's hit Thomas!" Ailan cried out.

Thomas continued and reached Ailan, flinging Liam onto his stomach and to the ground. "Thomas, he is hit!" Ailan repeated.

"I heard ya, Ail! Dun't worry!" Thomas replied.

In shock, Ailan angrily pushed by Thomas to get to Liam. He fell to his knees beside him and began to weep.

"Ailan, dear brother, he will be fine! Look at his back, lad!" Thomas said.

Ailan, wiping tears from his face, looked down at his beloved brother. There, on his back, was a large French shield with four arrows in it.

"Oh, sweet Lord! How did ya know? What? Thank you, Lord! Thank you, Thomas!" Ailan managed to get out.

"Father Pat, where are ya?" Thomas shouted.

"Here, Thomas, I am here!" Father Patrick replied as he crawled up next to Liam. "I will attend to him."

"Thank you, Father Pat," Thomas replied.

Just then, the shower of arrows stopped as abruptly as they started. The silence was eerie and palpable.

Thomas arose and stepped upon the fallen tree and spoke to the Celts and knights: "Men, listen to me! This silence means only one thing: we have only minutes to prepare for the British Army to attack! Prepare yourselves. This will be a fight to the death! Assume defense formation!" With that, the Celts and the knights hurriedly took their places, forming a line of defense that stretched out close to a kilometer in length. They used the densely wooded forest as a shield but knew they were outnumbered by a thousand. Twenty-one of their men were injured by the Brit rain of arrows, but miraculously, none were killed. Father Patrick was more than enthused to let that fact be known to the many men within his earshot. "The Lord is good and has blessed us mightily with His divine protection and favor!" The father shouted as he burrowed underneath the large, fallen tree Thomas used as his soapbox.

"Maybe so, Father. But the day's not over yet!" Liam managed with a groggy, hoarse voice.

"Liam, me boy! You're awake!" Father Patrick shouted with joy. "Rest easy, lad. You have been out for a while . . . hit your head hard on the ground after . . . uhhh . . . after, you know . . . your horse—"

"My horse!" Liam shrieked. "My beloved horse! Those bastards killed my—" he said as he fell back into the makeshift bed Father Patrick had made for him under the tree. Out cold.

Ten minutes later, the blast from across the valley came. The trumpets of war rang out loud and clear, causing everyone in the Celt-and-knight side to fall silent in anticipation of the coming fury. The drums then began to pound out a rhythm and then the entire British Army began to chant, keeping time to the war drums. As Thomas and his army peered across the field, they saw the first row of soldiers advancing slowly and methodically. Thomas, knowing the Brits' battle strategy, ran to his horse, mounted him, and then rode from one end of their front line to the other, shouting instructions: "Wait for them to get close enough to get a sure kill. Archers: on my command, let your arrows fly but not until I give the command! We must present a united front and battle together, as one. Those of you with slings, be ready to maneuver quickly to take out as many as you can. This will be a battle for the ages, men! Be fierce, be strong . . . for if God is with us—"

Then, the entire army shouted together, "Who can be against us?!"

Thomas then returned to the middle of the front line, dismounted, and drew his sword. "Father, be with us," he whispered to himself.

Ailan, standing only an arm's length away, replied, "He *is* with us, brother."

The ground began to rumble, and the sound was like nothing the Celts had ever heard before. It was like the sound of a thousand hooves beating the ground. Out from the forest they appeared, a line of British soldiers that spanned the entire width of the enormous field. They moved as one as they marched in formation. After the first row of men were in the open, another row followed, and then another. Thomas gave the order to hold their positions. "Wait, wait . . . do not engage until I give the command!"

As the British Army neared the middle of the battlefield, still marching in perfect formation, Thomas raised his hand. "Archers, prepare!" he shouted. Over three hundred Celt and knight archers hurried to the edge of the forest and readied themselves to let their arrows fly upon Thomas' command.

"Steady . . . not yet. Not yet . . . wait!" Thomas shouted. "And archers, ready! Aim!" The archers moved in unison and drew their arrows back. "*Fire!*" shouted Thomas.

The arrows flew. As they rained down upon the British Army, half the front row of soldiers fell to their death, their shields proving to be near useless. But the remainder kept marching on. "Archers, prepare! Aaaand . . . *fire!*" Thomas shouted again. This time, the arrows took out two entire rows of Brits, making the Brit commander give the command for his archers to fire back. As the Brit arrows came flying at them, the Celts and knights covered themselves with their shields, which were fashioned to completely cover a man's body from head to toe while assuming a crouched position, hence forming a wall of protection around them. Only three men were hit, but no fatalities or severe injuries occurred. With that came a roar of shouts and clanging of swords on shields, in utter defiance.

The Brits kept advancing and when they had reached the exact point that Thomas knew was the best time to wage a counterattack, the order came. "Ready! *Attack!*" he shouted.

The entire army of Celts and knights drew their swords, spears, weapons of war and charged in a full sprint. As they broke through the Brit front line, the bloodshed was massive. In a violent rage, the Celts and knights attacked, piercing with spears, slashing with swords, and killing with more intensity than any British foe before them. The fighting was so violent, even the seasoned warriors on both sides were astonished at what they were seeing. Thomas and Ailan were fighting back to back as British soldiers rushed them. Thomas would slash each approaching Brit, and Ailan would finish them off. The battlefield was nothing new to Solomon's Knights, but even they were astonished with the fervor in which the Celts fought. All the years of having to defend themselves against many foes had paid off.

As the battle raged, Thomas noticed one of his closest friends from Clan Lynch was about to be slashed in the back from a Brit sword. He left Ailan and charged across the bloody field, toward his friend. As he drew close, a spear came flying at him. "Thomas, *spear!*" Ailan shouted. Thomas turned and dove to the ground as the spear came within inches of his head. He rolled quickly with agility, regained his footing, and launched his spear toward the Brit with such strength the impact caused the enemy soldier to fly several feet in the air before landing with a loud thud on the ground—dead. Thomas ran to retrieve his spear, much to the amazement of his friend, who stood in utter shock at what he had just witnessed.

"Duck," Thomas said as he shoved his clansman friend to the ground and launched his knife at yet another Brit charging them, hitting him directly between the eyes.

"T'anks, Thom!" Thomas' friend said with a matter-of-fact wink.

"Me pleasure, Sean!" Thomas replied.

Just then, Ailan screamed from across the field, "They have fire!" As Thomas turned to see what Ailan was screaming about, his heart sank. In the distance, at the tree line, they stood—three large catapults and, next to them, a fire. They were gigantic wooden war machines, standing over twelve feet high, mounted on wheeled carts. It took six men just to position them.

The Brits appeared to be starting several fires and lighting large balls of some sort. The horror intensified as the first catapult launched a fireball directly into the middle of the battlefield, followed by the next two within seconds. The fireballs landed and rolled over several men, catching them on fire. The screaming of men as they were running in circles, burning to death, was so terrifying several men simply fell to their knees in utter disbelief. As the second wave of fire and fury rained down upon the battlefield, Thomas shouted, "Take cover! Run!" But there was nowhere to run to.

A minute later, Ailan shouted again, "Thomas, look!"

Thomas looked at Ailan, who was pointing toward the catapults. As the smoked started to dissipate, Thomas could see several hand-to-hand battles going on behind the monstrous contraptions. "Who is it?" he yelled back to Ailan.

"Not sure but it looks like clansmen, brother!" Ailan replied.

"Clansmen?" Thomas repeated as he made his way toward the catapults. Halfway there, he could see clearer that the men who were attacking the Brits were indeed clansmen. Thomas could not believe his eyes. The clansmen who were supposed to be on their way to the other hideouts were now fighting the Brits with their fellow Tribes of Galway brethren.

As Thomas reached the enormous contraptions, two men from Clan Blake approached him. "We're flanking them, our brother!"

Thomas, mouth opened and in shock, replied, "But how did you know we—"

Before he could finish, one of the men interrupted, "Word from the Knights of Solomon's Temple reached our convoys yesterday. They have watchmen everywhere who saw these bastard British readying for battle. So they sent in spies to find out exactly what they were up to. They found out plenty . . . but right now, there are men from clans Blake, French, Martin, and Skerrett, who were on their way to the Giant's Causeway and from clans D'Arcy, Bodkin, Font, and Kirwan, who were headed for the Cliffs of Moher, along with knights who were accompanying them, all total: 2,235 clansmen and 837 knights, totaling 3,072 men flanking the British Army as we speak."

Thomas' eyes grew wider and filled with tears. "Father Patrick was right . . . God is truly good!"

"Aye, brother, that He is!" replied the Blake clansmen.

Thomas then turned to his left and saw the entire tree line surrounding the battlefield lined with 3,072 men. The battle that had been raging nonstop fell silent. The British Army was completely surrounded by the Tribes of Galway, joined by the fierce warriors of the Knights of Solomon's Temple. There were only a few men left from the British Army manning the catapults, and as Thomas turned back to look at them, they scattered as fast as they could to the woods, where they were killed swiftly. Thomas took advantage of the quiet to again address the large horde. Since the catapults were now in the hands of Clan Blake, Thomas climbed up upon one and spoke. "Men, as you can see, we have guests!" He began. The entire battle field erupted into shouting and clanging of weapons against shields. "We are over three thousand strong! To our enemy: lay down your weapons, and there will be no more bloodshed." Not one Brit moved. "Lay down your weapons *now*, and you will live to see another sunrise. Don't, and you will surely die here today," Thomas repeated as he drew his sword and jumped off the contraption.

Suddenly, a British soldier came running out from under one of the catapults where he had been hiding, wielding a sword and shouting, "For king and country! Long live England, long live the king!" He ran at a full sprint toward Thomas, who saw the charging Brit out of the corner of his eye. With one fluid, rapid motion, he grabbed his knife from its sheath that was attached to his belt and flung it, hitting the Brit directly in his right eye, piercing his brain. The impact stopped his sprint abruptly, and he flew back onto the hard ground with a violent thud. Dead.

When the British Army, Celts, and knights saw this, they all stood in amazement. But a second later, one British soldier grabbed his spear and ran toward Thomas as well, throwing his spear as hard as he could at the enemy Celt. The spear was in midair when Ailan launched a large rock from his sling at the Brit, hitting him on the left side of his head, knocking him off his feet. As the spear reached Thomas, he simply dodged it and ran to finish his attacker, yelling, "Attack, attack!" He grabbed the hair of the would-be Brit assassin, lifted his head, and sliced open his throat from ear to ear. When the surrounding army of clansmen saw that the Brits had no intention of surrendering, they drew their weapons and commenced with the worst slaughter the British Army had ever endured. As they tightened their circle, not one Brit escaped from their terror. The defeat was profound and gruesome.

After two hours of slaughter and mayhem, the British Army was thoroughly defeated. The last Brit standing was their commander, who spit in Thomas' face when Thomas asked if he had any last words. The battlefield fell silent as Thomas stood face to face with him. Thomas then wiped the Brit commander's saliva from his face, drew his knife, and stabbed him in his heart with so much brute force it even took Ailan aback. But as the last Brit fell to his death, a roar of victory erupted.

"We are victorious!" Ailan shouted.

Thomas found his way to a nearby stream, where he fell to his knees in utter exhaustion. He stared into the babbling water, silently. *Though the victory is sweet, war is hell*, he thought to himself.

# Chapter Fifteen

## The Whole Truth Is Told

After the invocation, the fourteen chieftains said in unison, "Amen."

Patrick Athy then stood and addressed the gathering: "You know why you have been summoned here upon this very historic night. The time has indeed come. Tonight, the whole truth will be told to our rightful king and leader, William Thomas Athy. He is my eldest son, heir, and rightful sovereign of our beloved Eire. May God Almighty grant us the wisdom to convey the truth, in love, to our king." With that, Patrick turned to Aiden Blake, who was seated on his right. Aiden handed Patrick a scroll. Patrick took the scroll, opened it, and began to read what was written therein:

> As the centuries unfold, Eire will endure much. Her sovereignty will be taken, her independence laid to waste and her very survival tested as her enemies trod upon her shores. But we are a strong people, we are a brave people, and we will rise up at the appointed time to take back what is rightfully ours. But Eire will endure much before she is fully vindicated. There will be war, famine, and pestilence. Many will perish and many will abandon her to seek refuge elsewhere. But God will one day redeem her to her rightful glory. When the generation of the horse comes of age, the Tribes of Galway will gather together again with their counterparts and brothers, the Knights of Solomon's Temple. At that time, the revolution will begin. The rightful heir to the throne will be my descendent, a man who bears my name and has the birthmark upon his left forearm. Protect him and keep him unaware until the appointed time, then raise him up, anoint him, and he will lead our beloved Eire to victory.
>
> For God and Eire, in Christ's love,

Thomas William Athy, chieftain of Clan Athy and your humble sovereign

As Patrick finished reading the last line of Thomas Athy's letter, William began to stir. Grace shot a look at Patrick. "He's coming around, love. It's time," she said.

The fourteen clan chieftains arose, along with Grace and Pat Jr.

Patrick then said in a loud voice, "Chieftains Blake, Font, Kirwan, and Lynch, prepare our sovereign to be taken to the meeting place."

The four chieftains gathered around William as Grace, Pat Jr., and the rest looked on.

They gently removed the blanket Grace had placed upon him. Aiden Blake then fetched a satchel from a large duffle bag lying next to his chair. He reached into the satchel and retrieved a robe. He unfurled it and shook the wrinkles out of it. Embroidered on the back of the robe was a large rendering of the Clan Athy coat of arms and family crest. It was a long flowing robe dyed a dark purple, with white fur trim that ran its entire length. Sean Font, Robert Kirwan, and Patrick Lynch then positioned themselves around William, taking both his arms carefully and raising him to a sitting position. William, eyes still shut, stirred a bit and mumbled something unintelligible. "Careful, lads," said Patrick Athy quietly.

Aiden Blake then carefully placed the robe around William's broad shoulders and tied the cord loosely at the front of his neck as the other three chieftains lifted him to a stand. Two other chieftains brought a very old but beautifully handcrafted wooden chair that had been sitting in the corner of Patrick Athy's office for decades, hidden in plain sight. The inscription on the back of the chair, which had faced the wall, thus making it invisible, read

Throne William, King of Ireland agus na hOileáin Cheiltigh.
Translated: Throne of William, King of Ireland and the Celtic Isles.

The chieftains then lowered William onto the chair, picked him and the chair up swiftly, and followed Patrick Athy, Pat Jr., and Grace Athy, along with the rest of the chieftains, through the bookcase door and into the massive underground hideaway.

"Paddy lad, please stay behind and show our friends the Knights of Solomon the way." asked Patrick. "They will be here any minute."

"Sure thing, Da," Pat Jr. replied.

As the group descended the stairs, a knock came from the side door of the Athy family pub. Pat Jr. hurried to the door, opened it, and was taken aback by the large group of men standing there: over twenty men, dressed all in black, with large black backpacks. Pat Jr. awkwardly said, "Uh, good evening! You must be the knights I've heard so much about!" The men didn't make a sound and just stood there, glaring at Pat Jr. intently. "Oh, I am Patrick Athy Jr.," he offered.

"Oh, bonjour!" the man in front replied. "Indeed, we are them! I am Jean-Rene Vichier, at your service!" he said as he abruptly approached Pat Jr., hugged him, and gave him a kiss on both cheeks. "Very happy to meet you, m'sieur!"

Pat Jr. smiled awkwardly and motioned for the knights to come in. "Please, come in. We are headed down to the hideout now."

"Hideout? That sounds so IIA-esque!" quipped Jean-Rene, oozing sarcasm.

Pat Jr. had no idea what Jean-Rene meant and shot him a curious look.

"IIA. It stands for 'Irish Intelligence Agency'? Your MI5 equivalent?" explained Jean-Rene. "Never mind."

"Yes, I know what the IIA is, sir," Pat Jr. replied soberly.

"Oh yes, of course you do!" Jean Rene said with a hint of sarcasm. "You just don't find my French sense of humor very funny. Ha!" he said under his breath.

As the knights descended the stairs to the hideout, Pat Jr. stood at the top of the stairs, making sure no one was left behind. After the last knight entered the pub office, Pat Jr. shut and locked the side door, entered the hideout foyer and closed and secured the bookcase door behind him, and joined the gathering in the large warehouse belowground after he had scanned the office for any stragglers.

"There you all are! Welcome, brothers, welcome!" Patrick Athy said in a loud voice. For the next ten minutes, the knights and the clan chieftains greeted one another with hugs, handshakes, and the French custom of kisses on both cheeks. There was an intrinsic bond between these two groups of men, a bond that was centuries old, cemented in an abundance of trust, fellowship, and true brotherhood.

The spacious room had been cleared of all clutter, and a large oval table sat in the middle with enough seating for fourteen clan chieftains, twenty-one knights, and William Thomas Athy. Grace and Pat Jr. were to be seated on a small settee nearby. William had been placed on the Celtic throne, which was at the head of the table. And this was no ordinary table either. It was an enormous masterpiece carved out of Irish black alder wood. The legs were carved in the shape of fourteen spears, bound together by cord and the top was etched with a large map of the Celt Isles. And forming a circle around the map were carved fourteen coats of arms for each Tribe of Galway. The craftsmen used gold, silver, and precious jewels, inlaid so perfectly it looked like a painting. And there was a protective polyurethane layer, applied by Patrick's father decades prior, to preserve the astonishing work of art. The hand-hewn table was normally kept against the back wall of the enormous warehouse, covered with velvet and several tarps. It was not just a table, for in it and upon its surface were hidden and etched secrets, some holding proof of a Celtic history stolen.

"Sir Jean-Rene, it is time," said Patrick.

Jean-Rene Vichier approached William and stood directly in front of him. The Frenchman stared at William for several seconds in silence, then reached into satchel that was slung across his chest. He pulled out a small glass bottle, unstopped it, and dabbed its contents on a handkerchief. After sealing the bottle and returning it to his satchel, he slowly moved within inches of William's face. "So you are the one. You are the one my ancestors spoke of." With that, Jean-Rene bowed his head and began to pray aloud. "Father in heaven, I am your humble servant."

Pat Jr. cleared his throat and raised his eyebrows, which brought several glares upon himself from knights and Celts alike, and a swat from his mother, who was sitting next to him. "Sorry," Pat Jr. whispered, with a shrug.

"Father, we ask You to anoint this man to be the leader You have chosen," Jean-Rene continued. "Give him wisdom beyond his years and uphold him by Your sovereign right hand." He then placed the handkerchief under William's nose, causing him to gasp for air and his eyes to open wide and abruptly. He began to flail around and tried to stand up, but two knights held him by each arm, whispering into his ears, "Calm down, sire."

William sat back and shook his head in an attempt to clear the cobwebs from his mind, blinking his eyes slowly. "Where am I? What is all this? What did you do to me?!" he managed in a hoarse voice as he grabbed his neck and winced in pain.

"Sire, I am Jean-Rene Vichier, your humble servant and appointed guard," Jean-Rene said as he bowed before William.

"What? Yer who? And why are ya callin' me sire? I'm no sire, I assure ya! Da, what in the name of all that is holy is goin' on here?" William said, still groggy. "Wait! You drugged me!" With that, William tried to stand, his face turning red. But the two knights held his arms. "What are ya doin'? You can't hold me prisoner!"

"You are not our prisoner, you are our sovereign," said Jean-Rene softly. "You, William Thomas Athy, are king!"

The room erupted in shouts: "Long live the King of the Celts!"

"Yer all crazy! I am *not* yer king!" William replied, struggling to get his arms free.

"Indeed you are, sire. Please, allow us to explain," Jean-Rene said as he motioned to Patrick, who reached under the massive table and pulled a lever that caused the entire table to shift slightly and then the middle raised up, revealing a large circular bronze chest. Etched upon the entire circumference of the chest were the names of Clan Athy chieftains in chronological order, from 944 AD to present day. Fifty-three names spanned 1,074 years.

William's eyes narrowed as he peered at the bronze marvel in front of him. "What is this? What does it mean?" he asked intently.

"Will, look closely. There, next to my name," Patrick said as he pointed to the chest.

William cocked his head to one side and then managed to step closer to the table. As he scanned the names etched upon the bronze chest, his eyes grew wider. There, next to Patrick Athy's name, was none other than his own name: William Thomas Athy. William stared at the chest in disbelief and then noticed something. "Wait. What is that?" William asked as he pointed at the chest. "What is that writing next to my name? I can't seem to make it out. Is that Latin?"

"Yes, Will, it is Latin," answered Patrick.

"Why is my name the only one with something written after it? And why in Latin?" William pressed as he felt faint and fell back into his chair. "Why is *my* name on that apparatus to begin with? Somebody had better start explaining what the devil is going on here!"

Jean-Rene Vichier moved next to Patrick and nodded. Patrick nodded back, and Jean-Rene drew a sword from under his ankle-length overcoat. William's eyes grew big, and he yelled, "No!" thinking the Frenchman was going to kill his father. Jean-Rene then stepped to the halfway point of the large table, directly across from the bronze chest. He placed the tip of the blade of his sword into an opening on the chest and then abruptly shoved the blade in until the chest lid opened and a small section of the enormous table parted. The opening in the table allowed Jean-Rene to move close enough to the chest to remove the lid. He then reached into the chest and lifted out a large book, bound in aged leather with the Clan Athy coat of arms on its face. He gently sat the book on the table, in front of Patrick. Patrick glanced at William and nodded with a look of assurance.

"In answer to your first question: Your name is on the chest because you are the next in line to be chieftain of Clan Athy. Secondly, the writing after your name is indeed in Latin. It is thus because that is the language spoken by Gerbertus Aureliacensis or Sylvester II, Leader of the Church, AD 946–1003, His Eminence, Pope Sylvester II. This is his Bible and journal. In it is documentation and irrefutable proof that our clan, Clan Athy, are the rightful heirs to the throne, that the House of Windsor is a farce and that these isles, which are called British Isles, are actually the Celtic Isles, whose original monarchy were from the House of Athy! And you, William Thomas Athy, are the chosen king! For, there, beside your name, etched into the bronze chest in Latin, it says, "Et ait rex noster Future," meaning "Our Sovereign and Future King.""

William shook his head swiftly. "How can this be? Da, what is the meaning of all this? Why me?" he asked in a confused, exhausted voice.

"William, son, it has been ordained since the ancient times. You were to be the one to bring the truth to the world. It was foretold there would be fifty-three generations, spanning 1,074 years.

## Chapter Sixteen

## The Show Must Go on, But Will It?

Jarvis Ranch was swarming with local and federal law enforcement, all investigating the apparent attempted murder of Roy Jarvis. The cast and crew of Star Gaze Productions were doing their level best to continue with production of their movie, *The Nire*. But it was a daunting task, as every time Rudy Gallo yelled, "Quiet on the set!" inevitably, the crime scene investigators would either interrupt or one of their walkie-talkies would sound off and ruin the scene. So Colin Wohl and Larry Davis made an executive decision to halt production for a few days, to allow the investigators to do their jobs, unencumbered. Plus, the constant interruptions of police radios blaring and vehicles coming and going were making it impossible to film. So production stopped, but in an effort to maintain the amazing creativity flow that had been happening among the cast, the production team decided to shoot some indoor scenes that were not supposed to start until the following month. The indoor sets had already been built, furnished, and were ready to go. So the change of plans seemed the best decision. After the umpteenth time that Rudy yelled, "*Cut,*" because of interference from police radios, it was a no-brainer to everyone that they needed to go with a plan B.

The sets were built in a small field a quarter mile from the barn, toward the densely wooded area of Jarvis Ranch. From the outside, it was obvious that the buildings had been erected in a makeshift manner—unpainted plywood held up by exposed support beams. But it was quite a different story on the inside of each building, made to look like thirteenth-century dwellings. The artistry involved in making these rooms authentic was amazing. The attention to every small detail, including even the cutlery and wall art, was astonishing. There were five buildings total that were erected: one to serve as the home of Thomas Athy; three staged to look like a pub, a church, and a town center ballroom; and the last was the largest, standing three times as high as the others, built to look like the inside of a large cavern. And when the cast entered the large building, they were astonished into silence as they gazed up at the enormous faux cave that, for all intents and purposes, looked exactly like the real thing.

"The set decorators, artists, and builders have outdone themselves!" Angus said as he stood in the very center of the makeshift cavern.

"Absolutely incredible, isn't it?" Colin said.

"It is, indeed. The detail . . . it even smells like a cave!" Angus agreed.

Larry Davis entered with Rudy Gallo. Both had already seen the sets and were all business.

"Okay, people . . . can I have quiet on the set?" said Rudy through his megaphone. "We were driven out of the ranch, but the show must go on! No time to waste. Time is money! I asked you all to study the Cavern Scene last night, and hopefully, you all did. We will be filming here at the sets for the next week. We had planned on filming here in the early fall, but that all changed when the cops showed up and we lost our ranch! So please, quiet on the set! Places! Aaand, *action*!"

Just then, a loud thump coming from the roof of the faux cavern startled an already on-edge cast and crew. Before anyone could react, a large rock the size of a soccer ball fell and hit one of the cameras, knocking off the lens and damaging its face. Several men, including Angus, Colin, and Larry, dashed for the door in an effort to catch whoever caused the bolder to fall. Angus kicked open the door as the group rushed outside and ran quickly, surrounding the large set. As Colin reached the other side, he saw a figure dressed in black running and disappearing into the nearby wooded area.

"Hey! What the hell are ya doin'? Hey! Stop!" Colin shouted. "There's someone over here! Angus, Larry! Over here, near the woods!"

By the time the others joined Colin, there was no sign of the dark figure. Angus, who had picked up a large club meant as a prop, looked intently into the woods and said. "I'm catching the bastard. Who's with me?" Colin nodded, Larry shrugged, and all three men ran headlong into the dense woods. Angus shouted, "Colin, go left! Larry, go right! I will go straight on! If you find him, yell!"

So Colin veered to the left and ran as fast as he could. Larry, although considerably slower, ran to the right. Angus, a man of large stature, was surprisingly swift of foot and managed to plow through the heavily wooded forest with relative ease. Larry found himself in a clearing five minutes later, where he stopped to catch his breath. Suddenly, he heard footsteps behind him. He hastily grabbed a large branch that had fallen to the ground and spun around to face his would-be attacker. As he peered in the direction of the footsteps, he suddenly sighed and dropped the large stick.

"Lillie! What in God's name are you doing here? Don't you know there is someone trying to kill us roaming around out here?" Larry said as he approached and hugged his fiancée.

"Yes, Larry, I know, but I needed to know you were okay. I am not going to lose you!" Lily replied as she kissed Larry several times on his cheeks. "The police are on their way, so you need to just come back to the sets now, please!"

"Okay, Lil. Let's head back," Larry said with a relieved tone.

The two walked quickly, hand in hand, toward the sets. As Larry began to tell Lillie of his bravery in running toward danger, the ground gave away beneath them, and they both fell abruptly into a deep, dark pit. Lillie cried out for Larry, but he did not answer. She then heard approaching footsteps upon the ground above.

"Colin? Angus? Is that you? *Help!* It's me, Lillie! *Please help!*"

A few seconds later, Lillie was struck on her head, rendering her unconscious.


Angus had been running for over twenty minutes when he reached the river's edge. As he stopped abruptly, breathing heavily, he looked about his surroundings and saw Colin downriver.

"Colin, over here, chap!" Angus managed to shout.

Colin responded with a wave and ran swiftly toward Angus, who was kneeling to splash his face with cold water from the river. Colin reached Angus within seconds.

"Well, aren't you cheetah-like and not even winded! Are you even human, lad?" Angus said as he fell back onto the moist ground next to the river.

"I was an athlete in school. Try to stay in shape by running every day. You okay, chap?" Colin replied.

"I will be. Where is Larry?" Angus said, as he sat up and scanned the surrounding area.

"I don't know. He went right, I went left, and you went straight. He should be to our south, also by the river," Colin responded.

"Well, we had better find him," said Angus.

And with that, both men headed south, keeping to the river's edge. After twenty minutes of walking, they found no trace of Larry.

"Well, lad, we've found neither hide nor hair of him, and it will be getting dark soon. We should head back to the sets. Larry is more than likely there," Angus said.

"I agree. Let's head back," Colin concurred.

The two men arrived back to find police swarming and yellow tape surrounding the sets. The Jarvis boys were talking to police, and most of the cast and crew had headed back to their trailers. As Angus and Colin approached, Jennifer Sweeney and Rudy Gallo rushed to meet them.

"Where have you two been?" snapped Rudy. "Where's Larry?"

"We were going to ask you the same thing!" said Angus. "We looked everywhere but couldn't find him."

"What do you mean? Wasn't he with you?" pressed Jennifer.

"Yes, he was, Jen, but he vanished," answered Colin.

"Vanished? What do you mean, he vanished?!" Rudy shouted, obviously frightened.

"We all ran into the woods together. I went left, Angus went straight, and Larry went right. Angus and I ran until we came to the river. Angus ended up just north of me. We met up but never found Larry anywhere. He vanished," explained Colin.

Rudy screamed out, "Larry Davis vanished! He vanished! I feel faint . . ." as he wobbled and fell backward into Angus' arms.

"Medic!" Angus shouted.

# Chapter Seventeen

## A Reluctant King

William Athy woke up in his bed, his head still cloudy, and feeling exhausted. The sun was beaming in through his bedroom window, which usually made him awaken with a sigh of well-being and anticipation for the start of a new day, but not this morning. As his mind began to clear, he remembered the events of the night before and wondered if it had all been a dream, a strange, bizarre dream. He sat up slowly and turned to place his feet on the floor as he wiped the sleep from his eyes, stretched, and yawned. Suddenly, he realized he was not alone. There, in his bedroom, standing in front of the door, was Jean-Rene Vichier.

"Sweet Jesus, Mary, and Joseph! What are ye doin' in my room?" William spat, angrily.

"Good morning, sire. I am Jean-Rene Vichier, your humble servant and appointed guard."

"Well, Jean-Rene, I dun't care who ya are. Get out of my room! *Now!* And stop callin' me sire. I am not yer sire! I am not anyone's sire! I am just plain ole Will Athy!" William spat as he walked to his closet and put on a T-shirt and sweatpants. "If I were your sire, I'd thump ya for invading my privacy!"

"I do apologize for invading your privacy, sire," Jean-Rene replied.

William winced at Jean-Rene's refusal to stop referring to him as sire.

"I am here to protect you, not to harm you or cause you to be stressed, sire," Jean-Rene continued. "You may not like it and you may not want to be our sovereign, but you are, and the sooner you accept this, the better, si—sir."

"Well, my French guardian, if you dun't get out of my damn room, you will be the first of my subjects to be executed!" William shouted. "And where are my children? What have you done with my children?"

"I will step outside your door, into the hallway. But that is the best I can do. For your own well-being and protection, I must guard you with my life from now on. Your children are safe and with your parents," Jean-Rene replied quietly as he opened William's bedroom door and slipped into the hallway, closing it behind him.

William sat back down on his bed, head in hands, frustrated with his new, unwanted companion. He thought of ways to escape from his own home. He felt trapped and angry—angry at the situation and angry at his family for betraying him in this way. He arose from his bed and padded to the en suite bathroom, where he stripped and entered the shower. He stood under the strong pounding of the hot water for over ten minutes—each minute helping his head become clearer, each minute concocting a plan of escape.

*I am not going to be anyone's sire. I am not going to be a prisoner in my own home*, he thought.

He slipped out of the shower quietly, leaving the water running, dried off, and crept to his closet. There, he hastily dressed himself in jeans, sweatshirt, a pair of sneakers, and a baseball cap. He then grabbed his wallet, keys, and a pair of sunglasses from his bureau and quietly moved to the window, slowly opening it. He climbed out onto the porch and moved swiftly around his house, keeping close to the outer wall. As he approached his garage and driveway, his heart sank. There were four black SUVs parked in his garage and driveway, surrounding and blocking any possible escape route via his Range Rover. He stood there, his back against his home's eastern wall, trying to figure out what to do next. Finally, he decided to try to steal one of the black SUVs that were parked in his driveway. He crept slowly toward the black vehicle and was pleased and shocked to find it unlocked. William slowly opened the vehicle's driver's side door and slid into the leather seat, quietly closing the door behind him. He ducked under the dashboard, forced the protective panel off, exposing several wires. He reached into his pocket and pulled out his small pocketknife, using it to cut away the plastic protective wire covers, exposing the metal wires. Before he attempted to start the vehicle, William peeked up from the floorboards and scanned the outside area. Nothing. So he joined two wires together, causing the starter to spark and the SUV to roar to life. Before anyone in the area knew what was happening, William threw the tanklike black monster into reverse, backed into his yard, threw it into drive, and floored it.

Jean-Rene was opening William's bathroom door. "Sire, are you alright? You have been in there quite a while now, and I need to make sure you are okay. Sire?" Jean-Rene pulled back the shower curtain to find an empty shower. He turned the water off and heard the sound of a vehicle speeding away outside. He saw the window was opened and knew. "Merde! He has escaped!"

William managed to keep the large SUV from crashing as he made his escape. He knew that his French friend would be hot on his trail, so he sped toward the coast, where he knew he would never be found—at least, not right away. A year after William and his beloved wife were married, they had invested in some property on the Irish coast, near Waterford. An hour away from the Nire, the large parcel was remote and private, with a good-sized cabin sitting at the top of a small hill overlooking a spectacular view of the Atlantic Ocean. William had not been to the property in years, and as he stopped at the locked gate, memories came flooding back—memories of a time before children, before careers, jobs, and the business of life, a time when he and his beloved shared precious alone time together. As William pulled up to the cabin, he swallowed hard. There on the porch sat two wooden rocking chairs. It was a log cabin, built with local trees and beautifully finished in a dark stain with cream trim around the windows. The front door was painted a rusty red color, as were the accents and flower boxes under each of the eight front windows, four on either side of a double front door. The two rockers were handmade with the same local wood and stained to match the cabin.

"Will, we are going to grow old together right here, watching the ocean and rocking in these lovely chairs you made for us." William could hear his beloved wife Emma's voice as if she were still alive and there with him. He walked slowly toward the stairs to the porch, stopping to turn and take in the view of the Atlantic. "Oh, how I wish you were here, love," he whispered to himself. He climbed the stairs and glanced over at the two empty chairs. It was harder than he had anticipated to see this place again—their place. There was a large terra-cotta flowerpot, whose inhabitant was long since dead, that stood to the right of the front door. William squatted, reached behind the pot, and retrieved a small ceramic bird. The bottom of the bird opened to reveal a key. He let himself in and shut the door behind him. "Solace." William sighed.

Everything was just how they had left it, except for the dust that had accumulated over the years. He stood there scanning the room, which was large but cozy, with high, vaulted, open-beamed ceilings. There was one large brown leather couch and two leather recliners that matched. Across the large room, on the opposite side from the front door, was a small kitchen. Will made his way there, retrieved the cleaning products that were under the kitchen sink, and began to clean. Several hours went by, and the cabin was spotless. William even changed the sheets on the queen-size bed in the only bedroom—not an easy task, what with them being the same sheets he and his beloved wife had slept on. The memories were painful but, at the same time, sweet. The years had made the pain more tolerable, and William was actually able to smile and laugh at some of the treasures he found while cleaning. An old hat bought at the local flea market that said, "I'm with stupid!" and had a finger pointed to the right—Emma had worn that hat home from the flea market, laughing the entire time. William laughed to himself as he reminisced about the abundance of laughter he had shared with his beautiful Emma. The day they bought that silly hat, Emma told William she was pregnant with their first child.

After the cabin was livable again, William found the key to the root cellar. He unlocked the large wooden door that was between the kitchen and laundry room and descended the stairs, flashlight in hand. Fortunately, there was still an abundance of food and household necessities as well as light bulbs. William changed the cellar light bulbs and flipped the switch, which illuminated the room nicely. Made mostly of cinderblock and Irish stone, the cellar was quite a large room, packed with several shelving units and cabinets. The room was dark, cool, and earthy-smelling. It had three adjacent rooms also stocked full of all manner of survival supplies.

He had forgotten how much Emma and he had packed down there and was pleased to see everything he needed to stay as long as needed. Batteries, two solar generators, toilet paper, toiletries, medicines, first aid kits, bulk and canned foods enough to last an army for over a year. There was also a large cache of weapons, ammo, traps, and snares for hunting as well as fishing gear. The cabin had a well that produced crystal-clear, clean water abundantly and a septic system that also was a waste recycling unit. William felt safe, secure, and peaceful. After he had brought up some food and supplies, William opened a Guinness that had been stored in the cellar's wine cabinet, which was basically a natural refrigerator, and headed to the porch, where he settled into his rocking chair. As he looked out over the Atlantic Ocean, he remembered Emma's uncle who had left his amazing cabin in the woods to his beloved niece. After he died, Emma and William made it their pet project to fix the place up to suit them. Ironically, nobody knew about the cabin except William, Emma, her uncle, and Emma's sister, Samantha. It was completely off grid and able to function independently. The land was off the beaten path and remote enough that nobody had found it in all the years since it was built. Equipped with solar panels, a state-of-the-art water filtration system, security system, and bug-out shelter, the cabin in the woods was a dream fulfilled by Emma's uncle, who was a weekend survivalist. He had even equipped the place with satellite television and a security camera system. The bug-out shelter was just a few steps away from the cabin but completely invisible to the naked eye, as it was built into the hillside and the entrance was camouflaged with shrubs. It was built to house five adults for one year and was accessible from the front entrance as well as from a tunnel that connected it with the cabin root cellar. The shelter was thirty feet belowground, hewn into the Irish stone.

William was on his second beer when the chirp of a cell phone jolted him back into present-day reality. "Who could that be?" he mumbled to himself as he padded slowly inside to retrieve his phone. The caller ID said "Jenn." William hesitated but then decided he had better answer, but not before he figured out how to use the cell phone signal scrambler left by Emma's uncle. Once connected, it made it impossible to trace the cell signal. Will made sure it was on before he answered.

"Hello, Miss Sweeney. Long time no see."

"Hello there, stranger!" Jennifer Sweeney replied. "I was sitting here, all dressed up, waiting for my knight in shining armor to show up for our date, and lo and behold, he stood me up! Any clue why?"

Will was taken aback but quickly remembered he indeed had asked Jenn on a date. "Oh no! Jenn, I am so, so sorry, love! I have been ummm . . . well, preoccupied as of late. Can you find it in your heart to forgive me?" Will pleaded.

"I suppose I could make an exception this one time. But you owe me big-time, mister!" Jenn replied.

"Jenn, I'm afraid I will be out of town for a while. I had to get away to clear my head. I hope you know, I miss you," William offered.

"William Athy, how are we supposed get to know each other better if you are gone? Where are you, by the way?" Jenn asked.

"Uh, I am out of town . . . umm, but I will try to get back soon and take you on the best date of your life, guaranteed!" William said, trying to sound normal.

"Will, are you okay? I am truly worried. Your dad called an hour or so ago, asking if I had seen you. Is everything okay? Seriously," Jenn replied soberly.

"Everything is fine, love. I was just feelin' a bit overwhelmed is all. Nothin' to do with you, beautiful girl," William replied, equally sober.

"Men always say that 'It's not you, it's me' stuff when they're about to break up with you," she challenged.

"Miss Sweeney, I would have to be out of me mind to break up whatever this is we have! I have waited a very long time for someone like you to come along. Trust me, love. I am not breaking up anything, okay?" Will replied adamantly.

"All right, I believe you. I miss you a lot more than I want to, just FYI," Jenn whispered.

"Oh, sweet woman, I miss you as well. I will call you tomorrow, promise," William said earnestly.

"Okay. I look forward to hearing your sexy voice again tomorrow, then," Jenn replied in a sultry voice.

"You are driving me wild, Miss Sweeney. A man can only take so much, you know. We'll talk soon. Good night," William said. And he ended the call.


William watched the sun set and then went inside to prepare a much-needed meal for himself. He locked and bolted the front door before making his way to the kitchen. The solar generator came alive as he turned on the kitchen lights. It just needed to be primed and charged, which he had done that afternoon. Will knew he could power all the appliances for over two hours each night, which gave him the ability to cook, wash dishes, and take a shower before bed. After a satisfying supper of pasta a la Athy, which was linguini noodles that had been stored in seal fresh bags, with Emma's canned pasta sauce and some pickled vegetables also prepared with love by his dearly departed wife.

After William cleaned up the dishes and kitchen, he took a hot shower and fell into bed. He had enjoyed four bottles of Guinness that evening, and they had helped him relax quite efficiently. Sleep came surprisingly fast even after the events of the past forty-eight hours. William slept soundly.

The sun was just peeking over the hillside of the oceanfront property when William was jolted awake by pounding on the cabin's front door. He quickly grabbed the twelve-gauge shotgun he had leaned against the wall next to his bed and ran into the front living room. He stood there, wearing only boxer briefs and listened intently for several seconds: *bam bam bam bam*, the loud knocking again. Will crept toward the door, shotgun pointed directly at the door. Silence. Will listened and heard mumbling. A man's voice. Familiar.

"Da?" he whispered to himself. *What? How can it be me da? He has no idea this place exists*, Will thought to himself. Slowly, he crept closer to the door and peered through the peephole. "What the . . . sweet Jesus, Mary, and Joseph! How did he know I was here?" Will whispered to himself.

"Will, it's Da. Son, open the door . . . please," Patrick Athy pleaded as he stood on the front porch, eyeing the peephole.

William lowered the shotgun, unlocked the door, opened it, and glared at his father. "What the hell are ya doin' here, Da? How did you even know about this place?" William asked in an irritated voice.

Just then, Will noticed his father was not alone. Jean-Rene was standing next to the black SUV he had "borrowed" the day before. William then aimed the shotgun directly at Jean-Rene and shouted, "You had better put your hands up and walk your French arse over here, where I can see you!" Jean-Rene slowly raised his hands and walked toward the cabin porch. "What are you two doing here? How did you find this place? Nobody but Emma, her uncle, sister, and me even know it exists!"

"M'sieur, we only wish to protect you. We are not the enemy. We are your loyal subjects. There is a tracking device in the SUV you stol—borrowed. We simply gave you some time and then followed the signal here," Jean-Rene replied.

William lowered the gun, gave his father an angry look and proceeded to stomp back into the cabin, and slammed the door behind him.

"William, please, son . . . let us in. We are only here to help you! Please—" Patrick pleaded but was abruptly interrupted.

"The door is unlocked, Da! Sheesh!" William yelled from the kitchen, where he was making coffee as noisily as possible.

Patrick opened the cabin door slowly and peeked his head in first. "Will, you okay, son?"

"No! No, I am *not okayyyy*! I am fuming! Do ya really blame me, old man? I mean, you lie to my face for years and then expect me to simply accept some utterly outlandish story of our family being royalty and me being king of the Celts or some such nonsense! I think you all are insane! I want nuthin' to do wit' yer secret-society crap!" William spat angrily as he walked toward the two men.

"William, I understand your concerns and your anger, son. I truly do," Patrick offered.

"*You* understand, do ya?" William spat back.

"William, I know you're upset, but do not disrespect me! I am still your father!" Patrick said soberly.

"Oh, I understand feeling disrespected! You showed me no respect by jabbin' a needle into my neck and druggin' me, dear Da! Respect? *Ha!* You have to *earn* respect, old man!" William retorted as he walked back into the kitchen and poured himself a mug of coffee.

"M'sieur—" Jean-Rene started.

"And *you*!" William shouted as he pointed his finger at the Frenchman. "*You* shut the hell up! I dun't even know you! How dare you impose your will on me! Get out of my house! *Now!*"

"Perhaps I will take a walk and give you two some much-needed alone time," Jean-Rene said softly as he carefully made his way to the front door and quietly let himself out.

"Will, Jean-Rene doesn't deserve your ire. Focus that anger on me if you must, but that Frenchman risked life and limb to be here to protect and serve you!" said Patrick as he made his way to the couch and sat down slowly.

"I dun't know anything about why he is here, but—" started William.

"Exactly!" interrupted Patrick. "You know nothing, and we are trying our best to change that, son! If you would just set yer anger on the back burner long enough to listen! *Please*, William. You must be informed . . . your life and the life of our entire family depends on it!"

"What? How is my family's life in danger, Da? Do you know how crazy you sound?" replied William.

Suddenly, Jean-Rene burst through the front door, causing William to grab his shotgun. Jean-Rene closed the front door abruptly and yelled, "Get down! Get down *now!*" He had barely gotten the words out of his mouth when the air erupted in what sounded like fireworks. William and Patrick slammed to the floor, hands covering their heads as they realized the sounds were not fireworks but gunfire and they were the targets! So many bullets were flying through the cabin, all the three men could do was take cover.

As the bullets flew, breaking and destroying everything in the room, William managed to get Jean-Rene and Patrick's attention. He pointed to the cellar door. Both men nodded back to Will and the three managed to crawl to the door, open it, and slip down the cellar stairs swiftly. William managed to also engage the large metal safety door that his uncle-in-law installed in case of an apocalypse. Will thought, *This is as close to an apocalypse as it gets in Ireland!* The entire door and frame shifted, and from beneath the floor, a large metal shield-like door arose. The exterior of the cellar door, which could be seen from inside the house, between the living and laundry rooms, became completely invisible and looked like just another wall. The engineering was remarkable. Patrick and Jean-Rene were standing at the foot of the cellar stairs in complete shock.

"What did we just witness?" mumbled the Frenchman.

"Yes, Will . . . what in God's name? What *is* this place?" Patrick asked, obviously in shock.

"We are being attacked and shot at. Perhaps you two could save the questions about me cabin fer later, eh? Now, *who the hell is shooting at us?*" William replied.

"More than likely, MI5," Jean-Rene said matter-of-factly.

"What? MI5? What the hell is MI5? *Why is MI5 shooting at us?*" William shouted, now red-faced.

"We told you that your life was in danger, sire," said Jean-Rene as he checked the clip in his 9-mm handgun.

"I think we need to focus on staying alive and ask questions later, boys. Listen!" said Patrick.

"What? Listen to what?" William replied.

"Silence," Pat said.

"What does that mean?" Will asked.

"They will be storming into the cabin any second," answered Jean-Rene.

Suddenly, there was a large boom, then the sound of cans hitting the wood floors above.

"Tear gas," Jean-Rene said. "We need to get out of here!"

"This cellar is airtight. There is no way any gas is getting down here. Hurry, grab weapons and ammo, and follow me!" William said as he ran toward the arsenal.

"Sweet Lord! Where . . . what . . . how?" stammered Patrick as he stood in the doorway of the large arsenal.

"Em's uncle was a survivalist," William replied as he pointed to the gun locker. "Grab what you need and follow me!"

Jean-Rene smiled and said, "A survivalist? More like a mercenary!"

"Yeah, whatever . . . used to think he was crazy . . . not anymore," replied William as he led the way through the large tunnel to the bug-out shelter.

It was only a three-minute walk through the tunnel to the shelter. Once all three men were inside, William closed yet another large metal door. The room was large and dimly lit by outdoor solar lights that were placed at the baseboards, every twelve feet.

"Your uncle was a serious survivalist, sire! That is a military-grade, blast-resistant door! Nobody is getting in here . . . not even an MI5 bomb would penetrate that door!" Jean-Rene said, astonished.

"He was Emma's uncle," William replied. "He was more than just an enthusiast if you ask me. There were rumors he actually worked for the CIA. Everything in this compound is high-quality, military-grade, top-of-the-line equipment. There's enough ammo and munitions in this place to stage a world war!"

William then walked across the dark, cavernous shelter and opened a wall panel, flipped a switch that turned on three large overhead lights, and then walked to a large metal cabinet, opened it, reached in, and retrieved a bottle of Jameson Irish whiskey.

"Uncle Sean was a serious survivalist and maybe even a CIA foreign agent, but mostly, he was an Irishman through and through! There is nothing we can do but wait now. Those MI5 agents meant to kill us, and there is no way the three of us could win a battle against them. The only way we will survive this is if we stay put until they're gone. I figure they will search the cabin, find nothing, and leave," William said. "Now, you two want to tell me what the hell is goin' on and why MI5 wants us dead? I'm all ears!"

## Chapter Eighteen

## Man Down!

It took over two hours to organize a search, but IIA (Irish Intelligence Agency) and local police finally put a large team together, and as the sun went down, over sixty were scanning the woods, in search of Larry David, Star Gaze Production Company's production manager. Each searcher was given a flashlight, walkie-talkie, map of the area, and a half-hour safety briefing by Ireland's finest IIA agents and local constable. They staged a base camp next to the sets, consisting of three large open tents, filled with food, drinks, batteries, first aid kits, and other necessities. Each tent also housed several desks with laptop computers where police and federal agents were busy coordinating the manhunt. The list of civilian volunteers was over thirteen hundred, quite remarkable since the Nire Valley's population was just over that.

The evening brought a damp chill into the valley that permeated everything. Heat lamps were also set up in each tent to help warm those working diligently to find Larry Davis. And as the search party scanned the woods where he was last seen, rain began to fall, and then, only a few short minutes later, the storm hit in earnest. The satellite radar showed the storm, but it was moving faster than first predicted.

Driving wind began to make any rescue effort impossible. And as the weather only got worse, an all-points bulletin went out so that everyone with a walkie-talkie heard: "Attention, all search teams: Because of the worsening weather, we are postponing search efforts until daybreak. Please return to base camp ASAP. We repeat: return to base camp ASAP."

Meanwhile, back at the Jarvis Ranch, the IIA and local police had taken over several outbuildings not only serving as a base for the ongoing investigation of the attempted murder of Roy Jarvis but now serving as a search command center for Larry Davis. The Jarvis indoor arena served nicely as command central, with concrete floors, plenty of square footage, and central heating. The arena was normally used for local and regional equestrian events and had state-of-the-art upgrades, including satellite

Internet, top-notch lighting, a full-service kitchen, and two twenty-stall bathrooms. The floor of the oval show arena itself was pressed dirt, but wood pallets had been brought in and laid down on top of the dirt floors and then plywood and finally, an industrial-grade carpet.

The Jarvis family opened their ranch home to all law enforcement as well as Star Gaze employees and generously only asked in return that people be respectful of their home and clean up after themselves. The arena, or command central, was bustling with people, mostly law enforcement working on the disappearance of Mr. Davis—screening phone calls on the local police tip line, filtering through testimonies of eyewitnesses, putting together a timeline, and other duties. So when Jennifer Sweeney and Colin Wohl walked in, they were hardly noticed.

"Jenn, you need to tell one of them what you told me," said Colin.

"Okay, yes. But who?" Jenn replied.

"Well, he looks like he may be in charge or at least knows who is," Colin replied as he pointed to a dark-haired man sitting at one of the many desks set up on the arena oval. He looked to be in his thirties, slight build, wearing black-rimmed glasses and an IIA jacket and badge.

"Okay, he will do," Jenn said, shooting Colin an uneasy look.

"Hello," Jenn said as she approached the man's desk.

Without looking up, the man said, "Fill out one of the MP-38 forms over there and leave it with any of us agents. We will get to it ASAP. Thank you," as he nodded toward the table next to him, eyes still on his computer.

"Uhh, umm . . . I am here to report a missing person," Jenn said timidly.

The man started his speech again but was interrupted.

"Hey! Can you at least look up? This woman is trying to report a missing person who may have been with Larry Davis! Hello?" Colin said, bordering on nasty.

Jennifer glared at Colin, wide-eyed and mortified.

"Colin, there's no reason to be rude!" she said, attempting to hush her overzealous boss.

The man finally looked up and saw Colin, whom he all but ignored and then turned to Jennifer, who caused him to do a double take.

"Uhhhh . . . oh, sorry. Hello," he said, straightening his hair and standing. "I'm Agent Paulson, IIA. How can I help you?"

"Well, I need to report a missing person. My friend Lillie Adams has vanished," Jenn said.

"And according to your friend here, this Ms. Adams may have been with Mr. David?" Agent Paulson asked.

"Yes, yes, that is correct. She and Larry are engaged, and she left this note on my desk, in my trailer. We are roommates, staying here while the movie is being made," Jenn explained as she handed a note written on a sheet of yellow post-a-note paper.

> WENT TO CHECK ON LARRY.
> BE BACK SOON.
> LET'S GO OUT FOR DINNER!
> L.A.

"L.A. is Lillie Adams?" Agent Paulson asked, causing Colin to sigh.

"Yes, L.A. is Lillie Adams. That's how she signs all her office correspondence," Jenn answered.

"And when was this note written?" Agent Paulson pressed.

"I'm not sure when it was written, but I found it roughly an hour ago," Jenn replied.

"Okay. Wait here," Agent Paulson said as he held his hand up and then walked across the arena floor to a media area where several large screens were set up. One screen had a large map of the Nire Valley, the other a photo of Larry Davis. Directly in front of the screens were four desks arranged in a semicircle. Agent Paulson approached the desk, where a woman sat, and handed her the note.

"Looks like that's the boss lady, eh?" Colin quipped. "Not bad-lookin' for a cop!"

"Colin, will you stop? Show some respect, boss!" Jenn spat back. "Shh, here they come."

The two agents made their way across the arena, talking quietly.

"Hello, I'm Agent Stacia O'Malley, IIA. Agent Paulson briefed me on what was goin' on. When was the last time you saw Ms. Adams, Ms. Sweeney?"

"Well, the last time was this morning as I headed out to work. She was still in the shower, but I yelled, 'Have a nice day!' and she yelled back, 'You too, beautiful!' She calls me that," Jenn replied, now blushing.

"Okay. And Ms. Adams and Mr. Davis are engaged to be married?" Agent O'Malley asked.

"Yes, they are," Jenn replied.

"And you found this note about an hour ago?" asked Agent O'Malley.

"Sweet Lord! Yes! Yes! Yes! She already told Clark Kent here all of this! When are you going to find her and Larry?" Colin blurted out, frustrated.

Agent O'Malley turned to face Colin, cocked her head slightly, and raised one eyebrow. "I'm sorry . . . you are?" she asked, oozing sarcasm. Stacia O'Malley was a striking woman, with light blue eyes and strawberry-blonde hair that she kept neatly up in a bun. She was of average height with a well-proportioned figure and fair Irish skin. Wearing the customary IIA jacket, white button-down shirt, a pair of black, figure-hugging leggings and black ankle-high work boots, Stacia O'Malley was a force to be reckoned with.

"I am—" Colin began but was interrupted.

"Come with me, Ms. Sweeney. We will need you to fill out a few forms and give us a written statement," Agent O'Malley said as she shot Colin a narrow-eyed glare.

Jennifer and Colin followed both agents to a small side room where there were three tables set up and several folding chairs. Agent O'Malley gathered a tablet, a pen, and several forms and placed them on a table. "Here you go. When you're done, just bring these forms plus your written statement to me. I will be at my desk."

"Okay, thanks," Jenn replied, apprehension in her voice.

Colin watched Agent O'Malley and Agent Paulson return to their desks. As he scanned the large arena from the doorway of the room Jenn was in, he noticed something strange. On the third large screen, located next to Agent O'Malley's desk, was a picture of William Athy. Colin didn't fully comprehend what he was seeing from across the arena. *How did I not see that earlier?* he thought to himself. So he said to Jenn, "You okay, love? I am going to go find a restroom. Be back in a flash." Jenn nodded as she continued to fill out forms. Colin slowly made his way closer to the large screen where he saw his best friend's picture displayed. As he crept closer, unnoticed, the writing on the large screen under William's picture came into focus. It said, "William Thomas Athy, WWM, 6'3", 185 lbs., last seen driving a stolen black SUV. Armed and extremely dangerous."

"Wanted? Extremely dangerous?! WWM? White, widowed, male? What the hell?" Colin said under his breath. Then, he quickly snapped a pic of the screen with his cell phone camera.

"Can I help you, Mr. Wohl?" blurted out Agent Paulson, which made Colin jump and curse.

"Yes! Yes, you can! Why is William Athy's picture on the screen?" Colin managed, heart pounding.

"Well, sir, he is wanted by IIA and the local police for questioning," replied Agent Paulson.

"For questioning? About what exactly?" Colin pressed.

"That is official police business, sir. Now, can I escort you back to Ms. Sweeney?" Agent Paulson replied as he gestured toward the room where Jenn sat, filling out forms.

"No, no. I can find my way just fine, thank you," Colin said as he hurried back to Jenn, Agent Paulson watching the entire time.

"Psst, Jenn, hurry up! We need to get the hell out of here now! They're after Will!" Colin whispered loudly.

Jenn stopped writing and let what Colin just said to her sink in. "Wait, what?" Jenn asked, eyes narrowing as she looked at Colin. "What do you mean 'They're after Will?' What makes you say that, Colin?"

"Look. Over there, on the third big screen." Colin replied, nodding toward the screen. "Discreetly! Don't let our friendly IIA agents see you!"

Jenn got up and moved to the doorway slowly, checking the room for onlookers. As her eyes fell upon the big screen, she gasped. "What on earth? Why? What is Will doing on the IIA's TV screens?" she asked, concerned.

"It says he is wanted for questioning. Whatever the hell that means. We need to get out of here now! I have a bad feeling," Colin replied, bordering on panic.

"Well, should I finish—" Jenn started.

"No! Jenn, we need to leave now. Grab Lillie's note, leave the rest, and let's go! Hurry, love!" Colin said abruptly.

With that, Jenn grabbed Lillie's note and took Colin's hand.

"Okay. We need to leave without Clark Kent and Uma Thurman seeing us!" Colin whispered.

"What? What are you talking about?" asked Jenn, confused.

"Never mind. Just stay close to me, eyes down, quietly. I will get us out of here," Colin replied.

"Okay," Jenn said, and the two exited the room and walked quietly but swiftly along the wall, into the foyer and out the front doors, undetected.

"We did it! Now, let's get over to the Athys' ASAP!" Colin said as the two ran to Colin's rented SUV.

Once inside, Colin grabbed his cell phone and immediately dialed William's number as he sped off.

"No answer. Dammit, Will. Where are you?!" Colin shouted.


Agent Stacia O'Malley made her way to the small room where she had left Jennifer Sweeney and Colin Wohl. She looked around and stepped into the doorway. "Agent Paulson? Can you come in here, please?" she shouted across the arena.

Agent Paulson hurried across the room, where the crowd was dwindling as agents were called out on possible Larry Davis sightings. He entered the small room to find Agent O'Malley looking over the forms she asked Jennifer Sweeney to fill out. "What's going on, Agent O'Malley?" he asked.

"Did you do as I asked?" she said.

"Yes, ma'am. The device was planted on Mr. Wohl's rented SUV. We watched them leave, and two agents are following them as we speak," he replied.

"Good. Let's hope they lead us to Mr. Athy," she said as she threw the papers Jenn filled out in the trash. "He is priority one!"

"And what about Mr. Davis?" Agent Paulson asked.

"As our MI5 and IIA bosses stated, collateral damage, Agent Paulson. Our main objective is to capture William Athy—dead or alive."

Lillie Adams awoke blindfolded, her hands and feet bound. She had no idea where she was or what was going on. She could only hear people at a distance talking. She tried to yell but realized she was also gagged. The panic set in a moment later, and she tried to struggle free but could not move. She tried to calm herself and slow her breathing down, but the terror of the situation made it impossible. The voices drew closer, and she could hear them clearly. They had British accents and were discussing Larry. She acted like she was still unconscious and listened intently. She heard two British male voices.

"It was a mistake, chap, okay? He is a rookie and didn't mean to kill him. But what's done is done! There's nothing we can do about it now except cover our asses. Larry Davis was collateral damage."

Lillie tried with all her strength to hold in her emotions, but she hyperventilated and passed out. She had just overheard that her beloved fiancé was dead.

Awakened again a few moments later, Lillie managed to regain consciousness. She was in a vehicle that was traveling at a rapid pace on a very bumpy road. She realized that she was no longer bound or gagged but still blindfolded. With her hands free, she removed the blindfold and could see she was in the trunk of a car. It was so bumpy her head hit the top of the trunk several times, causing her to bleed profusely. Lillie tried desperately to wipe the blood from her eyes and head, using the blindfold. Suddenly, the car came to an abrupt stop. Lillie decided to put the blindfold back on and act as if she were still unconscious. The trunk flew open, and she heard the same two British male voices.

"She dead?"

"Nearly."

"Should we shoot her to be sure?"

"No, chap, our orders are to dump her here and leave. And that's exactly what we'll do!"

With that, the two grabbed Lillie by the arms and ankles and lifted her out of the trunk and threw her into a gully alongside the dirt road. The wind was knocked out of her as her slight body hit the ground hard. She remained conscious and heard the men close the trunk, turn their car around, and speed off. Barely able to move, Lillie managed to peel the blindfold off her bludgeoned head and sit up. She winced in pain and realized her ribs were likely broken. A storm was raging, and Lillie was being pelted by rain and wind. All she wanted to do was lie down and give up; every inch of her body was riddled with pain. She tried to draw in a deep breath, but the pain was too excruciating.

"You have to get up, Lills!" the voice inside her shouted. "Get up and move, or you're dead!" She realized it was Larry's voice inside her head, telling her to survive. So she mustered every ounce of strength in her battered body and managed to stand. Although wobbly, she stood and looked about the area. Nothing. No lights, no sign of civilization whatsoever. She took a step and then another. "One foot in front of the other, Lills. You got this."

Lillie slowly made her way back the same way the two Brits sped off in their car. She knew eventually she would find civilization again.

"It must be late. It's so dark," she whispered to herself. Then she remembered. "I have a watch!"

Lillie stopped and pulled back her shirtsleeve to reveal her cheap 1980s Casio Cosmic Flight watch that Larry had gotten her as a gift when they first started dating. They both had a fascination with the 1980s, and Lillie adored her watch. She pressed the button on the side of the watch face, illuminating it.

"Eleven o'clock?" she said. "I can do this. I have to do this."

Lillie walked for what seemed to her like an eternity. She was getting weaker and weaker with each step, and it was getting harder and harder for her to breathe.

*I must have punctured a lung*, she thought to herself.

An hour went by, and just as Lillie was about to give up and collapse to the ground, she saw them—lights. Lights from a town and they were close!

"Oh my gosh, oh my gosh . . . people! Help!" she managed.

She kept moving toward the lights, and after several more minutes, she reached a building. As she managed to reach the front doors, she realized the establishment was closed and dark inside. So growing weaker by the second, she slowly continued to the next building and then the next. Finally, she came to a pub where she saw people getting in their cars and leaving. She tried to yell to them for help, but she could not draw in enough air to even speak. No one saw her as they were too busy and too inebriated to notice anything. So she kept walking until she reached the front door of the pub.

Patrick Athy Jr. was washing out the last of the beer from the sink when the front door of his pub flew open and she staggered in, soaked to the bone and shaking like a leaf from obvious exposure to the brutal storm outside. "Is there a phone?" she asked in a weak, shaken, hoarse voice.

"On the back wall." Pat Jr. nodded toward the back of the establishment, where a phone set on a small table, next to the back door. He watched as she walked shakily to the table and picked up the phone. Not more than a few seconds later, she dropped to the concrete floor, out cold.

Chapter Nineteen

The Long Road to the Nire

The air was thick with the smell of death, and Thomas Athy knew that the British king would surely not take his army's sound defeat from the previous day lightly. The Celt and knight army had fought a formidable foe and won. Without the help from the other Galway clans, the result surely would have been different. The Celts and knights who were originally headed to the Giant's Causeway and the Cliffs of Moher were already mounted up and ready to resume their trek as well.

The task at hand was to get all the caravans to the Nire Valley, Giant's Causeway, and the Cliffs of Moher as quickly as possible and to become invisible to the British scouts that were surely monitoring their every move in hopes of exacting revenge. The Celts had not been unscathed, with twenty-seven fallen men, nor the knights, who lost sixteen brave warriors. After their dead were buried and they said farewell to their brothers in arms, Thomas addressed his battle-weary army.

"Men! Will you gather around?" he began and then waited for the large group to draw closer. "Come closer! Closer. Good. Celts and knights, you fought bravely and fiercely yesterday. I have never seen such passion and determination in all of my years. Ya made me proud!"

A cheer rose up, and Thomas lifted his hands to quiet them again. "Men, I know you are weary and I know you need rest, but I am asking you to overcome your weariness because we must, *must* get this caravan to the Nire Valley as quickly as possible. King Henry will receive word soon that his army was annihilated." More cheers erupted. "So we need to move swiftly and get the important cargo in our wagons delivered and stowed into safekeeping. Sir Renaud, other clan chieftains, my clan members, and I have devised a plan to hopefully elude any further attacks by the British. We must split up and take different routes to the Nire. Our brothers who are headed to the Giant's Causeway and the Cliffs of Moher also helped us come up with this plan. The cargo will be dispersed among all of us, which will help keep it safe. We must travel in disguise as well so that we are not recognized. Groups no larger than twenty each must be formed, and you must hide any recognizable signs that you are a Galway clan member or knight. Stow your tartans and crests. Blend in with the locals and attract no attention. We will all travel in various routes and then meet at the Nire in three days. Some will take a direct route, some will circle back, and some will travel north first and then south as to throw off any British scouts. Me bruther Ailan will see to it that each group receives enough food, drink, and gold to make the trip. Now, each clan chieftain has instructions and route information. So find your clan and prepare quickly. We depart in two hours. And, men, may God be with us."

Each clan met, received all necessary information and supplies, loaded up their share of the cargo, split into smaller groups, and began their journey to the Nire Valley.

Thomas led a group of twenty-three men who were to take the highland route to the Nire, keeping to the mountains until they reached Clonmel, in County Tipperary, and then begin their descent into the valley. The journey from Galway to the Nire Valley was over 180 kilometers, which would normally take twenty-four hours, but they could not all simply take a direct route for fear of being spotted by the British. Each small group posed as either a band of merchants, a group of thespians, and even traveling apothecaries selling potions. Thomas' group was posing as traveling minstrels. Since he, his younger brother Ailan, Father Patrick, and his dear da all played an instrument, it was an easy guise. And so, they were on their way.

Meanwhile, King Henry III was anxious to hear of his army's victory late the next evening as he paraded around the streets of Winchester, England, enjoying the Festival of Music, followed by his usual entourage and a military guard. Henry was made king of England at the age of nine. He was also known as Henry of Winchester. He was charitable and cultured but lacked the ability to rule effectively. As a diplomatic and military leader, he proved to be arrogant, cowardly, ambitious, and impractical.

"I hope you all know I am about to receive word that my army obliterated those foul, filthy Celts in Ireland quite handily. I am the leader of the fiercest army in all of Europe, you know!" Henry boasted as he spilled wine all over himself. "I would have been there, but my duties as king here made that impossible!"

As King Henry rounded a street corner, followed by his patsies and armed guards, a British scout approached, obviously shaken.

"Your Royal Highness, sir, word from Ireland!" the scout said as he bowed and offered a rolled parchment.

Henry stopped abruptly and looked at the scout down his nose, as he offered his hand. The scout looked up from his bow and grabbed the king's hand and kissed his ring. "Steady, you cretin!" Henry yelled as he then wiped his hand on the clothes of the person standing next to him. "No need to be overzealous!" Everyone stood frozen as the king of England glared at his loyal assistant, Frederique. "Well? Read it, you utter ignoramus!" Henry said, seething condescension.

"Yes, sire," Frederique said as he grabbed the parchment from the scout. He cleared his throat as he unwrapped the message. Henry sighed impatiently.

"To Henry III, Lord of Ireland, Duke of Aquitaine, Sovereign and Royal King of England."

Henry flashed a juvenile smile and shrugged. "That's me!"

Frederique glanced at Henry and continued reading. "From Sir Thomas Athy, Baron Atheney, Rightful King of Eire, Rightful Sovereign and Royal King of the Celtic Isles."

Henry's smile was erased abruptly and replaced with a look of utter shock. "What? What is the meaning of this?!" he bellowed. "Who gave this parchment to you? Where are you? Where did that scout go?" The group looked about frantically, but the scout had disappeared. "Give me that!" Henry spat as he grabbed the parchment from Frederique's hands.

"I cannot read the rest! It is gibberish! What does it say? What does it say, you fool?!" Henry screamed and shoved the letter back to his assistant.

"I do not know, sire. It looks to be written in a foreign language. Gaelic, perhaps?" Frederique offered.

"Gaelic?" Henry pressed.

"Well, it is from Sir Thomas Athy, the Irishman who—" Frederique started.

"I know who Thomas Athy is, you idiot! Find me someone who can read Gaelic—*now*!" the king of England shouted as he threw his glass of wine in the street and hurried to his carriage. "Take me to the palace! Frederique? Come on! We have several Irish swine drudges slaving away at the palace. Surely, one of them can translate that letter for me!"

With that, King Henry and his entourage were whisked away in the royal carriage, headed for Winchester Castle.


As the small group of Celts and knights meandered through the mountains of beautiful green Ireland, Thomas Athy smiled atop his trusted steed. "Ailan, me dear bruther, do ya t'ink our scout delivered the letter to jolly ole King Henry yet?" he said, holding back a laugh.

"Well, bruther, I do believe it is around dat time!" Ailan replied. "Dun't ya wish you were a fly on the wall in Winchester this bonny night, Thom?" And the two burst out laughing.

# Chapter Twenty

## They Shoot Celts, Don't They?

William repeated, "Da, you want to tell me what is goin' on and why MI5 wants us dead?"

Patrick Athy paused for a moment to collect his thoughts, set his handgun and twelve-gauge shotgun down on a table, and turned to William. "Son, you are who they are after. They found out you are the chosen one, and they want you dead."

"Wait, what? How did they find out about all this king nonsense?" William pressed.

"William, do you seriously think MI5 would be tryin' to kill ya if there wasn't something they needed to keep quiet? They cannot allow you to live because if they do, the entire British monarchy would be in ruins! Dun't ya understand, son? Your very existence could bring down the House of Windsor!" Patrick replied as he moved to within inches of his son and rested his hand gently on his shoulder.

"Da, I didn't ask for all this!" William replied, sounding very frustrated.

"I know, son. But it is the hand that life has dealt ya," Patrick replied sympathetically. "Will, let me say this: I know that this is all very frustrating, confusing, and unsettling, but you must think of Eire." William sighed and started to say something. "Let me finish, William, please. This battle is centuries old and deeply rooted in our ancestry. They, those men out there," Patrick continued, pointing to the front of the hideaway. "They do not want the truth to come out, and they will do whatever it takes to protect their lie. And it isn't just MI5! There are people in high places, powerful people who also want to protect this secret. Trillions of dollars have been invested in keeping the lie protected. The Bilderberg meetings that take place in America . . . one of their top priorities is to protect the House of Windsor. There are many powerful families globally who have a vested interest in keeping the Windsors protected. William, you are the rightful heir to the Celtic throne, son. Without you, all the documentation is null. You are the definitive, most important piece of this puzzle, and you need to come to grips with the fact that you are king—king of these Celtic Isles, king of a dynasty that is thousands of years old. If you refuse to step into your rightful place, all will be lost. All the centuries of Celts who fought and died to protect this vital information will have died in vain. You are he who is spoken of by Thomas Athy himself when he wrote his chronicles. He spoke of a descendent who would carry the torch and lead the final battle. He said his distant son that will be born in the twentieth century will be the chosen one. Like a modern-day Moses, if you will. Thomas Athy spoke of *you*, William. *By name!* 'William Thomas Athy will lead our people to their rightful place in history. He will bring justice to the long-suffering Emerald Isle and what they will call the British Isles.' William, you are divinely appointed for this centuries-old, foretold mission! You cannot turn your back on your destiny, son!"

William was now pacing; the words of his father rang true in his mind and spirit. He knew at that moment that he needed to stop resisting and step into his rightful place. But he was scared. Not for himself but for his precious children. "What will happen to Ian and Fiona?" he finally managed.

"They will be taken to a safe place, in America," Patrick answered.

"America? *No!* I will not allow it! I cannot be without me childrun, Da!" William said, visibly shaken.

"Sire," Jean-Rene interjected. "May I try to help?"

"Uh, okay, but I am not sure how helpful you *can* be, considering!" William said, finding a chair and sitting.

"Sire, your children are of the utmost of importance to all those involved in this on our side. They, specifically Ian, are your heirs and will take your place," Jean-Rene said carefully and gently.

"*What? No!* You *will not use me chuldren*!" William shouted, tipping his chair over as he stood abruptly.

"William, Jean-Rene is only trying to help," Patrick offered.

"*Help?* Me son *is not* involved!" William spat back.

"He is involved, William, or he will be when he is older. It is the natural order of things. There has been a plan in place for centuries for you and your firstborn son. All the arrangements have been made, and Ian will be safe, as long as you allow those whom you rule over to do their jobs!" Patrick explained. "Everything has been arranged, Will. Trust those who call you sire."

"Sire, His Royal Highness, Prince Ian will have the best protection possible, as well as Her Royal Highness, Fiona," Jean-Rene added.

"His Royal Highness, Her Royal Highness? *Ha!* I will *never* be able to live wit' dem if ya call dem dat!" William replied, now a bit more at ease. "Tell me about this protection for me kids, Frenchman!"

"Yes, sire! There is a global network that has been in place since Thomas Athy's time. It started with simple safe houses and underground societies that keep the corrupt globalists at bay. It went from a mainly Europe endeavor to an enormous global one the last 242 years. When America became a nation in 1776, many of their founding fathers were from the Knights of Solomon and Celts themselves. They knew the truth and were dedicated to keeping our truth protected until the chosen one came of age in the twenty-first century—you, sire. There are loyalists all over Europe and in America. They have infiltrated the CIA, FBI and most American law enforcement and government agencies. We have several in MI5 as well. There have been several American presidents, of Irish ancestry, who also know the truth and are loyal to our cause. Those who oppose globalization and the New World Order are our friends and have vowed to protect you as well. Ian and Fiona will be sent to a prepared place in Maryland, USA, to a small town whose inhabitants are all our loyalists. They will be educated and well taken care of until the final battle is over and you are appointed the king of the Celtic Isles, before the entire world."

William sat back down slowly, deep in thought. As he began to speak, a huge boom came from outside the hideaway, toward the cabin. All three men grabbed their guns and headed for the escape tunnel.

"What was that? A bomb?" William said.

"Yes, definitely an explosion," Patrick answered.

"Sire, I believe that was propane, perhaps?" Jean-Rene offered.

The men ran, single file, through the tunnel and back into the cabin basement, to assess any damage. William hurried to check the reinforced door that led into the cabin itself. It was completely intact.

"No damage here at all," William said.

"Shh, listen!" Patrick whispered.

The three men stood at the foot of the basement stairs and listened intently. It was muffled, but they could hear gunfire. It sounded like World War III above them.

"Is that helicopters?!" William said, in shock.

"I believe so, sire. I believe we are being rescued!" Jean-Rene said as he climbed the stairs to listen closer.

William followed Jean-Rene to the top of the stairwell and stood alongside him. "How do ya know we're being rescued, JR?" William asked quietly.

"JR, sire?" Jean-Rene asked, one eyebrow lifted.

"If we're gonna be in battle together, I cannot keep having to call you Jean-Rene! JR is an abbreviation of yer name, Frenchman!" William answered, with a hint of sarcasm.

"I would prefer French to JR, sire. Respectfully," he quipped.

"OK, French it is! T'ank da Lord! You French and your hyphenated names! Sheesh," William replied with a hint of a smile.

"Yes, sire. You can call me whatever you like! If French is better for you, so be it!" Jean-Rene said, adding a slight bow of his head.

Just then, there were four loud knocks on the metal door.

"Aha!" shouted French. "It is our rescuers, indeed. But let me confirm."

French then used the butt of his shotgun to knock on the door.

"Morse code?" William asked.

French nodded, holding his index finger to his lips. "Listen, sire."

More loud taps. "Open the door, sire! It is them!"

# Chapter Twenty-One

## Commotion at the Pub

Patrick Athy Jr. rushed to the woman who had just fainted and fallen to the floor of his family's pub. "Ma'am? Ma'am! Are you okay? Obviously not. Hello?"

Pat Jr. tried to rouse the lady on the floor, but she was not responding. He arose from the floor and rushed to the nearby table to retrieve the phone, which had fallen onto the floor as well.

"Hello, this *is* an emergency! A woman just fell in me pub, and she won't wake up!" Pat Jr. shouted. "I am calm! Just get here and hurry!"

He then grabbed a clean bar rag from the shelf behind the bar, moistened it with cold water, and placed it on the woman's forehead. "There, there . . . everyt'ing will be okay, love. The ambulance is on its way!" he said as he pressed the cold rag upon her head. Pat Jr. looked down and assessed the woman's face, noticing several bruises and cuts on her face, neck, and hands. As he scanned the rest of her body, he noticed she had no shoes on and was in bad shape. *Probably hypothermic,* he thought. He then arose and ran to the pub office to retrieve a wool blanket from the couch. "Where is it?" he asked himself as he searched the room, opening drawers and cabinets. Finally, he spotted it on the back of his father's chair. He rushed back to where the stranger/lady was lying and was surprised to see no trace of her. "What in the . . ." Pat Jr. said to himself. "Did the ambulance get here and take her already?" Then he heard commotion outside the front entrance of the pub and went to investigate. As he opened the front door, he saw two men carrying the woman and placing her in a black SUV. "Hey!" Pat Jr. screamed.

One of the men, who was hurrying to the driver's side of the SUV, stopped suddenly, drew a weapon, and fired upon Pat Jr., who heard a pop like the sound of a firecracker, then felt extreme pain in his chest. "What the . . .

what was that?" Pat Jr. mumbled. He looked down and noticed blood on his shirt. "I've been shot? I've been shot!" he said as he could feel the life drain from his body. His knees buckled, and he fell to the ground just as the ambulance he called pulled up to the pub.

## Chapter Twenty-Two

## Woman Down!

Lillie Adams awakened with a start and gasped. "Where am I? What's happening?!" she mumbled.

All she could see was bright lights passing by overhead. As she became slightly more lucid, she spotted several people in uniforms. She realized she was on a gurney, in some sort of cement hallway.

"Please, help me!" she cried.

Just then, a person in a white lab coat whispered in her ear, "Shut up, or you'll die!" as she used a syringe to put something in Lillie's IV. Lillie struggled to yell but could not move. The lights faded. Out again.

# Chapter Twenty-Three

## The Rescue

William hurried down the stairs to a power panel, opened it, and pressed the button. The enormous metal door jolted to life and then began opening.

"Take cover, boys!" Patrick yelled. "Just in case it isn't who we think it is!"

"No need!" French said. "Bonjour, nos frères d'armes! Je savais que c'était toi. Vite, nous devons mettre notre roi en sécurité!" Translated: "Hello, our brothers in arms! I knew it was you. Hurry, we must get our king to safety!"

As the large metal door opened, several people in all-black attire stood, heavily armed with machine guns, faces covered, and no identifiable markings on any of them.

"Ya better be damn sure they are our rescuers, French, or your *king* will be a wee bit perturbed!" William whispered as he leaned closer to his French companion.

"Oui, monsieur! Or, I mean, sire! They are the Knights of Solomon's Temple!" French said confidently.

"How can you be sure, JR—I mean, French?" William quipped, "They look like ninjas to me, all in black, faces covered . . . excuse me if I seem a bit shaken, but I'm a bit shaken!

"Ahhh, Jean-Rene! C'est toi mon ami! Dépêchez-vous, nous devons obtenir notre roi et vous hors d'entendre! MI5 et Dieu sait qui d'autre enverra des renforts d'une minute à l'autre! Dépêchez-vous! L'hélicoptère attend!" Translated: "Ahhh, Jean-Rene! It is you, my friend! Hurry, we must get our king and you out of here! MI5 and God knows who else will be sending reinforcements any minute! Hurry, the helicopter is waiting!"

One of the masked men shouted as he motioned for the three men.

"What? What is he saying, French?" William said, still feeling uneasy.

"He speaks French, sire!" French offered.

"Yes, French, I know!" William replied, bordering on impatience.

"You speak French, mon roi? Fantastique! Maintenant, nous n'aurons pas à parler anglais . . . un langage si laid et non poétique! Je préfère discuter en français, sire! Ooh-la-la . . . Quel soulagement! Ha!" Translated: "You speak French, my king? Fantastic! Now we won't have to speak English . . . such an ugly, unpoetic language! I would much rather converse in French, sire! Ooh-la-la . . . what a relief! Ha!"

The same leading masked man rambled as he peeled the mask off his head. His name was Jean-Pierre-Yves Martin; he went by the name Yves. A thirty-five-year veteran knight, his middle age showed on his face. But, as it is with most older men, his maturity lent him a certain je ne sais quoi. Jean-Pierre-Yves was a striking man with long, wavy dark brown hair. His eyes were light green, and he wore a neatly trimmed goatee. His hair was gray around the edges, which gave him a look of maturity, but he was extremely fit and quick-witted.

"What in God's name is this Frenchman goin' on about, French? Lord Almighty, he speaks as if I know what he is sayin'!" William spat as he shook his head.

The unmasked French knight then smiled broadly. "My mistake, sire. I thought you meant you spoke French!"

"Oh . . . no, no. I do not. Maybe a little high school French, but that's it," William replied as he, French, and Patrick climbed up the stairs, through the metal door, and into what was once a cabin living room. All that was left was the walls around the basement opening, which were reinforced. Most of the front of the cabin was blown away and still smoldering. Several knights surrounded William, placed a blanket over him and Patrick, and hurried them off, through piles of debris. Once outside, William scanned the area. The black SUV he had driven to the cabin was destroyed. The gas tank had exploded, which left a crater and a pile of metal in its place.

Trees, grass, and vegetation had been singed, and smoke filled the air. As he gazed out over the Atlantic, William noticed an approaching fleet of boats, speeding directly toward them.

"Are they with you?" he asked and nodded toward the water.

Just then, automatic gunfire rang out from the shoreline. Dozens of knights opened fire on the approaching armada. The boats, numbering over a dozen, tried to dodge the barrage of gunfire. But half were hit immediately, two exploding into flames that caused the boats behind to crash into each other. Still, two boats continued to move swiftly toward the shore as bullets tore holes in their bows. As the boats zigzagged toward the shore, French shouted, "They are unmanned! Hurry, get on the helicopter now! We must get out of here!"

Everyone on shore stopped firing their weapons and ran to waiting vehicles. William, Patrick, French, and three other knights ran as fast as they could to the helicopter. As they boarded, a surface-to-air missile was fired from one of the boats, hitting only twenty yards away from them and causing Patrick to stumble and fall hard onto the charred ground.

"Da!" William screamed as he was forced into the waiting helicopter. "Help him!"

French saw Patrick fall and ran to his side. "Come, my friend, I will get you out of here!" he said confidently as he lifted Patrick onto his shoulder and began to run. Just then, another rocket was launched, heading directly at the two men.

"French, Da, *get out of there! A missile is heading straight for ya!*" William screamed. But it was too late. The missile hit only a few yards from them, exploding forcefully.

"*No! Da! Da!* Get up! Get out of there! *Da!*" William screamed, tears running down his face. "*No!* You have to help them! That's me da!"

"Sire, we must leave now! They are gone. We lost them, sire. I am sorry," Yves said, trying to console his king. But William wouldn't listen. He struggled to try to run toward his father, but the knights subdued him, one plunging a needle into his neck. "I am sorry, sire, but your life is our priority."

William looked at the knight in disbelief. "Not again," he managed. Then he lost consciousness.

# Chapter Twenty-Four

## Meanwhile, Back at the Ranch, Again

The old International Scout meandered slowly down the driveway of Jarvis Ranch, coming to a stop just in front of the family home. Sue Jarvis exited the driver's side and walked around to the passenger side and opened the door.

"Come on, love. Let's get you inside so you can lie down and rest," Sue whispered lovingly to her dear husband.

Roy Jarvis was a shadow of his former self. The cancer had wreaked havoc on him, so much so that the poison he had ingested nearly killed him. He had been in the ICU for a week and then was finally moved to another room a few days prior to his release. The doctors were actually quite amazed that Roy, no young man, survived at all. After all, they gave him a 10 percent chance of living the night of the poisoning.

"Love, I know you are trying to help, and I appreciate it very much. But yer smotherin' me. Let loose of the reins just a wee bit, will ya, me dear?" Roy said, voice still very weak.

Sue shook her head and continued to help her husband into their house. Their housekeeper of thirty years slammed open the massive front door and came trotting out. Machiko was an older Asian woman, all of four foot nine and full of energy.

"Meester Jarvis! You are alive! Praise Jesus, you are alive!" Machiko squeaked with a broad smile on her face. "Come inside, I made your favorite soup!"

Now, with his wife under his right arm and his housekeeper under his left arm, Roy Jarvis begrudgingly obeyed the two women and slowly let them help him to his favorite easy chair. Once there, he gazed out the huge picture window in front of him. "I never thought I would ever see this place again," he whispered to himself.

After nearly two hours of Sue and Machiko fussing over him, Roy had enough. And as Sue approached with yet another pill to take, Roy let out a groan.

"What is it, love? Are you in pain?" Sue asked, concerned.

"Yes, my darling, I am in terrible pain! Would you help me to our bed? I . . . I need to rest a wee bit," Roy whimpered.

"Of course! Let's get you to bed, sweet love," Sue responded.

Machiko, hearing the commotion, came scurrying into the family room, in full panic mode. "Oh no, Meester Roy! Are you sick? Let me help you!" she said, practically shrieking.

"Okay, okay, ladies!" Roy said, rolling his eyes as the two women assumed their prior positions, under each arm. "Just get me to bed and leave me be for a bit. Thank you."

As they approached the king-size bed in their large master suite, Sue asked, "Love, do you need a pain pill?"

"Yes! Please," Roy responded, wincing in pain.

Sue hurried to the bathroom medicine cabinet as Machiko settled Roy into bed, fluffing his pillows and fussing with the blankets. "You okay, Meester Roy? Can I make you some tea? Or soup or—"

Roy interrupted, grabbing his loyal housekeeper's hand. "Machiko! Dear woman, I am fine. Now, please calm down and get me my silver flask. I believe it is in the top drawer of my dresser," he said as he nodded toward the opposite side of the room.

"But, Meester Roy—" Machiko started.

"No buts! No buts, dear. Please do as I ask," Roy blurted out, feeling his face flush in frustration.

"Yes, Meester Roy," Machiko replied, scowling.

"Thank you," Roy said, visibly exhausted.

"Roy Jarvis, you do not need that!" Sue scolded.

"My darling wife, either I get a swig from my flask or I jump off the nearest cliff!" Roy replied, desperately.

Sue looked across the room at Machiko, who was frozen in mid-stride, looking over her shoulder at Sue, who simply nodded. "Give this stubborn man his flask. But *one swig*, mister, or I'll throw ya off that cliff!"

"Thank you, love." Roy sighed in relief.

Once the two women had fussed, changed his head bandage, given him a pain pill, and closed the bedroom blinds, Roy was finally alone. He took in a deep breath and let the darkness surround him. "Peace," he whispered. "Finally."

He closed his eyes and tried to sleep, but his thoughts would not stop tormenting him. The questions "Who poisoned me? Who would want me dead? Why me?" kept running through his brain, over and over again. Finally, he had had enough. Roy grabbed his flask and headed to his walk-in closet. He flipped the closet light on and scanned the area, then gathered clothes, a belt, hat, work boots, and a jacket. He took them into the bathroom, shut the door, and proceeded to change. Once dressed, he managed to sneak out the bedroom French doors. Once outside, he drew in a deep breath. "Ahhh, fresh air, I missed ya!" he whispered.

Knowing that Sue had left the keys in the old Scout as usual, Roy quietly made his way to his prized vehicle, slowly opened the door, and slid behind the wheel. He said a little prayer that the ladies inside, at the opposite end of the house, would not hear him as he started the engine. It came to life on the first try, which made Roy smile. *That a girl*, he thought.

In a few short minutes, he was on the road, headed toward the river. Although weak from the relentless disease in his body, with a massive headache from his fall and the effects of the poison he ingested, Roy was determined. He had to know what had happened to him and why.

He drove slowly, as every bump caused him pain. Taking a swig every few minutes from his flask helped and by the time he arrived at the scene of the crime, the pain had eased considerably. He stopped the Scout between the river and the campfire site, the same place where he had passed out. As he opened the door and managed to get out slowly, he noticed several deer only a few yards away. "Well, good evening, ladies," he said. "And a lovely evening it is." The deer only looked up briefly, then continued to graze on the lush vegetation. Roy made his way to his favorite spot by the fire pit and sat down. He just sat and stared at his favorite part of his massive ranch. The green, rolling hills, rushing river, and majestic woods were just what he needed. He closed his eyes and breathed in the clean, crisp air, listening to every sound as he finally relaxed. After a half an hour, Roy felt almost human again. He stood up and drew in another long, deep breath as he stretched his tired body. *Well, before Sue and Machiko discover I have escaped and send a search party, I had better get on back home*, he thought to himself. He took one more long look around his beautiful surroundings but this time saw something out of place. It was late afternoon now, and the sun was beginning to fall behind the dense forest. So the lighting was dim, but he saw what looked to be a spear with paper on the tip of it on the edge of the woods, close to the place where they found the last one. "Not again," he said to himself.

Roy managed to hurry to the Scout and retrieve his rifle, flashlight, and walkie-talkie, then headed toward the edge of the woods and the mysterious spear. As he approached the sight, he drew his gun up, readying himself for anything. Narrowing his eyes, he scanned his surroundings thoroughly. Then, he crept up to the spear and grabbed the paper that was placed on its tip. Upon the paper, there was writing, just as the first but a different verse:

Caitheann na carraigeacha amach
le pian searbh.
Bhuaigh cathanna
gan aon ghaois a fuarthas

Translated:

> The rocks cry out
> with bitter pain.
> Battles won
> no wisdom gained.

*Well, now. I am guessing whoever planted this spear is also the one who poisoned me,* Roy thought.

He then rolled the note up and put it in the breast pocket of his coat and hurried to the Scout.

"I'm goin' to get to the bottom of this right now!" he said as he took another swig from his flask, started the engine, and headed for the ancient burial site. Once there, he parked and started the ascent up the hill, flashlight in his pocket, rifle in hand, flask in pocket.

Winded from the hike, Roy paused at the top of the hill and drank two large gulps of whiskey, wiped his brow with his hand, and continued to the burial grounds. As he approached the site and drew closer to the large stone, the hair on the back of his neck stood up. He could hear a low, humming sound coming from the giant stone with the Gaelic poem written on it. He was paralyzed with fear and froze in his tracks. "I need some liquid courage about now," He whispered to himself. He took his flask out of his coat's breast pocket, opened the lid, and took three more large swigs. "That ought ta do it," he whispered again. With that, he mustered up enough courage to draw closer to the stone, and as he made the turn to approach the front of the stone, where the message was etched, he couldn't believe his eyes. "Oh my God! No! Who could've done this?" he whimpered and collapsed to his knees. There, on the front of the massive stone, was a man naked, covered in blood, hanging by his neck. A rope was thrown over the top of the stone and attached to a tree several feet behind it. So many flies were swarming around the scene, it sounded like a horrible symphony of out-of-tune violins and cellos. As Roy lifted up his head and forced himself to gaze upon this horrible sight, it came to him. He recognized this poor man's face. "Larry Davis! Oh my God, *no!*" Roy cried out in a loud sob. "Why? Who did this?"

---

As Roy wiped the tears from his eyes, he tried his best to stand up. The effects of the whiskey and pain pills were hitting him hard, and he struggled to stand and steady himself.

"I need to get him down from there," he said. But he froze again when he heard footsteps approaching.

Without realizing it, he had dropped his gun several feet away. He looked quickly around, spotted it, and as he took his first step, he lost his balance and fell to the ground. The footsteps drew nearer. Roy's heart was pounding in his chest. He managed to crawl to his rifle, and as he was within inches from it, a large boot stomped on his arm, pinning him down. "Aaaayike, what . . . what are you doin' on my property?" he managed. He struggled to try to free his arm, but the weight was too much. He looked up to see who had trapped him but only saw a dark figure and then the blade of a sword as it swung toward his neck.

# Chapter Twenty-Five

## Reunions Are Sweet

As the helicopter flew over the Irish countryside, William slowly regained consciousness. He had been carefully placed in a seat by a window, with a blanket over him.

"Sire, are you okay? The effects of the sedative should be completely gone in an hour or so. Here, drink this. It will help," said Yves as he handed William a bottle of water.

"Where are we goin'?" William managed in a hoarse voice as he took several sips of water.

"We are headed to a safe house, sire," Yves replied. "And may I say, I am so sorry about your father and Jean-Rene. If only I could have gotten to them," he said, visibly shaken.

William stared out the window, emotionally numb, his face tearstained, his heart broken. He had just seen his beloved father die as a missile hit only a few yards from him. William was in shock, trembling and semi-unresponsive to the knights who surrounded him.

An hour and a half later, the helicopter began its decent into a large field. William, although still dazed and in shock, was regaining his physical strength and mental clarity.

"Where are we?" he asked Yves, who was seated next to him.

"We are near Galway, sire. This will be home for a while," Yves replied.

Galway was the birthplace and home to Clan Athy, one of the oldest families of the Tribes of Galway. William felt a certain draw to this area and was surprised to actually be excited about what was unfolding in his uprooted life. It wasn't so much that he was now resigned to all the changes, but he was changing on the inside. He had experienced several dreams that were so real he could no longer ignore them, dreams that gave him a different perspective. He had been fighting against his newfound reality but was beginning to comprehend the enormity of the situation. It wasn't just about him; it was so much bigger than that.

The helicopter pilot announced they were about to land over the cockpit ICS (intercommunications system). William leaned toward his window, straining to see what was below them. As they approached a clearing in the large field, William spotted a group of vehicles and several people standing next to them. He narrowed his eyes as they drew closer. "Wait, is that—" he started.

"Yes, sire. That is your mother, Miss Jennifer Sweeney, your brother, sister-in-law, and Colin Wohl," Yves replied.

William's heart sank. "Does my mother know—"

"No, sire. We thought you should tell her of your father's fate," Yves interrupted.

William could barely contain his emotions as he saw his mother's face outside his window. The helicopter touched down and everyone commenced with unbuckling and gathering their personal items. William sat frozen, staring out his window, trying to find the words to say to his dear mother. He swallowed hard and exited with Yves and two other knights escorting him. Grace Athy hurried to her son, tears in her eyes, and wrapped her arms around him, which actually made William stumble a bit. For a small woman, Grace Athy's hugs were fierce.

"My son. My dear, sweet son, you are finally here! Give yer mum a kiss, love!" Grace managed.

"Hello, Mum. So good to see you too," William replied, fighting back tears.

The two held their embrace for several seconds until Jenn cleared her throat quietly and smirked just a bit. William let go of his mother, and he kissed her on the cheek.

"Love you, Mum." And his attention was drawn to Jennifer. "Hello there, beautiful. Fancy meetin' you here," he said as he opened his arms.

Jennifer Sweeney rushed into William's arms and wrapped her arms around his waist tightly.

"Oh, Will . . . I was so worried. I am so happy to see you . . . I missed you," Jenn said, losing her composure.

William held her tight and whispered in her ear, "I missed you so much too," as he kissed her neck.

"What, no kisses for yer best friend and real king?" Colin Wohl quipped, forever the comic relief.

"Ahh, Sire," William replied as he let go of Jenn and turned to his dearest friend and extended his arms wide.

The two lifelong friends embraced.

"Who would have thunk . . . *you*, royalty!" Colin whispered in William's ear.

"Who told ya, Sire?" William asked.

"Oh, there's a story for ya, Will! Ha. They basically kidnapped Sam and me—" Colin started.

"Sam? Where is she?" William asked, looking for his dear sister-in-law.

"She's with the kids, love," Grace offered.

"Oh my gosh . . . my children! Take me to them now, please!" William pleaded, looking at Yves.

"Yes, sire. Right away," Yves answered.

"Sire? That's about as much irony as I can take! Haha," Colin joked as the entire group loaded up into the waiting vehicles.

"After you, bruther." Pat Jr. said, motioning to William, his left arm in a sling.

"What happened to you, Patty?" William asked.

"I will fill you in later, Will but I will be OK." Pat Jr. answered as he made his way to one of the waiting SUV's.

William and Jenn cozied up to each other in the first vehicle, among the knights' security detail. Yves had not left William's side since they met at the coast and sat on the other side of his sovereign. William put his arm around Jenn and kissed her forehead as the vehicles moved swiftly in a row toward the safe house. And what a safe house it was! As the convoy of vehicles rounded a corner, the expanse of the Atlantic Ocean came into view. The road they were on was not paved, and there were no other houses to be seen. After driving for ten minutes, they turned into a driveway that meandered down to the Oceanside property. The enormous gates in front of them opened, and they passed through as armed guards stood at attention. William shot Yves a look, eyebrows raised.

"They're KST, sire," Yves said.

"KST? Knights of Solomon's Temple?" William questioned.

"Yes, sire. Sorry. They will be everywhere you go now," Yves replied.

The vehicles snaked along the oceanfront driveway for another five minutes and finally came to another, smaller gate that was unmanned and opened. As they drove through, the safe house came into view.

"Sweet Jesus, Mary, and Joseph! Ya didn't tell me it was a full-blown castle, Yves!" William said as he leaned forward, eyes widened.

"Yes, sire, this is your castle," Yves answered, with a half-smile. "This was the home of Baron Thomas William Patrick Athy. Welcome to Atheney Castle, sire."

William's mouth fell open as they pulled up directly in front of the most spectacular castle he had ever seen. And as an Irishman, William wasn't easily impressed. There are over thirty thousand castles in Ireland, and William had seen over half of them, as every weekend while he was young, Patrick and Grace Athy would load their sons up into their family van and "have an adventure," as Patrick used to say. They explored almost every square mile of the Emerald Isle but somehow missed Atheney Castle.

The group departed their vehicles and stood in front of a grand entrance. Atheney Castle was absolutely stunning. It had obviously been well taken care of, as its walls were still white and pristine. Medieval castles in Ireland were made of cut stone with a lime plaster coating on top and then skillfully whitewashed. Atheney Castle was originally erected in 1250 and was then only a fraction of the size it became over the centuries. It was nestled in a grove of tall fir trees and surrounded by lush gardens and several small lakes. The River Clarin emptied out into the Atlantic on the northern side of the property, just a hundred yards from the castle.

The square footage of the original was only three thousand feet; it was comprised of only two towers, eight main rooms, and twelve outbuildings. As the centuries unfolded and the castle was inhabited by each new generation of Clan Athy, it was renovated and built onto multiple times. The castle that stood before the Athy family now was over twenty-five thousand square feet.

"What . . . how . . . where . . . when?" William stammered.

"I said the same thing when we arrived here, Will," Colin quipped. "This place is incredible. Even more incredible is that no one really knows about it except these weird secret-society, 007 *Spy Who Loved Me*, Knights of the Round Table dudes who have very little in the way of a sense of humor!"

William shot Colin a look. "Why are *you* here? I mean, I'm glad to see ya, Sire . . . don't get me wrong. But isn't this putting his life in danger . . . all of their lives in danger?" Will said, turning to Yves.

"All your questions will be answered in good time, sire. For now, let's get you inside. There are some people who are anxious to see you!" replied Yves.

So the entire group headed up the massive stone stairs toward the front entrance. As they drew closer, the door to the castle opened, and two very excited children bounded out and ran directly to William, who fell to his knees, tears streaming down his face.

"Awww . . . loves of my life, there ya are!" he managed. "Oh Lord, I missed you so much."

The three embraced and cried together, which caused the rest of the group to tear up; even the rough-and-tumble knights were trying to keep composed.

Suddenly, Fiona stopped hugging and backed away from her father and brother. She crossed her arms in front of her and gave William a scowl. "How dare you leave us like that, Da! I was worried sick. You have to promise to never leave us again or I'm . . . I'm . . . I'm gonna run away!" she spat and then turned her back and cried in anger, chin down, brow wrinkled.

William got up, winked at his son, walked over to his precious daughter, bent down, and grabbed her up into his arms, hugging her with the ferocity of his own mum.

"I love you, Fiona Emmanuel Athy, and I promise to never leave you without telling you why again. I may travel here and there, and you will have to stay home. Or we may travel together to faraway places. But I will *never* leave you for very long. Okay?" William offered, kissing Fiona on both cheeks, several times.

"Hmm. Okay, Da," she said, still scowling, tears running down her face.

"So now I need that Miss Fee smile!" he quipped. Nothing. "Pleeeease, Princess Fiona Emmanuel, yer da is tryin here!" William said as he gave his daughter his famous puppy-dog pout. A slight smile started at the corner of her mouth. "There it is . . . yep, I see it coming . . . you can do it, Princess . . . smile in 3 . . . 2 . . . 1!"

With that, Fiona burst out laughing, hugged her father around his neck, and kissed his cheek.

"Yer forgiven, Da. But pleeease, dun't leave me with Ian again!" She smirked.

"It's a deal, Fee," William responded, with a smile and sigh. "Tanks fer forgivin' me, Fee. It means a lot."

William then walked over to Ian and said, "And you, son? Are you needin' to scold yer ole da too?"

"No, Da. I am old enough to understand, and I am a prince! Princes dun't whine!" Ian replied and gave his father another hug.

"T'ank ya, son. Or should I call you, HRH?" William said with a grin.

"Ian is fine, Da."

"Sam!" William said with an apologetic tone. "Sorry, love . . . so much going on. How are you?"

"I am still in shock but okay, Will," Samantha replied as she embraced her brother-in-law and gave him a peck on the cheek. "You won't believe who I'm seeing now."

William hugged Samantha tightly and then raised one eyebrow. "Seeing? Yer seeing someone? Who is this lucky guy?" he pressed.

Samantha smiled, blushed, and shot Colin a look. William surmised the situation and glared at Colin. "We'll talk later, Wohl," he warned.

"Uh, okay," Colin replied, raising his eyebrows at Samantha.

"Let's see these new digs!" William said to his children with a broad smile. Then he looked at Jenn and offered her his hand.

They stepped inside the massive door and stood for a good two minutes while William simply gazed in awe at his surroundings. The foyer was as big as most houses at over fifteen hundred square feet. The ceiling was forty feet high and handcrafted out of dark hardwood. In contrast, the floors were a light Irish river stone inlaid in mortar with a layer of clear sealant. The craftsmanship was astonishing. The walls were the original cut stone with lime finish and also sealed. Four large fountains were placed in a row in front of the main entrance, each one hand-hewn out of Irish stone. The sound of water flowing inside was pleasing to William. A grand staircase was directly in front of the main door, beyond the fountains. It was made of a rich, dark wood like the ceilings, except more polished. Four chandeliers made of Waterford crystal hung from the ceiling, directly over each fountain, casting a prismlike light over the entire foyer. Two enormous fireplaces were on the walls to the left and right, made of River Clarin rock. A grown man could walk into these fireplaces without having to adjust his posture. The walls were covered with beautiful paintings: landscapes, portraits, impressionism, and even abstract art were carefully placed and accented this glorious room. Limestone life-sized statues of Irish warriors lined the wall on either side of the staircase, an imposing sight to any visitor. William could hardly breathe as he scanned the entire foyer. Awestruck and exhausted, he sat down on an old wooden chair that was placed just inside the door.

"I can't believe me eyes. This is *mine*? How can this be?" he managed.

Yves stood alongside William, gazing up at the magnificent craftsmanship before them. "Yes, sire. This is your new home. However, only for a short time."

"What? Why only a short time, Yves?" William asked.

"In good time, sire. Tonight, we feast, drink, enjoy family and rest. Tomorrow, you go back to school," Yves replied. "You have a lot to learn in very little time, and all your questions will be answered then. Next month, we are America-bound. Safety is our first priority and Ireland is becoming less safe with each passing moment."

William sat, his body utterly spent, his mind reeling from the events of the day. "I am going to trust you, Yves." William sighed. *How do I tell me mum that her husband was killed? I dun't know the words to use to tell her*, he thought to himself as he relaxed his head back on the chair.

The children, Jenn, Grace and Pat Jr., Colin, and Samantha headed up the long staircase to the family area, where there were all the modern conveniences imaginable. William and Yves lagged behind in the foyer.

"Sire, I know your father is weighing heavy on you and—" started Yves, when his cell phone chirped from inside his breast pocket. "Excuse me please, my Lord," he said as he answered it: "Bonjour, c'est Yves. Oui. Oui. Oh, c'est toi, Jean-Rene? Vous êtes en vie? Remercie le Père céleste! Et M. Athy? Oh, Bravo! C'est un miracle! Bien. Oui! Nous vous verrons bien tôt! Oui, gloire à Dieu! Alors, heureux mon frère! Au revoir." Translated: "Hello, this is Yves. Yes. Yes. Oh, it is you, Jean-Rene? You are alive? Thank the Father in Heaven! And Mr. Athy? Aww, bravo! It is a miracle! Okay. Yes! We will see you both soon! Yes, all glory to God! So happy, my brother! Goodbye."

"Who was that?" asked William.

"Sire, brace yourself! Your father is *alive*!" Yves said, eyes wide, smiling.

"What? Are ya serious? Oh God. Really? How? I mean, I saw him—" William stammered.

"Yes, sire. He is alive! That was Jean-Rene! They are both alive! Battered, cuts and bruises, but *alive*!" Yves said, close to shouting with joy.

William arose, tears streaming down his face. "I can't believe it, Yves. Me da is okay!" he said as he hugged his guardian knight and wept uncontrollably. "He's okay. And I dun't have to tell me mum her beloved husband is dead."

"Yes, sire. What fantastic news! They will be here in an hour or so. Perhaps you would like to compose yourself and get cleaned up?" Yves offered.

"Yes, yes, I need to pull me self together, Yves. Maybe a shot or two of whiskey and a hot shower? I'll be right as rain after!" William replied, clearing his throat and wiping the tears from his face.

"Yes, sire! Whatever you wish. I will have everything prepared for you. Now, let me show you around and get you that shot of whiskey!"


Ian, Fiona, Grace, Jenn, and Pat Jr. were enjoying the video arcade that was next to the massive family room. All of them had been instructed by the Knights of Solomon regarding William's new role. And although it was hard for them to grasp the magnitude of the situation, they supported their beloved father, son, brother, boyfriend, and friend completely.

William, on the other hand, was finding it overwhelming to be the subject of so much attention. Yves, who had been observing the young man who would be king, realized the best thing he could do for William was to give him some space. And so, Yves arranged for his king a one-hour escape. The master suite of Castle Atheney was a 2,000-square-foot apartment, equipped with not only a bedroom, en suite bath, and sitting area but also a bar, kitchenette, sauna, whirlpool bath, and high-tech entertainment center. William was left in complete privacy after the castle staff had prepared the master suite for him. He stood under the hot water of a luxurious shower for over fifteen minutes, allowing the rain-shower faucet to wash the dirt and his cares away. Then he eased himself into the whirlpool tub to soak his sore muscles and tired bones. The relief and joy that the news of his father being alive brought was profound. And as he padded into his bedroom after his soak, wrapped in a robe with a Clan Athy coat of arms on the breast pocket, he said a little prayer of thanks: "Lord, I am overwhelmed by Your grace and mercy. Thank You for sparing my father's life. Thank You for watching over my children and family. Give me strength to do Your will in this life. I dun't know how to be a king, but I know if it be Your will, I can do all things. Amen."

He then stepped into his closet that had been stocked with every possible clothing necessity. As he walked through the 500-foot closet, he was amazed at the detail taken to choose his attire. "They even knew my favorite rugby team?" William said to himself as he pulled a sweatshirt from one of the shelves. "Unbelievable," he whispered. An hour had passed quickly, and as William pulled on a pair of jeans, there came a knock at his bedroom door.

"Yes, who is it?" he yelled across the room.

"It is Yves, sire. Just wanted to let you know your father and Jean-Rene will be here any minute," the voice outside the door replied.

"Come in, Yves," William said.

Yves opened the door slowly and peeked his head in first. "Are you doing well, sire? Everything to your satisfaction?"

"Everything is amazing, Yves. I am feeling human again, thank you. And please, thank the staff. I cannot believe the thoughtful details . . . they truly did their research!" William answered.

"Yes, sire. You will have a chance to thank them yourself, tomorrow," Yves replied.

William smiled and nodded. "Great. Looking forward to meeting them."

Yves' cell phone rang out loud, which caused both men to jump slightly. "Whoa, why so loud, friend?" William said, with a laugh.

"Sorry, sire. I turned it up when I was outside, patrolling the grounds. With the river and ocean sounds, it is hard to hear," Yves replied as he brought his phone to his ear. "Hello, this is Yves. On our way!"

"Who was that?" William asked.

"Your father and Jean-Rene are here! Shall we?" Yves asked as he motioned for William to go ahead of him.

"Ah, great!" William replied as he hurried out into the hallway, followed by Yves.

As William and Yves bounded down the stairs, the front door opened and Jean-Rene appeared, head bandaged, face scraped up, walking with a limp. William hurried to greet him but couldn't help but look past him. There, just outside the castle door, on the front step stood Patrick Athy, looking up at the castle before him eyes wide, mouth opened, shaking his head. "Oh my sweet Jesus . . . look at this place! Will, you must've shit a brick when you saw this, eh, son? Haha . . . look at the size of it, would ya? You could have the whole feckin' Irish rugby team here and still have enough room for our entire town!" Patrick slurred loudly.

"Da! Yer alive! Thank the Lord!" William shouted as he approached his father, arms opened.

"Well, of course I'm alive, son! Dun't be a feckin' eejit!" Patrick replied, staggering a bit.

William looked at Jean-Rene. "French? What the hell is wrong with me da?"

"Sire, I am so sorry but the knights' medic administered morphine to your father. He has a significant back injury from the fall. We will be getting him the very best medical attention posthaste. Uh . . . and . . . well, he had a few sips off my flask as well . . . to calm his nerves. We were nearly killed," replied Jean-Rene, sounding a bit defensive.

William raised one eyebrow at French and shook his head. "No worries, I am glad you are both okay," Will replied. "Da, let's get you inside, cleaned up, and a bit more sober before Mum sees you!"

"Mum? Yer mum is here? Where is she, Will? That woman still lights me fire, ya know what I mean, son? Hahahaha . . . whoa, what a body," Patrick said, barely able to stand.

"Whoa, Da! TMI!" William replied, with a tight-lipped smile as he put his father's arm up over his shoulder to help him inside.

"I gotta lie down, son. The room is spinnin' in circles, and I want off this carnival ride! Haha! Whoa, look at this foyer! Holy shi—" Patrick managed.

William interrupted, "Okay, Da! Enough of the profanity—yer grandkids are upstairs, and we dun't want them to hear their grandfather talkin' like a McGregor!"

William and Yves helped Patrick inside, and Yves motioned toward a large painting on the left side of the staircase. "Head to that large mural, sire. It's a door to the basement," said Yves.

"Of course it is!" William replied sarcastically.

As they approached the mural, Yves stopped. "Wait here," he said as he veered to the right and grabbed the side of the painting. It opened up like a door, to reveal a staircase. "Downstairs we go," Yves said.

As they descended, William could hear sounds and voices coming from below. They became clearer as they approached another door. Yves punched in a code on a keypad next to the door, and it opened, allowing them to enter a hallway.

"This is the basement, sire. You will have a full tour tomorrow, but it is basically the central nervous system for our entire operation, equipped with a state-of-the-art communication system, security system, satellite system, and much more. It is a completely self-sufficient city down here," Yves explained as they made their way down a corridor. "Okay, we need to go in here."

They entered an unmarked door on the left.

"Wow. A hospital?" William said.

"Yes, sire. Your father will be well taken care of down here. May I suggest he stay here until he is sober, cleaned up, and assessed by our doctors?" Yves offered.

"Yes, absolutely. I dun't want me mum to see him like this," William replied.

# Chapter Twenty-Six

## Alas, the Nire

Thomas Athy and his band disguised as minstrels arrived in Limerick in the early afternoon, weary from their travels. The plan was to get a few supplies and camp out of town so as to not be noticed. That plan was quickly revised when Ailan was approached by the town mayor while purchasing salve for his horse's leg injury. On the narrow road from the dome hideout to the Nire Valley, there were several narrow passageways to maneuver, and horses were getting their legs injured. The route they were forced to take was treacherous, and at one point near Ennis, the wagon's wheel got stuck between two rocks and it took hours to remove it and repair the damage.

Now, all the men wanted to do was rest, eat a hot meal, and drink cold ale, but that was not to be. Thomas and his men were in the process of setting up camp, when Ailan rode up with three strangers, also on horseback.

"Brother, these men are here to talk to you!" Ailan shouted as he dismounted.

Thomas, who was busy making sure their precious cargo was safe, turned around abruptly, scowling at his younger brother.

"What say you, brother? Who are they?" Thomas said, visibly irritated.

"These fine men are Limerick's mayor, sheriff, and deputy! They noticed me whilst I was purchasing salve for our horses. I, being a stranger, piqued their interest. Haha," Ailan said, shooting Thomas a nervous look. "They asked who I was and what I was doing in town."

"What business is it of theirs why you are in town?" Thomas snapped back, glaring at the men.

"Now, brother—" Ailan started but was interrupted by the Limerick mayor.

"Now, now, we do not mean any harm, sir. It's just that your delightful brother here informed us that you were a band of minstrels!" the mayor said gleefully. "And we are in dire need of your services this very night! You see, we are having the Limerick Harvest Ball tonight, and the minstrels we hired have gone missing! So you see . . . we need you!"

"I'm sorry, mayor, but we are weary from our travels and are not prepared at all—" Thomas started.

"I really *must* insist!" the mayor said as twenty more men on horseback surrounded them.

"What is this?" Thomas said, eyeing his sword that was leaning against the wagon.

"Like I said, we are in dire need of music for our ball!" the mayor repeated.

"So you surround us? We are simply musicians . . . tired ones." Thomas offered as he crept toward his sword.

"Stay where you are! I know exactly who you are! You are the Celts who beat the king's army!" the mayor said.

"I dun't know what yer talkin' about!" replied Thomas.

"Yes, I think you do, Thomas Athy! Or should I call you the Terror?" the mayor argued.

"What? Haha. I am no terror, just a lowly minstrel!" Thomas quipped. "You have the wrong man, mayor!"

"No, I don't. You see, I am Alexander Lynch, of Clan Lynch. I cannot believe you did not recognize me, Thom!" the mayor replied as he dismounted, removed his hat, and held his arms out.

Thomas narrowed his eyes and stepped closer. "Allyn? Is that *you?*"

"Yes, Thom, it is! You filthy Athy pig!" the mayor screamed in laugher.

Thomas and Alexander "Allyn" Lynch were boyhood friends. Their families lived close to one another, and they used to play together nearly every day until the Lynch family moved to Limerick.

"You fat bastard! Look at you!" Thomas replied. "Mayor? When did that happen? You gave me a start, Allyn, I'll tell ya that!" And the two old friends embraced.

The rest of the men dismounted and began to introduce themselves to one another.

"Good to see ya, Thom. I saw Ailan in town, and he told me what you all were doin'. We're here to help in any way we can," Allyn said.

"Good to see you too, old friend!" Thomas replied. "But me baby brother has been told not to say a word to anyone!" Thomas replied, shooting a look of anger at Ailan.

"It's Allyn, Thom! There is no need to worry about Allyn, surely!" Ailan replied.

"Young Athy! You ought not to be telling *anyone* else! Thom is right—the less who know, the better. That said, I truly *do* need you to play at our town's ball," Allyn said, matter of fact.

"Allyn, it is indeed good to see ya, but we are exh—" Thomas started.

"I know, I know," Allyn interrupted. "You are weary! But we are desperate!"

Thomas sighed and looked around at his men. They all seemed to already be enjoying each other's company. "Perhaps an evening of music and friends will do us good," he replied.

"Good!" Allyn shouted. "It's settled!"

Later that evening, Thomas and his men arrived at the Limerick Assembly Ball. The building in the public square held over four hundred people, and tonight, there were well over that in attendance to celebrate the harvest of barley. Thomas, Ailan, Dermot, Father Patrick, and Liam were joined by several other clansmen, in the orchestra pit of the Public Assembly House. They began their first set with an upbeat, lively tune to which hundreds crowded the dance floor. Thomas led on the cittern, a small stringed instrument with a harmonic tone. Liam played the recorder and thus the melody. The others played various instruments, including a shawm, which was a woodwind that livened up every song. After two full hours of playing, with only two ten-minute breaks, Thomas and the rest of the musicians were exhausted. As Allyn, the town mayor, announced that the last song was next, the dance floor was completely packed with people. And as the music began, the front doors of the Public Assembly House slammed open, and twelve armed British soldiers rushed in, causing screaming, running, and panic to ensue. Several people were being trampled, as most knew that the British never showed up unless they were there to wreak havoc. Thomas and his band of "minstrels" knew the British more than likely were there to capture or kill them. The orchestra pit was on the opposite side of the room from the front doors, so Thomas knew their only hope of escape was through the back doors, behind the stage. The orchestra pit was directly in front of the stage. As the Brits pushed their way through the large crowd, many of the locals started to form a wall by linking arms. They also knew the soldiers were likely there to capture their fellow Irishmen from Galway. Many knew exactly who Thomas was and were intent on protecting their national hero. Ailan was the first to dash toward the back doors, and he made it without being seen by the Brits. Then suddenly, there arose a commotion from the townspeople outside the front doors. There was shouting and a mock scuffle, which caused the Brits to run back outside. That was the diversion Thomas and the others needed. They hurried to the back doors, slid out unseen, and were mounted on their horses before the soldiers ever saw them. Thomas grabbed a lit torch and led them all out of town and back to their relatively safe camp.

"Whew. Glad we got out of there with our lives, Thom! Those soldiers surely were looking for us," Ailan said as he poured himself a cup of ale from the supply cart.

"Yes, I believe they were told where we were . . . someone must have recognized us. We must depart before first light and backtrack a bit so as to throw those bastards off our trail!" Thomas replied. "We will need to sleep in shifts as usual, but instead of just two watchmen, we will need four. Ailan, easy on the ale, lad. You, me, and two other volunteers will have the first watch."

It had only been two hours since most of the men drifted off to sleep, when three horsemen carrying torches bounded up to the camp on horseback. One yelled, "Wake up, Celts! Wake up! The British are coming fer ya! Get up!"

The entire camp was awakened abruptly, several instinctively grabbing their weapons and assuming battle stances. Ailan had his sling at the ready but realized the horsemen were friend, not foe.

Thomas approached them cautiously and recognized the men as townspeople. "These men are our countrymen and friends. Put down yer weapons. Thank you fer the warnin'. Do you know where the British are exactly?"

"Not more than two miles away, headed this way!" the second horseman answered.

"You heard him, men! Break camp now! Cover our tracks! We leave *now!*" shouted Thomas.

Thomas then summoned his brothers, knowing they had to come up with a plan to evade the Brits.

Ten minutes later, the entire camp was erased, and Thomas' small caravan was headed back toward the town of Limerick and straight at the approaching British.

"Okay, this is a good place!" Thomas said in a low voice. "Ailan, make sure the horses are well enough away from the road. Father Pat, you're with me on the wagon. Everyone else, take cover and have your weapons at the ready."

Father Patrick, dressed in his priest robe, climbed onto the wagon and took the reins in his hand. Thomas took dirt and rubbed it all over his face and clothes, disheveled his hair, poured a cup of ale, and joined Father Patrick on the wagon seat.

"All right, Father. I hear the British approaching. Stay calm and play the part as we planned. Oh, and say a prayer," Thomas said as he gulped down some ale. "Here they come."

Thomas began singing an old Irish drinking song as Father Patrick prodded the horses. The Brits approached abruptly and surrounded the wagon, several holding lit torches.

"Halt! Stop your wagon at once!" the head officer shouted.

"Aye, sir!" Thomas slurred as he stood up and saluted and then fell back onto the wagon bench clumsily.

"Who are you and what are you doing traveling at this hour?" the officer pressed.

"I am Father Patrick O'Conner, and this is Sean Brady. We are taking these supplies to the monastery near Limerick. May I offer you and your men a spot of ale or perhaps some Irish whiskey to warm yer bones?" Father Patrick said, laying on a thick Gaelic accent.

"No! We do not want any of your ale or whiskey. Have you seen anyone else on the road tonight?" the officer replied.

"No . . . only daft people are traveling at this hour, sir!" Father Patrick said. "Beggin' yer pardon, I didn't mean you."

"Why are *you* traveling at this hour?" the officer repeated.

"Well, we didn't plan to be, but our wagon wheel broke and my vicar's assistant here took a long while to fix it. I refuse to sleep on the ground at me age . . . I have a bad back, you see . . . and he is a good lad but

216

enjoys the spirits a wee too much, dun't ya, Sean? And—" Father Patrick rambled.

"All right, all right. Be on your way! You are of no help to us," the officer said impatiently.

And the Brits continued on their way as Thomas and Father Patrick remained in character until the last Brit soldier was out of sight.

Ailan, Liam, Dermot, and the rest all reappeared slowly from the surrounding woods, Dermot clapping and smiling. "Bravo, Patty! Bravo, son! You two were magnificent. Haha . . . but Father Patrick, hopefully, the Lord will forgive your lyin'!" Dermot quipped and burst out laughing with the rest of their group.

"T'ank ya very much, adoring crowd!" Thomas joked as he stood up, bowed, hiccupped, and fell back on Father Patrick's lap. "Haha . . . that was truly satisfying! To pull one over on the British Army is always a treat!"

After a brief laugh, Thomas stood, brushed himself off, wiped his face with a cloth, and became more serious. "The plan worked well! Now, let us waste no more time. We will have to head east for a wee bit to continue to throw the Brits off. And then, we will resume our trek to the Nire Valley. Let us not forget our most important mission: delivering this precious cargo."

And deliver they did. After a long, arduous journey, the band of "minstrels" arrived at the Nire Valley. Road-weary and in need of a hot meal, bath, and a pint of ale or two, the group met up with the rest of the clans at the appointed place: a small village called Ballymacarbry in County Waterford. Just a mile away was the spectacular, remote valley of the Nire. Large, green mountains cascaded into smaller hills and eventually met the expansive valley floor, where the Nire River snaked the entire length and disappeared into the hillsides to the south. Thatched-roof cottages dotted the valley floor, emitting smoke from their fireplaces, causing a foglike blanket to hover over the entire area.

The clans gathered at the northern entrance to the valley, atop a small hill. Their journey finished but now a new adventure began. This was where a third of the Tribes of Galway would settle, guardians over a priceless treasure, along with the Knights of the Temple of Solomon.

"Ahh, heaven on earth, lads. I look forward to our wives and families joining us in a few months." Thomas sighed. "By then, we will have most of the necessary work done, the cargo stowed safely underground, our cottages built, and our crops planted."

Thomas dismounted and drew in a deep breath. "Well, lads . . . this is where we 'bury the past to be resurrected in the future.' Welcome to the Nire, our new home.

# Chapter Twenty-Seven

## Tragedy

Sue Jarvis was chopping scallions for dinner as her housekeeper and friend Machiko prepared a stir-fry meal on the stove.

"Chiko, could you please use jasmine rice instead of the brown?" Sue asked. "It's Roy's favorite."

"Of course, no problem, Suzi-san," Machiko quipped in an exaggerated Asian accent, something she enjoyed doing to make Sue laugh.

"Haha, you keep me smiling, dear one," Sue replied. "I'm going to go wake up Roy. I'm surprised he hasn't smelled your cooking already and yelled for a plate!"

"Haha . . . he will like stir-fry, Miss Sue!" Machiko answered.

Sue cleaned up her mess from the kitchen counter, rinsed off her hands, and slowly padded back to hers and Roy's bedroom, quietly opened the door, and stuck her head in.

"Roy? Dinner is almost ready. Chiko is making your favorite," she said softly. Nothing.

"Roy? Roy . . . time to wake up, dinner is almost done, love!" she said louder, walking into the bedroom and turning on the overhead light. The bed was empty.

"Roy, where are you, dear? I didn't think you would sleep this long. Are you in the bathroom?"

Sue looked in the bathroom, walked out onto the back porch through the French doors, and scanned the area. Nothing. She came back into the bedroom and looked in the closet. Her heart sank when she saw that Roy's favorite hat, jacket, and boots were missing.

"No, he surely wouldn't . . ." Sue rushed to the front window of the house and looked out onto the driveway. "No Scout . . . *No Scout?* Machiko? Machiko, hurry!" Sue shouted.

"Yes, Miss Sue," Machiko answered as she trotted into the living room, wiping her hands on her apron. "Mr. Roy okay? You okay?"

"No, Mr. Roy is gone, and I am most certainly *not okay*!" Sue snapped back. "I'm sorry, Chiko, but Mr. Roy seems to have escaped and driven off in that damnable Scout! That man is going to be the death of me, Chiko!"

Sue picked up the phone and dialed Roy's cell number. It went directly to his voicemail. Then, she hurried to the kitchen and grabbed the walkie-talkie off its cradle, noticing one was missing. *He had one in the bedroom with him*, she thought. But after several attempts to reach Roy, she gave up.

"Where on earth can he be?" Sue sighed.

Again, she picked up the phone and dialed, but this time, she called her son Robert. Sue told Robert everything, and the oldest of the Jarvis sons was there within a few minutes.

As he drove up, Sue met him in the driveway. "Oh, son, thank you for coming," Sue said, and she hugged Robert. "I can't imagine where he's gotten off to!"

"Well, Mum, you know Da . . . he's always going somewhere or busy doing something. He'll be back soon, I'm sure . . . especially when he smells Machiko's cooking!" Robert offered reassurance to his mother.

"You're right. He probably just went down to the river. That's his 'at peace' place, as he says," Sue agreed.

"Maybe we should take a drive though and look around a bit," Robert suggested.

Sue already had her jacket on and was out the door before Robert finished his sentence.

"Mum, wait up!" Robert shouted. "Sam is on his way."

"Oh, good, three sets of eyes are better than two," Sue managed.

Mother and son loaded up into Robert's Jeep and waited for Samuel. Robert tried to keep his mother calm, but with each passing minute, she became more worried.

Samuel sped up the driveway and came to an abrupt stop next to them. He nodded at Robert, grabbed a few items from his car, and hopped in the backseat of his brother's Jeep.

"Any word yet?" Samuel asked as he slid inside.

"No, not yet, but I'm sure he is fine and will be back any minute," Robert replied, nodding at his younger brother and looking at him, wide-eyed through the rearview mirror.

"Oh, uh . . . yes, I'm sure Da is just havin' a swig of Jameson down by the river!" he replied, winking at Robert.

"That's what I said, Sam. T'anks fer comin', son," Sue said, reaching back and squeezing her youngest son's hand. "I am sure he is fine . . . but he won't be after I get ahold of him!"

Both boys snickered as Robert backed out of the driveway and headed for the river.

As the three pulled up to the campfire site at the river, they saw nothing at first. Robert was about to drive off when Samuel stopped him.

"Wait. Stay here. I'll be right back. I just want to have a look around," Samuel said.

He then exited the Jeep and walked over to the campfire area. He squatted down and looked closely at the ground.

"What is he doing?" Sue asked.

"Just having a look, Mum. Looking fer tracks or a sign Da was here," Robert replied, patting his mother on the hand.

Samuel stood up and walked back to the Jeep and got back into the back seat. "Yes, he was definitely here. His tracks are fresh and headed downriver."

"The burial site!" both brothers said in unison.

With that, Robert headed toward the old Gaelic burial site. As they drew closer, Sue yelled, "There he is! There's the Scout! What a relief."

Robert pulled up next to his father's old Scout. "Well, his Scout is here, but he's not," he thought out loud.

"What on earth . . ." Sue said, sounding worried.

"I'm sure he's just checking out the site, Mum. Stay here, and Sam and I will go find him. It is cold and mistin' out," Robert said adamantly.

"I am comin' witcha, son—no arguments!" Sue responded.

"Mum, for once in yer life, would you please just listen to *me*!" Robert spat. "Sam and I are good at this, and you will only slow us down. No disrespect meant, but *please*, stay in the Jeep. We'll be right back with Da."

"All right," Sue replied soberly.

"T'anks, Mum. We will bring him back," Robert said, leaning to give his mother a kiss on the cheek.

"Be careful, boys," Sue said as she peered out the fogged-up window.

"Yes, ma'am," both boys replied.


Robert nodded to Samuel as they exited the Jeep. "I have my flashlight and nine-mill in the back," he whispered.

"Okay, I'll wait while you get them," Samuel answered.

While Robert retrieved his items, Samuel scanned his father's Scout thoroughly. "Hmmm," he said to himself as he opened the driver's side door.

"Did ya find something, Sam?" Robert asked as he approached.

"He left his walkie-talkie here." Samuel replied.

"Well, that's not like him," Robert said, eyes narrowing. "He has told us a million times to always have a radio on us!"

"I know, not like him at all," Samuel agreed, shaking his head. "I dun't like this, Rob. Something is off."

"What do ya mean, Sam? I'm sure he is just up there checking things out. Now, let's go get him!" Robert said, trying to reassure himself.

"He just got out of the hospital. He is weak. He should not—" Samuel started.

"I know, I know, Sam! But I prefer to remain positive," Robert interrupted.

"Okay, fair enough." Samuel replied.

Once armed with light and firepower, the two Jarvis brothers headed up the hill to the burial site. As they approached the top of the hill, Samuel stopped abruptly, looking toward the large stone.

"Something is *not* right, Rob! We need to get out of here *now*!" Samuel said, panic in his voice.

"Sam, calm down! We need to find Da!" Robert replied.

So the two slowly crept forward, guns drawn, flashlight illuminating the path in front of them. The humming sound caused the two brothers to pause and look at each other. Robert motioned to keep forging ahead. Suddenly, Samuel saw something in the clearing by the front of the large stone. He gasped. "*Da!*" he shouted and ran toward the object.

"Sam, *nooo*!" Robert yelled. "It's not safe!"

As Samuel drew closer to the object on the ground, it came into focus. "That's Da's jacket," he whispered to himself. Then, another object that was near the woods caught his attention. It was a spear, and upon the top of it was a round object. Samuel took a few steps toward it, dropped to his knees, and let out a bloodcurdling cry, "*Nooooo!* Da! Da!"

Robert hurried to Samuel's side and squatted down to check his brother, not seeing anything else. "Are you okay, Sam? What did you see?" Robert said as he too looked toward the woods. "What is that?"

Samuel was hyperventilating but managed, "It's him. It's Da."

"What? No, it's a stick or a spear with a . . . a—" Robert started.

"A head on the tip," Samuel cried. "It's Da, Rob. It's Da!"

Robert narrowed his eyes and strained to see it. He took two steps forward and froze. "No! It can't be!"

Samuel managed to get up and stumble toward the figure on the ground. He fell again as his knees once again buckled. "*Rob!* His body is over here!"

Sue sat in her son's Jeep impatiently waiting for her boys to come bounding down the hill with her beloved husband in tow. She rolled down her window to get some fresh air when she heard a loud scream.

"Samuel?" she said to herself. "*Samuel!*" Now shouting, she quickly opened her door and dashed up the hill. Another scream.

"Samuel, what is it? Where's your father? Samuel? Robert?!" she yelled as she reached the top of the hill. She saw a flashlight stream beaming from the ground and ran toward it. Before they could stop her, Samuel and Robert watched their mother run at full speed, tripping over the remains of her husband and landing on the ground on the other side.

"Mum, *no!*" Robert screamed.


Sue had landed face-first on the ground, not yet comprehending what had happened. She groaned in pain and rolled over onto her back. "Boys? Boys? What is happening? Only I heard you shouting. Where's your father? Roy? Roy, where are you?" she managed.

Robert knelt next to his mother and helped her to sit up. He took off his jacket and put it over her shoulders and said, "Mum, keep your eyes on me, okay? Dun't look to the right or the left. Look at me."

Sue was confused but did what her oldest son asked and stared into his face. But what she saw in his eyes did not comfort her. Robert's face was ashen, tearstained, his eyes filled with terror. He glanced over at his father's torso and then realized he shouldn't have. Sue then knew in her heart, something was horribly wrong. She started to turn her head toward Roy's remains, but Robert grabbed her and drew her into his chest, keeping her face away from the horror behind her. But as her son held her, she looked over his shoulder and saw her youngest son also kneeling, and in front of him, she saw the spear and then focused her eyes upon it. When it finally clicked in her brain what she was looking at, she let out a heart-wrenching groan and lost consciousness. Robert continued to hold his mother tight and sobbed uncontrollably. Minutes later, Robert, still holding Sue, managed to retrieve his cell phone from his breast pocket and call the police.

"Sam, help me get Mum to the Jeep," Robert managed. "*Sam!* Compose yerself, li'l brother! Mum needs us!"

Samuel, in utter shock, slowly arose from the ground and tried to move toward Robert and his mother but fell to his knees again and vomited on the ground.

"Oh, Sam . . . lad, I'm sorry. You're in shock. God help us, please!" Robert wept.

He no more got those words out of his mouth than headlights illuminated the grisly scene. Robert looked toward the lights, squinting. *Is this the police already?* he thought to himself.

The vehicle stopped, headlights pointed directly at the large stone. The driver's side door opened, and a figure got out and walked toward Robert, Sue, and Sam.

"Mr. Robert? Mrs. Jarvis, Sam? What has happened? I heard the police scanner say they were on their way to Jarvis Ranch and the old burial site."

Robert, still blinded by the headlights, couldn't see who this person was. But the voice was that of a man and the accent sounded Irish.

"Who are you?" Robert asked, still unable to see.

"It's me, Connor Aberdeen. Chief Constable," the voice replied.

"Oh! Oh my God, Connor! They killed Da! Me mum passed out, and Sam is in shock. Thank God you are here. Help us, please," Robert replied in desperation.

"They?" Connor asked as he approached Robert.

"They, he, she—I dun't know! But whoever it was cut me da's head off and put it on a spear, over there," Robert said, tears streaming down his face.

Connor squatted next to Robert and looked about the scene. "It is a horrible scene, isn't it, lad?" he said, with a half grin.

Robert looked at Connor's face and felt he was looking into the face of the devil himself.

"Why . . . why are ya smilin', Connor? Do you know who did this?" Robert asked, now feeling pure fear.

"He just couldn't leave well enough alone, Rob," Connor replied, taking a handkerchief out of his jacket pocket and wiping his forehead. "He had to find out for himself. Yer da couldn't just keep his nose out of it."

Robert looked over at Samuel, who was motionless but listening to every word. He looked up at Robert and slowly raised his index finger to his lips. Robert nodded slightly and tried to keep Connor engaged in their conversation.

"Connor, whattaya sayin'? Who killed him? Who did this?" Robert pressed, voice raised.

Samuel quietly arose from the ground and crept slowly toward Connor, who had his back to him. As Samuel took his third step, Connor with one fluid motion, grabbed his gun from a side holster, spun around, and fired directly at Samuel. The bullet hit with such force, it knocked him to the ground.

"*No!* Samuel!" Robert shouted. "You bastard! Why are you doin' this, Connor?"

"Just like yer dead da, eh, Sam?" Connor said in a low growl. Then he turned the gun on Robert, still sitting on the ground, his mother in his arms.

"One wrong move and I'll kill you and yer mum too," said Connor as he walked backward, toward Samuel. "Need to make sure yer little brother is dead, lad! Haha."

Connor turned and looked down at the youngest Jarvis son, kicked him in the side, and laughed again. "Yep, he's a goner too!" he said. Just then, the air became filled with the sound of loud popping and Connor groaned as several bullets hit him in the back. He looked down at his chest and saw that his shirt quickly became soaked with blood. "Well, this may ruin me day," he said. Then he fell forward and landed on Samuel's legs, dead. Robert looked toward where the shot rang out and saw several figures drawing closer.

"The police! Thank God. Samuel?!" he shouted. "Help—me brother was shot!"

Over a dozen police officers surrounded the area and began to assess the crime scene.

"Sir, can you tell us what happened here?" one officer said to Robert.

"That monster you shot . . . he killed me da and me brother. And more than likely, that man up on the rock too," Robert replied.

Two paramedics then rushed up the hill and attended to Samuel. One knelt down and examined him. "He's still alive! Looks like the bullet missed his heart—he'll live, but we need to get him to the hospital now!"

Another EMT attended to Sue, who was starting to awaken. He looked at Robert and said, "Before she wakes to see this horrible scene, I am going to give her a sedative. She is probably already in shock."

Robert nodded and stood up slowly and allowed the EMT to attend to his mother.

A police officer approached Robert and put his hand on his shoulder. "Are you all right, sir?" he said.

Robert looked at the officer with glazed-over eyes and said in a strained voice, "No, I am not all right. I will never be all right again."

## Chapter Twenty-Eight

### The End, Until We Begin Again

The cast and crew of Star Gaze Productions were gathered outside the Jarvis barn, as the commotion coming from the burial site had them all worried. The police were not answering their many questions, so Angus and two other actors, Douglas Fairchild and Rodney Jones, decided to find out for themselves what had happened. With Larry Davis still missing and no word on Lillie Adams' whereabouts, the cast and crew were more than a little nervous.

"All right, lads . . . let's take the four-man ATV and head up to the burial site. If the authorities won't keep us informed, we will find out what is goin' on ourselves," Angus said.

"You three aren't goin' nowhere without me!" said a determined Molly Taggart. "And dun't even try to argue!"

"Argue with you? We'd have to be daft or under the influence, my dear! Get in!" Angus replied sarcastically.

The four were then on their way to the burial site. When they arrived at the foot of the hill, an ambulance was leaving the scene. There were several police vehicles and emergency crews on scene as well. Angus parked away from the crowd of vehicles, and the four actors headed up the hill to the burial site on foot, evading any law enforcement. Once they reached the top of the hill, Dermot held his hand up. "Stop. We don't want to be seen. There . . . let's head to that outcrop of bushes and observe from there," he said, motioning to a grouping of furze bushes.

The four ducked behind the outcrop and gazed upon the busy scene, none of them knowing what had transpired there. Then, as Molly scanned the area, her eyes fell upon the large rock, which caused her to let out a loud gasp. "What on earth? Who . . . oh my, that isn't? *It is!* That is Larry Davis! Oh my, oh my," she stammered and fell back to the ground from a squatting position onto her backside.

Angus looked at Molly, puzzled, but then focused on the large rock, through the blinding floodlights that had been erected. He held his hand up to his brow to shade his eyes. Suddenly, the gruesome scene came into focus. "Oh holy, sweet Lord, no! Who did this?" Angus said, also visibly shaken.

The other two actors followed suit as they too cast their sights on the horrible scene.

"What happened here? Who would kill Larry? Why?" Angus managed as he continued to look upon his friend, strung up upon the large stone. As he forced himself to look elsewhere, another object came into focus: the spear. Angus could not believe what his eyes were seeing. He grabbed Molly and drew her into his chest. "Dear Molly, please don't look! We need to get the hell out of here. Whatever happened here was pure evil," Angus said, noticeably upset.

"Angus! I am a grown woman. I can handle this just as well as any man," Molly said, pushing away from Angus and looking over his shoulder. When she saw the spear and realized that there was a severed head of someone atop it, her countenance changed immediately, and she grabbed Angus to steady herself. He held Molly close. "Let's get out of here now!" he whispered, and the four actors hurried back down the hill to their ATV.

They were completely silent as Angus drove them back to the parking lot, near the barn. Several people from the cast and crew gathered around them, asking what they had seen.

Angus held his hands up to quiet everyone. "Please, please quiet down. What we have just witnessed up there is nothing short of terrifying," he started, which caused an uproar. "Please, please, *quiet!*" he shouted, angrily. "You all need to remain calm, please. I will tell you everything just as soon as I can gather my composure."

The crowd fell silent. Most of them knew that if Angus was shaken, whatever he witnessed must have been horrible.

The mountain of a Scot reached into his vest pocket, pulled out a flask, and took a long draw of whiskey then let out a sigh. "What we just saw up there at the burial site was hell and could have only been done by the devil himself. Folks, Larry Davis is dead, and whoever killed him slit his throat, stripped him naked, and strung him up on the large rock up there."

The crowd let out a loud collective gasp, many screaming, "*No!*"

Angus again held up his hands. "That's not all! Quiet please. That is not all. There was also another spear found. This time though, instead of a note attached to its tip, there was . . . there was . . . a . . . a severed head."

The crowd went into full panic mode, weeping and screaming. Angus took Molly by the hand and led her to his trailer. "Come on, love . . . let's get you to a warm, safe place. Tomorrow, we head home. This movie will not be finished until the authorities get to the bottom of whatever happened up on that burial ground."


As the crowd began to disperse, a black unmarked SUV pulled up into the parking lot. Two plainclothes law enforcement officers got out of the two front doors, made their way to the rear passenger-side door and stood. The door opened, and out stepped Lillie Adams, wrapped in a blanket. The officers escorted her to her trailer, where she packed a few of her belongings and followed her escorts back to the vehicle. Angus saw her from across the parking lot as he was headed to his trailer with Molly. "That's Lillie! I need to—" Angus started.

"Go, see if she's okay. I will be fine, meet you at your trailer," Molly replied.

Angus made his way toward Lillie, but the officers with her stopped him. "What happened, Lil?" he asked as they stopped him from approaching her.

"He is my friend, no need to worry," Lillie told her escorts. "Angus, it is so good to see you," she said, wrapping her arms around his waist.

"Where ya been, love?" Angus asked.

"Long story," Lillie replied. "I just want a hot bath and to find out where Larry is. They won't tell me anything!"

Angus' heart sank. The two officers looked at each other and then diverted their eyes elsewhere.

"You didn't tell her? Seriously?" Angus said in disbelief.

No response.

Angus hugged Lillie tight and whispered in her ear, "Lillie, love. Larry is gone."

"I know he's gone, and they need to find him!" Lillie replied.

"No, love. He's dead. They found him hours ago," Angus continued, not letting Lillie push away.

"What? He's what? *No!*" Lillie screamed and wept loudly. "How? What happened, Angus?"

"Love, I will tell you everything I know, but we need to get you some place warm," he replied.

The two officers stepped closer; one, speaking quietly, said, "Miss Adams needs to come with us, sir. She is under protective custody."

"Protective custody?" Angus replied. "Well, protect her, then, by telling her the truth!"

"Sir, we had planned on informing Miss Adams just as soon as we arrived at the safe house," the officer replied.

As the news of Larry's death sank in, Lillie became more and more distraught, weeping uncontrollably and screaming, "Larry!"

"Love, you need to go with these officers. They are taking you to a safe house," Angus said.

---

"No! I am not leaving with them! I want to see Larry! Where is he?!" Lillie screamed and started flailing around.

"Get a medic here *now*!" Angus shouted as he tried to keep Lillie from thrashing about. "Calm down, love."

The company medic came running and helped Angus escort Lillie to the medical tent near the stables. The two officers followed, one talking to someone on his cell phone.

As the group arrived at the med tent, one officer said to Angus, "We cannot force Miss Adams into protective custody, but she has been abducted twice and rescued once already."

"I understand. What if I assure you I will take full responsibility for her safety?" Angus asked.

"It is up to Miss Adams," the officer replied.

"Well, she is no shape to make any decision right now," Angus snapped.

"We will wait until she is," the officer replied. "But if she refuses protection, we cannot be held responsible for what happens to her."

"My priority is her safety and well-being. You two can do whatever you need to. Just don't cause her any more stress," Angus said adamantly.

Once in the med tent, Lillie was given a sedative. Angus then addressed the two law enforcement officers: "This woman has been through enough. I will talk to your supervisor and do whatever it takes. But she is coming with me back to my trailer, where she will be surrounded by friends who love her. If you need to get her permission when she is more lucid, fine. But you are not taking her anywhere without me!"

"We spoke with our superior officer, and she gave us permission to leave Miss Adams in your custody. But we will need to record a verbal agreement on my phone before we take off," the officer said.

"Fine," Angus replied.

Molly opened the door of Angus' trailer as he and Lillie approached. "I was watching for you. Tea is ready," Molly said.

Angus, who had Lillie in his arms, said, "We're gonna need something a wee bit stronger than tea, love."

Colin Wohl's cell phone rang out as he was just about to pour a brandy for him and William. Atheney Castle was teeming with various people, preparing for the new king's departure to America. Colin was excited to be a part of his best friend's ascension to royalty and was in a jovial mood. That changed abruptly as the voice on the other end of the phone told him of the gruesome deaths of his friend and boss Larry Davis and Roy Jarvis. Colin's face became as white as a sheet. William glanced at his dear friend from across the large sitting room and knew he had just received bad news.

"Colin, what is it? Who was that?" William asked as Colin slowly laid his phone down on the bar.

"That was the Tipperary Police. Larry Davis and Roy Jarvis are dead, murdered. They want me to get back to Clonmel as soon as possible to make sure our cast and crew are taken care of and to halt production of the movie. I guess I am acting head and CEO of Star Gaze Productions," Colin managed as he found a chair and sat down abruptly.

"Who would kill those two? Why?" William asked.

"They said the suspect is also dead. They, the police, shot him at the scene. It was Connor Aberdeen," Colin replied, shaking his head.

"Connor Aberdeen? What? But he's the chief constable!" William replied as he sat down next to his dear friend. "I am so very sorry, Colin. Is there anything I can do?"

Colin looked at his friend and replied, "Well, yes. The Tipperary Police said that the incident happened because of you. Will, you need to do exactly as the Knights of the Temple of Solomon tell ya. Your life depends upon it. Connor was apparently working for MI5. He was assigned to assassinate the Celtic king and to stop production of a movie that would tell the world the truth. My dear friend and king, you must go to America."

# Chapter Twenty-Nine

## Land of the Free, Home of the Brave

William and a small contingent of knights turned bodyguards escorted Colin and Samantha to the waiting helicopter.

"Thank you, William. Or should I call *you* sire?" Colin quipped. "I have to admit, this whole thing is still very surreal. *You*, king? I mean, seriously crazy stuff!"

Samantha smiled and nodded in agreement.

"I know, Sire! It is pretty nuts. But it is my reality now. *Our* reality," William replied.

"William, you must stop calling *me* Sire! Not fitting of a king," Colin said as he hugged his oldest friend.

"You're right, of course, but old habits are hard to break," William replied. "Now, after you have tied up all the loose ends back home, a plane will be available for you. You and Samantha are expected in Maryland in two weeks. Dun't be late!" William said.

"Thank you, William. I will make sure we are on that plane in two weeks. I have closed my veterinary practice in Clonmel. You now have both of our undivided attention, Your Royal Highness," Samantha replied with an awkward curtsy.

William smiled and kissed his sister-in-law on the cheek. "HRH? Really, sis?" he whispered in Samantha's ear. "What would Em say about all this?"

With that, Colin and Samantha boarded the helicopter and were off to Jarvis Ranch.

As William and his entourage arrived back at Atheney Castle, they were met at the front steps by Yves, Jean-Rene, and Patrick.

"Ah, good morning, sire! Did your friend and sister-in-law get off okay?" asked Yves.

"Yes, they are on their way back home to tie up all the loose ends. I guess Larry Davis' remains are being flown back to California tomorrow and Roy Jarvis' funeral is tomorrow afternoon," William replied. "I really should be there to pay my respects to Roy's family."

"Son, you know you cannot go there. It is just too dangerous," Patrick said.

"I know, I know. I'm just sayin'," William said, frustrated.

"I don't mean to change the subject, sire, but today is your last day of training here at Atheney Castle. It is important that we get started straight away," Yves said, determined.

"This week flew by, Yves. I really do appreciate everything, but you must obey my orders, correct?" William pressed.

"Yes, sire. Your wish is my command," Yves said.

"Well then, I wish to be flown to the Nire Valley and Jarvis Ranch tomorrow. Shall we get started on today's training?" William replied as he patted Yves on the back, winked at his father, and bounded up the stairs and through the front doors. "Come on, lads, we've got work to do!"

After a week of intense physical training and hours of pertinent history lessons, William's head was swimming. He received more in one week than most receive in four years at university. From sunup until well after midnight, William was barraged with information.

"Sire, we only have two more weeks to prepare you for Maryland. I do not think a trip to Mr. Jarvis' funeral is a good idea," Yves pleaded.

"Yves, my dear chap, three hours is all I ask," William replied. And as Yves looked like he was going to press the issue, William continued, "There is no more to say! Make it happen!"

"Yes, sire," Yves replied, bowing his head slightly and glancing at Patrick.

"William, son, you are putting not only yourself at risk but also all those who have to protect you. You have seen how determined our enemies are! They have killed two innocent men, your beloved, prized mare, and attempted to kill us! I beg you to reconsider," Patrick said sternly.

"I am the king here, Da!" William spat but instantly regretted it. "I mean . . . well, you know."

Patrick then widened his eyes and drew closer to his son. "William Thomas Athy, king or no king, I am your father! Dun't you *ever* speak to me like that again! You aren't king of anything just yet! Your coronation is in two weeks! I still have time to whup yer arse if need be! Now, stop yer damn whinin' and listen to Yves and me! Goin' to Jarvis Ranch is out of the question!" Patrick said in a low, stern voice, only inches from his son's face.

William swallowed hard and was transported in his mind's eye back to his boyhood. The few times Patrick talked like that to him and his brothers, it made an enormous impression on them all. When Da was really mad, his voice deepened, and a sound whuppin' was next.

"Yes, sir," William replied.

The matter was over.

Once down in the gigantic basement of Atheney Castle, William changed into workout clothes and joined eight other men in the gym. Yves and Patrick stood in an office that overlooked everything. Five of the eight men were knights, and three were Clan Athy cousins, all well trained in self-defense. Their job was to prepare their sovereign for any threat that might arise.

———

First was strength training, then hand-to-hand sparring. This day was different, however, since Yves had two special guests coming to assist in William's training: Arie Rosenstein and Simon Meltzer, two world-renowned IDF (Israeli Defense Force) experts on Krav Maga, a military self-defense fighting system based on a combination of techniques sourced from boxing, wrestling, aikido, judo, and karate.

For the next two weeks, William trained with the very best from all over the world. United States Special Forces secretly brought their expertise in sharpshooting and evasive maneuvers as well. Two weeks flew by for the young king, and on the eve of their departure for America, everyone was gathered in the family room. Jenn, William, the Athy family, knights, several members of the Tribes of Galway, and various Irish clan members were all enjoying food and drink. And as Yves tried to get everyone's attention, the door opened, and in walked Colin and Samantha.

"Ah, you made it! We were worried!" William said with a wink and a smile. "Just in time. Yves was about to make a toast! Please, Yves, continue."

Yves addressed the crowd: "Yes, thank you for your attention, please. Thank you, everyone. Tomorrow, we depart for America and begin a new chapter in this Celtic saga. Tomorrow, hundreds of people will gather at a compound in Maryland for the sole purpose of seeing the coronation of the rightful king and heir to the Celtic Isles. This gathering is done in secret for obvious reasons but know this: Those who will be attending are in full agreement with the truth of our mission. They are some of the most powerful and influential people in the world, heads of state and royalty, all gathering to see this man, William Thomas Athy, crowned king of the Celtic Isles. And this is not just a ceremonial gathering. No, my friends. It is a true coronation that will usher in the next phase of our quest, for 2020 will be the year the British monarchy is brought down and the Celtic reign begins. Our army is made up of millions who have been preparing for decades. But this quest is centuries old. You all know the true story now. So let us toast to this: To king, country, truth, and honor. To victory over our enemies, and to Eire, the true capital of the Celtic Isles!"

The End

To Be Continued

Made in United States
Orlando, FL
01 April 2023

31590148R00157